THE Heart Shot

Also by Emily Schneider

Ash & Smoke Series:

Scales of Ash & Smoke
Scales of Ice & Shadow
Scales of Sun & Storm

THE *Heart Shot*

EMILY SCHNEIDER

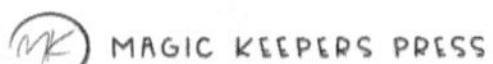

MAGIC KEEPERS PRESS

The Heart Shot

Copyright © 2023 Emily Schneider

For information contact:
Magic Keepers Press, LLC
magickeeperspress.com

Paperback: 9781737495796

Ebook: 9798988115601

First edition May 2023.

Edited by Amanda Chaperon
Cover Design by Ink & Laurel © 2023

For all the girls who have never felt treasured.
You are worth the fight.

PROLOGUE

Elsie

The right time to dump my boyfriend of four years probably wasn't while sitting at an expensive restaurant, surrounded by tables full of people, on the night I expected him to finally propose.

But I never claimed to be in my right mind, and I couldn't let this go on anymore. It wasn't worth it.

I sipped on a glass of ginger ale to calm my stomach, trying to breathe despite the tight red dress clinging to my body that was forcing all the air from my lungs.

Squeezing the non-existent life out of my cloth napkin with clammy hands, I closed my eyes, trying to shut out the din of chattering people that pounded into my head. Though the light fixture dangling above our table was dim, it radiated enough warmth that sweat beaded on my forehead and made my antiperspirant work harder to fight the threat of Niagara Falls pits appearing beneath my arms.

My boyfriend, Ben, sat across from me, alternating between cutting his steak into the tiniest morsels I had ever seen and tapping his phone screen to see if he had any notifications. As always, the relationship with his phone was far more important than the one he had with me.

It didn't matter how hard I tried, what I wore, or how much makeup I plastered on my face, my boyfriend was always glued to his phone. I probably could have painted my face like a clown, or better yet, sat here naked and he still wouldn't have given me the time of day, wouldn't have spared me a second glance.

My dad had set us up four years ago when I was a junior in college. Ben had recently graduated and received a job offer to be a marketing manager at the same retail chain my dad worked for. He thought we'd make a good pair, though I'm sure that was simply parent-speak for him liking the stability Ben offered. If my dad had bothered to ask what I actually liked in a man, he would've known that Ben was *not* it.

Sure, he was handsome, but he had a habit of acting entitled and rude; he never thought about anyone but himself. My dad didn't see that side of Ben, though. My boyfriend was an excellent faker, schmoozing his superiors as if that was the job he was hired to do. No one truly saw the man beneath the mask—the one that only I was privy to. My dad only saw the successful man with a stable job that could provide for his daughter.

It was too bad the guy turned out to be a turd bucket.

Yep, I just called my boyfriend a turd bucket.

Ben was the instant success story that everybody dreamed of emulating, and I was quickly lost in his shadow.

Meanwhile, I started my career by selling mini-donuts.

Yep. Mini-donuts.

I went to school to be a writer, but when you're drowning in student loans, writing doesn't always pay the bills. No one wanted to take a chance on someone fresh and untested. Now, two years after college, I was finally finding my place in the writing world, freelancing as much as I could, but it still didn't even come close to Ben's success.

I'm sure my dad meant well when he schemed to get us together—wanting me to be cared and provided for—but Ben's personality was...not for me. He cared only for himself, and what he could get out of everything and everyone. When he spoke to people, he didn't see their eyes, only dollar signs.

He hadn't even noticed that I ordered the shrimp risotto tonight—even though I was deathly allergic to shrimp.

Rubbing at my temple, I watched him check his phone for the umpteenth time.

Did he even remember I was sitting here?

I let out a frustrated breath, blowing the dark-blonde hair from my eyes as I glared at the bulge in his jacket draped over the chair. Ben had been dropping hints about proposing for the past week, but I hadn't been convinced he'd ever commit to doing it. At least, until we sat down at the table and I caught a glimpse of the box in his pocket when he took the jacket off.

That's when the panic set in and I knew I had to end things. Tonight.

When we first met, Ben was a sweetheart, buttering me up like he did with everyone else. But as time passed, his true colors started to show, and he didn't bother to hide his cruel side with me anymore.

Needless to say, marrying someone like him was not what I imagined for myself.

Maybe I would be happy once I saw the ring on my finger, maybe I'd adjust to being the wallflower for the rest of my life. I'd never admit to anyone that he made me unhappy. I was a people pleaser to my very core and had prepared to marry Ben, if he ever asked, because I couldn't envision saying no to him. That was the annoying thing about being me: I was so desperate to be wanted, to not be alone. Ben met that desire—even if it was only halfway.

Besides, no one ever said no to Benjamin Sallow.

At least until now.

Now, none of it mattered.

"How's your steak?" I asked, my voice drowned by the cacophony of voices filling the room. Ben's jaw clenched as he chewed, his eyes still fixed on his phone. No response. "Ben?"

His jaw froze mid-bite, eyes wide as he looked at me, before quickly swallowing and giving me a sheepish smile.

"Sorry, babe. Lost in thought." The phone clicked as he turned off the screen. "How's your dinner?" Of course, he didn't bother to look at my plate to see that I hadn't touched it, nor did he wait for my answer before tapping again on his phone.

I fought the urge to stick my tongue out at him like a child. I hated when he called me *babe*. To me, it wasn't a term of endearment but a demeaning nickname. It felt like I was an object and not a person. Anything would have been better than *babe*.

Why had my dad thought we'd make a good pair?

Though, he clearly didn't know what love was. Neither of my parents did.

That thought reminded me of why I was doing this and cracked straight through the lid on my irritation. I set my fork down with a clank. Ben didn't even look up.

"I think we should break up," I announced.

The words were plenty loud, albeit a little shaky, but Ben acted as though he hadn't heard them. Several seconds passed before he tore his attention from his phone and folded his hands under his chin.

"You know, Els," he said, ignoring my declaration, "I was thinking we could head down to visit my parents this weekend. They bought a new boat and—"

"I want to break up," I interrupted, shutting down

the wriggling worm of hope in my heart from the sudden invitation. In the four years we'd been together, I had only met his family once, and I was never invited to any of his family events.

I gave a small shake of my head. This changed nothing. It didn't matter how much I wanted his family to accept me.

A beat of silence pulsed between us.

"What?" he asked after a moment, mouth hanging open.

"You heard me." I tossed the napkin onto my untouched food.

"Funny joke, Elsie." He laughed half-heartedly, sitting back in his chair with crossed arms. The man, so used to getting his way, radiated arrogance.

Of *course* he wasn't taking me seriously.

"We're done, Ben." I stood from my chair, preparing to leave but, on par for the course of my life, the tablecloth snagged on my bracelet. As I walked away, the entire thing went with me, dragging the plates and glasses off the round table with a loud clash as they crashed to the floor.

My entire body froze like a deer caught in headlights.

The room quieted for a split second as every eye turned to me, and I was suddenly in a vacuum, all sound sucked away. All that remained was my pulse pounding in my ears. I wanted to melt onto the floor like a puddle. I hated being the center of attention. I didn't want to be

Ben's preferred wallflower but I didn't like to be front and center either.

With burning cheeks and shaking fingers, I fought to get the cloth unhooked from my metal bracelet while a handful of waiters rushed around, cleaning up the mess I had made. My empty stomach swirled and, for a second, I thought I might be sick.

Wouldn't that be the cherry on top of this entire night?

Ben sat there, watching me struggle to untangle myself, anger twisting his mouth into a deep scowl. He didn't bother to help.

Slowly, the volume of the room crept higher as people returned to their dinner and conversations, the staff still working to clear the mess from the floor. Frustrated, I gave up and yanked the bracelet off, chucking it onto the table. I didn't want it anyway. It had been a manipulative apology gift from Ben last year after he had forgotten our anniversary and went out with his buddies instead.

As I turned on my heel to flee, cold fingers grabbed my wrist.

"Now, hold on just a minute," Ben snapped. "What do you mean we're done?" He reached into his suit jacket and pulled out the little box I expected to be hiding in there. Popping it open, he set it on the table. "I was going to propose," he added. He had the audacity to sound hurt, like a whiny kid whose toy had been taken away.

The ring was stunning—and huge. It had a thin gold band and a circular diamond that was easily the width of my finger set in the middle. My decision wavered for a split second as I saw my future reflected in the facets of the jewel.

Ben and I were married with a beautiful home and family, but as I looked at the ring, I could clearly see that he'd always put his marriage to his career over our own. I would always be an afterthought. Our children would wonder why their father was too busy to spend time with them, and I would fade into the background, forgotten. We would spend years drifting apart, growing resentful toward each other, until one day, after decades together, we would snap and destroy everything in a divorce. I had seen it before.

As much as I hated the thought of being alone, the idea of putting myself through such pain and heartache was worse. My resolve hardened.

"Well, now you don't have to." I tried to pull away, but he tightened his grip.

"Is this about your parents? You know their divorce has nothing to do with—"

"Do *not* finish that sentence," I seethed, the anger I had tried to bury for months burning in my stomach.

"Elsie—"

"I don't want to marry you, Ben."

His mouth gaped like a fish, as if he couldn't fathom that someone could feel that way about him. He finally removed his bony fingers from my wrist.

"You're making the biggest mistake of your life, Els.

You'll never find anyone better than me."

I huffed out an unamused laugh, shaking my head, then looked Ben dead in the eye. "I don't want anyone better." I turned my back on my almost-fiancé, calling over my shoulder, "I don't want anyone at all."

Elsie

Four Years Later

This is the most ridiculous thing I have ever read.

A headache hammered against my skull as I sat at the peninsula in my kitchen, working on a blog article. If the article wasn't for a popular lifestyle website, I probably would have considered turning the job down. This particular writing gig was not my first choice, but I had bills to pay and the potential exposure from this website could be huge. That was the unfortunate part of being a freelance writer—I had to write what people hired me to write, even if I hated the content.

While the article was technically based on a true story, I could only see it as a work of fiction. This type of stuff didn't happen anywhere but in romance novels.

I sighed for the millionth time. This website was paying me far too much for me to do a subpar job, though, so I was going to grin and bear it by forcing my annoyance, irritation, and skepticism into a tight little box. Maybe those feelings would suffocate.

I rubbed at my forehead, staring at the first paragraph my fingers had rebelled against typing.

I mean, who wanted to read an article written about an unlikely meet cute between two strangers who fall in love at first sight? It was *ridiculous*. Those types of scenarios didn't happen in real life. It was probably a one-in-a-bajillion chance. And yes, bajillion was absolutely a real number.

If there was one thing I had learned in life, it was that love wasn't real. It was a nice notion in books, but in real life? Not a chance. These people I was writing about were delusional. Their supposed love-at-first-sight would end eventually, and then this article really would be a work of fiction.

If it was *my* story, the article wouldn't end with the characters getting together. It would end with them seeing reason—that love was nothing more than a cruel illusion—then they would go their separate ways, living happily ever after *alone*.

The blinking cursor taunted me as I stared at the screen. I let out a long breath.

Come on, Elsie. Just write the dang thing so you can get paid. You don't have to believe everything you write.

Something soft brushed against my arm, immediately soothing the jagged edges of anxiety pricking through my stomach. My cat, Rhys, whom I had named after my favorite fictional character, rubbed his body along my arm and shoulder, his soft purring calming me.

"You're the only man I need, Rhys," I murmured, giving his head a scratch. "At least I know that cat love is real." All it took was a little feeding and brushing and he would love me forever. Could I say the same thing about a man? Absolutely not.

A small meow was his only response before he jumped off my lap and scurried up the cat tree in the corner. My eyes tracked him across the room before scanning my little bungalow. It was cozy, yes, but also empty. As much as I didn't believe in love anymore, I couldn't deny that living alone was not my cup of tea.

I hated coming home to an empty house, but I wasn't willing to do anything to change it. Nor would I *risk* changing it. There were other ways to feel less lonely than being in a relationship with a man. Namely, my cat, Rhys. Who needed people when you had a cat?

Slamming my laptop shut, I shoved it into my backpack and headed for the door. While I was an introvert and preferred being by myself, sometimes the silence of my house was suffocating, and I needed to get away for a while. I grabbed the keys from the bowl next to the door and stepped out into the warm, fall day, repeating *I don't need a man* to myself the whole drive to the local coffee shop, where I would force myself to finish that blasted article once and for all.

"I'm sorry, you want me to do what?" I shoved the rest of the giant pretzel that served as dinner into my mouth, tossing the wrapper into a nearby trash can.

"Oh, don't freak out, Elsie," my best friend, Maya, said, arching a perfect brow at my outburst. "It's just a photoshoot."

I zoomed through the mall at what felt like supersonic speed to get away from Maya's begging, wishing I hadn't agreed to meet her as a way of procrastinating finishing that article.

"Elsie, slow down," Maya called, her tennis shoes squeaking on the tile floor as she struggled to catch up.

"I would hardly call this 'just a photoshoot,'" I snapped as my own sneakers squealed to a halt.

Maya rolled her eyes, putting her hands on her hips. "Honestly, Els, if I had another option I would take it, but I need *this* photoshoot, and you're the only person I can ask."

And by that, she meant I was her only single friend who could participate in such a shoot—one where I'd have to pretend to be in love with a stranger. On camera.

"It's just for an hour. Then you never have to see the guy again," she added as I rubbed my forehead, secretly hoping there was a chocolate store somewhere nearby where I could drown my sorrows.

I cursed the day when Maya decided to take photography classes at the local community college four months ago. She always loved taking photos, but a couple years ago she made the decision to turn her photography hobby into a career. Unfortunately, it was hard to grow a successful business in little Meridel, Iowa, a small town on the western edge of the state. Maya hoped the class would increase both her connections in the photography world and skills, which would open more doors for her.

I wanted my best friend to succeed, I really did, but if she hadn't signed up for the class, I wouldn't have her pleading for me to take pictures with a stranger.

What kind of an idea is that anyway?

It would be ten thousand levels of *awkward*.

I couldn't stand there taking lovey-dovey photos with a stranger. There was a reason I went into writing—I was no actress.

This was a disaster waiting to happen. It was the start of a bad joke, and my face in those photos would be the punchline. With my luck, the photos would go viral, and I would become the next great meme.

"Maya..." I whined, turning to walk into another store, not paying attention to which one it was, and groaning when it ended up being the lingerie section in one of the big chain department stores.

Ugh.

Maya laughed. "See, it's a sign!"

"I wouldn't take accidentally walking into a bra section to be a sign that I need to agree to this." I gave her my best scowl, pausing amidst the lacy unmentionables and crossed my arms.

"Come on, Els. I will absolutely get on my knees and beg you. Right here. Do you really want to cause such a scene?"

I scoffed. "Me? You'd be the one doing it."

"Please?" Maya dropped to her knees, proving she meant every word by wrapping her arms around my legs and staring up at me with puppy dog eyes. "I need this, and I need you to do it. Just don't even think about the guy. Although...you should because he's quite attractive."

I groaned, wobbling as I tried to maintain my balance with her holding my legs together. "You already have him picked out?"

"Better. He's already agreed to do this."

"*What?*"

"Yep. You're the only thing holding back this photoshoot now."

"Who is it? It's not one of your creepy exes, is it?" I gasped. "It's not *Gerry* is it?"

Maya rolled her eyes. "Oh please, Els. Like I would ever set up someone I care about with *that* guy."

I sighed dramatically. Maya had met Gerry on a dating app several months ago. Despite his pretty blue eyes, the body odor on that guy, akin to a pubescent boys' locker room, put an end to that date pretty quickly.

Maya squeezed me tighter. "I promise this guy isn't a weirdo, doesn't stink, and won't make you uncomfortable. Just say yes. Please?"

With a scoff, I pulled my legs free of her arms and speed-walked away, trying to find my way out of the maze of bras and thongs.

"Besides," Maya continued, hurrying after me. "When's the last time you did something random and fun like this? Ever since..." She paused, biting her lip, knowing she almost brought up the one thing I hated talking about.

She sighed. "You've been alone for a long time, and you usually turn down my invitations to get out of that little cottage of yours. Come meet someone new and have some fun. And at the end, if there's no spark, the photoshoot is done, and you never have to see the guy again."

"So, this is your lame attempt at matchmaking?" I retorted over my shoulder, hands balling into fists. The last time someone tried to set me up, I wasted four years of my life on a guy who never thought I was worth fighting for. "Why don't you focus on your own non-existent love life instead?"

Regret slammed into me as the words slipped past my lips. Maya had been on a handful of dates over the last few months, but nothing ever went further than the first. I didn't know if that was her choice or theirs.

She hurried to my side, violently shaking her head. The movement reminded me of a dog shaking water off after a bath. "You're right. My love life *is* non-existent, and not important right now. Believe it or not, I'm trying to help you. I can't do this photoshoot without you, but I've at least made it well worth your while. Help me out while giving your heart a shot."

"My heart doesn't want a shot." The words tasted bitter on my tongue.

Maya scowled. "Keep telling yourself that. I know you're lonely. You're terrible at hiding it from me."

Though I'd never admit it to her, she was right. It had been at least four years since I'd done anything that could be considered *fun*, but there was a genuine reason for that. It was better to keep everyone at a distance, especially men. Why would I break that streak now?

But on top of the little voice whispering for me to do the photoshoot, I had another reminding me how much I hated disappointing people, especially those close to me.

I groaned again, coming to a stop when I finally made it out of the bras...and entered the section of men's underwear. I snorted at my terrible luck, and Maya sniggered. I turned to glower at her, but the pleading in her eyes stopped me cold. Why couldn't I simply say *no*?

Worse, why did my heart want me to say *yes*?

What was happening to me? I was content to be alone and single. It kept me safe.

But still...

Would it really be so bad?

After all, it was only a photoshoot.

With a stranger.

There would be no flirting, or falling in love, or any danger to my heart. It was simply some pictures with a guy.

What could go wrong?

I dropped my head back and sighed. "Fine, Maya. But no kissing."

2

Jameson

I closed the door to my office as the last patient of the day exited the clinic, my entire body shaking with fatigue after the longest day of work ever. How I spent the last year working twelve-hour shifts six days a week, I wasn't sure.

Thankfully, today was my last day at *this* clinic.

I threw the last of my personal items into the box on the desk, then wiped down the table with an antiseptic solution. I didn't even bother looking back as I turned off the light and left the claustrophobic room that had been my life for the past year.

I tried my best to be optimistic in all things because why would anyone *choose* to be a negative Nancy? Life was hard enough without adding pessimism into the mix. Even though change was always challenging, I was determined to make the most of this. I was ready for bigger and better things.

My phone buzzed in my pocket and I fished it out, climbing into the cab of my truck. My sister's name flashed across the screen.

"Hey, Emma."

"Jamie! How's my big brother?"

"The better question is how is my little sister at her fancy college?" I expertly dodged the question. There was a five-year gap between us, but we had always been close, and watching our mom fight for her life had brought us even closer. Still, it was hard to admit to her that things hadn't been great. She didn't need *my* stress added to hers.

Emma laughed. "I don't think I'd consider Iowa State to be *fancy*."

"Anything is fancy compared to Meridel Community College."

"No argument there."

Emma's bright laugh eased the ache in my heart ever so slightly. That was one thing we had in common, despite all we had been through. We were great at keeping a good attitude and staying optimistic. Yet another reason why I didn't want to bring her down with how I was really feeling.

Emma had spent three years taking classes at the local college, but with Mom finally doing better, she decided to finish her bachelor's at a school that offered the degree she wanted.

"To what do I owe the pleasure of your call?" I asked, needing to shake those thoughts from my head.

"Oh, I just wanted to hear your voice. It's weird not having you and Mom close by at all hours. I miss you guys." And just like that, the ache was back. "Have you been up to anything fun lately?"

I snorted. "You know all I do is work."

"Maya mentioned that you're starting at a new clinic. That's a good thing, right?"

"Yeah," I said, letting out a long breath. "Today was my last day at the old one. I'm ready to put twelve-hour days behind me."

"Yeah," she echoed, something strange creeping into her voice. "And now you'll have more time for things like dating."

I choked on my spit, nearly coughing up a lung. "Excuse me?" I finally croaked.

Emma giggled. "It's well past time, brother."

"I've tried going on a few dates, and I don't think I'm made for the dating world. It's...scary out there." I had been on a few dates recently, and none of them were good.

"Why do you think *I'm* still single?" she replied, a smile in her voice. "But I know there's someone out there for you, Jamie. Probably closer than you think. You shouldn't give up yet."

I paused. "Emma, why does it sound like...do you know something I don't?"

"What?" she gasped, the sound far too dramatic to

be real. "I don't know what you're talking about."

"Are you hiding something from me?"

"Of course not. Why would you think that?"

"I don't believe you."

It was obvious she was grinning as she said, "Trust the process, Jameson. Trust the process."

"What the heck does that mean?"

"Oh, nothing! I should go. Lots of homework."

I sighed, knowing it was no use trying to get information out of her. Emma was usually an open book unless she had a secret, in which case she was locked up tighter than a goblin bank vault.

"Wait," I said, trying to keep her on the phone. It was my turn to pester her like a loving brother was supposed to do. "Have you spoken to Liam lately?"

A long pause filled the phone, and I checked to make sure she hadn't hung up.

"You know I haven't." Her voice had gone from cheery to ice-cold.

"Have you tried to call him?"

"Of course not. Liam made it perfectly clear what mattered to him, and I wasn't it. That's all there is to it."

I wanted to pry, to push her toward contacting him, but I didn't want to jeopardize our own relationship. Liam was Emma's childhood best friend, all of Meridel had expected them to get married someday, but ever since he got a record deal and moved to California last year, my sister wouldn't even talk about him.

"All right. I'll leave it alone." I knew when to accept defeat and back off.

"Thank you." I was certain she was sticking her tongue out at me. "I'll talk to you later, Jamie."

My thoughts spun in circles as I hit the red button to end the call, wondering why she felt the need to bring up dating and what she possibly could have been hiding from me. It wasn't something we ever talked about.

As tired as I was, the thought of going home to my empty house, and spending the evening with only my dog, had my stomach twisting. I did my best to view being single as an opportunity for growth rather than soul-sucking loneliness. Most of the time it was a losing battle.

Thankfully it was Wednesday, so instead of driving home, I went straight to Angel's Hearth. The weather was unseasonably warm for September, forcing me to wiggle out of my jacket as I walked up to the red brick building where my mother lived. On autopilot, I went through the motions of signing in, and ignored Rhonda the receptionist as she flung flirty looks my way. I turned down the hall-way, rode the elevator to the top floor, and walked to the end of the hall toward room 306.

It was still strange to me—her living here. When my mom had come to me a year ago saying it was time for her to move out of my house, it had shaken me. For ten years my life had revolved around taking care of her night and day, and then it just...stopped.

My mom was the strongest woman I knew, evident by everything she had fought to survive over the past decade, but it was hard to let go and let someone else take care of her. Though I knew she was in good hands at this assisted living home, it was still a struggle to turn off the part of me that wanted to care for her.

Now, I had too much free time.

I scoffed at myself. Who complained about having too much free time?

Apparently, I did, because it left my brain free to wander in anxiety over my mom and in loneliness because I was still single at twenty-nine.

The chaos of my life had settled as much as it could, and now all I wanted was someone to come home to each night other than my dog; someone to not only care for but to enjoy the life I had been forced to put on hold for so long.

Hence why, after years of not dating, I finally bit the bullet and tried one of those dreaded dating apps. Unfortunately, Meridel was a small enough town that I didn't think I'd ever meet my soulmate here.

Even more unfortunate was the string of truly terrible dates I'd been on over the last month. I cringed at the memories. One had body odor so terrible, I gagged into my elbow all night. One was still infatuated with her ex, another was only looking for a hookup, and the last was too engrossed in either her phone or flirting with the waiter to even bother conversing with me.

Clearly, I had been out of the dating scene for too long and an app was not the way to go. Or I was destined to be a bachelor for the rest of my life. It could go either way.

In the end, it was too much, so I deleted the app and called it quits—at least for now. If I met a girl down the road and we hit it off, so be it, but I wasn't going to actively search one out.

I blew out a breath as I arrived at my mom's apartment door, pausing to collect myself and shove those bad dates into a corner of my mind I couldn't reach. Knocking twice, I opened the door and immediately regretted it. A familiar blonde sat in the chair next to my mom, grinning her signature mischievous, scheming grin.

"Hey Jam-Jam," my cousin, Maya, called. Her voice reminded me of Emma's when she was hiding something. It was a little too high, too forced, and full of secrets. Instinctively, I went on alert as I nodded hello, holding back a cringe at the nickname she made up for me when I went through my guitar playing phase as a teen.

Emma and Maya had become close when my mom had first gotten sick. Maya was great—like a sister to me—but her personality was strong, and she loved to push each and every one of my buttons, which was a feat in itself because I was known for being calm and composed. She liked to go on these "quests," as she called them, where she tried to *better* me. Whether that was fixing my wardrobe, or finding me a job where I worked fewer hours, or—to my absolute horror—fixing me up on dates.

In truth, I appreciated her efforts, but I didn't need my cousin to fix me. I could do that all by myself. I had taken care of my mom and sister—and done a pretty good job of it—when everything went downhill. I was perfectly capable of adulting on my own, thank you very much.

"How are you doing, Mom?" I asked, kneeling in front of her chair.

She gave me a gentle pat on the cheek. "I'm just fine, dear. I'm glad you could come."

Since she moved out of my house, we had a standing dinner date every Wednesday. It had been her decision to move out, to let me get on with my life, but seeing each other regularly was important to us.

I only wished my cousin hadn't made a habit of joining us. Though, with Emma off at college, and Maya's parents essentially out of the picture, I had a feeling she simply wanted a place to belong.

"Ready for dinner?" I asked, avoiding Maya's watchful eyes.

"Yes, dear," my mom said as I took hold of her hand to help her out of her chair. While she was thankfully in remission, the medicine that helped cure the cancer had left her bones brittle and her body weak—which was why she lived here rather than on her own.

"Maya will be joining us," she added when we were halfway to the door. Maya gave me a saccharine smile, the perfect picture of innocence.

I suppressed a sigh, plastering a smile on my face despite the feeling of foreboding hanging over me as we walked down the hall to the dining room. What meddling would my cousin attempt today?

The scent of gamy meat overwhelmed my senses as we rounded the corner into the dining room. It was stew day, my least favorite of their questionable meals. Mom and Maya took a seat next to each other at the four-person table, and I plopped down across from them. As soon as we were situated, a nurse brought out bowls of stew, some bread, and a pitcher of iced tea and placed it before us.

Mmm. Brown mush. My favorite.

I poured myself a glass of tea and took miniscule sips to prolong not eating the stew. It wasn't that it was bad—it simply wasn't good.

Oh, who was I kidding? No optimism could save this food. It was awful, like eating moist dirt with vegetables.

It was some odd texture, too—like brown jello with thick chunks of tough meat and hard veggies. I lifted some on my spoon and fought down a gag, letting it fall back in the bowl with a *plop*. I politely played with my spoon in the mush, making it appear as if I were eating it, nibbling on bread, and sipping tea in even increments.

I had avoiding eating this stew down to a science.

Of course, Maya's shrewd eyes missed nothing, and she snorted at me more than once. My mom had no such qualms about the food and had already scarfed down most of her bowl. She was either used to the mediocre meals here or she wanted to finish it quickly and get it over with.

"So," Maya started, interrupting my stew swirling. "I have a favor to ask."

I blew out a breath, forcing the corners of my lips upward into a smile. Here came the meddling.

"I have an assignment for my photography class where I have to come up with a unique photoshoot idea and implement it." Maya paused, glancing at me for a reaction. When I said nothing, she continued. "Everyone else has super lame ideas, but I have the perfect one, and it'll really help my portfolio."

"And how does this include me?"

"I need you to be one of the models for the shoot."

I huffed out a laugh. "I'm not a model."

She barked a laugh of her own. "Have you seen yourself, Jam-Jam?" Maya shook her head as if I'd said something preposterous. "The concept is simple. Two strangers who have never met before—"

"Generally, the definition of a stranger."

"—doing a couples photoshoot where they have to pretend to be in love."

I choked on a gulp of tea. "You want me to do *what*?" I coughed out.

Maya gave me an innocent smile. "It'll be fun."

"By whose definition?"

My mom cleared her throat, setting down her spoon.

Her stew bowl was completely empty.

"Jamie, I think you should help Maya. Do the photoshoot."

My eyes narrowed, catching my cousin's glance at my mom. Usually, my mom stayed out of the scheming, but it almost looked like...was she in on it? What had Maya told her before I arrived?

"I can't pretend to be in love with a stranger," I said, rubbing at my temple where a headache was forming. "Especially not on camera."

"Come on," Maya begged. "It'll be fun. Elsie is amazing and I know that—"

"Elsie? As in your best friend, Elsie?"

I had never met my cousin's best friend, but Maya constantly talked about her, especially with my sister off at college. Her lips pressed together in a line as she nodded.

"No."

Maya's brow furrowed in outrage. "Come on, Jam-Jam. I already told her you had agreed."

The bread I'd eaten turned to ash in my stomach. "Why would you tell her that?"

Maya ran a hand through her blonde hair. "Because there's no one else I can ask to do this, and you're perfect for each other, and I want you two to meet."

At least she didn't beat around the bush.

I groaned. "Not this again." The last time she tried to set me up with someone—several years ago—the girl had been a psycho. When I tried to tell her I wasn't interested, she went nuts.

Handcuffs were involved.

I rubbed my wrist at the memory. The girl had handcuffed us together so I couldn't break things off with her.

After a single date.

There was no way to "optimist" my way out of that one.

I hadn't really been interested in dating back then and had only agreed to it because my mom and Maya had wanted me to.

I shook my head. "Didn't you learn your lesson last time?"

Maya winced. "Okay, I admit Freya wasn't a good fit for you, and I've apologized a thousand times." I couldn't help but cringe at the mention of the girl's name. "But that was four years ago. I've given you plenty of time to trust me again." She gave me a closed lip smile as she slipped a spoonful of stew into her mouth.

"Or maybe you should just not try to set me up with anyone." I narrowed my eyes. "Have you been talking to Emma about this?"

Her eyes widened and she batted her eyelashes. "Jam-Jam, whyever would I do that?"

I huffed out a laugh, somehow unsurprised that my sister and cousin were conspiring to get me back into dating.

"Jamie, be nice," my mother scolded. "She's only

trying to help you." Maya's head bobbed up and down in violent agreement.

Great, Mom is in on it, too.

It shouldn't have been surprising. She and my mom had become closer recently. Maya's dad had taken off when she was a kid, abandoning her, and her mother lost it as a result. She was no longer present in Maya's life, absorbed in herself and her career. Maybe my mom felt a need to be the parent Maya didn't have now that she wasn't fighting for her life.

Even so, I couldn't hold back an eye roll.

"This one is different," my cousin promised. "I know her personally, and she's incredible. I know you'll like her if you give it a chance. Bring back Mr. Sunshine and say yes."

I snorted at the nickname that most people in Meridel called me, wishing it was that simple. But there was something about Maya and her meddling that got beneath my skin, unveiling the version of me that only came out when I accidentally drank decaf coffee. I was a caffeinated ball of sunshine but a decaf grump.

I sighed. "You really think I'm going to go along with this after...you know who?" I couldn't bring myself to say her name. The girl wasn't dead, but I wanted her to rest in peace in my memory...and never come up again.

"Please, Jamie?"

Uh-oh. She stopped using that infernal nickname. Maya was serious about this.

"She already agreed," Maya added, her smile not quite

reaching her eyes. "I need two people for this photoshoot. I can't do this without you."

"Don't you have anyone else you can ask?"

She gave a violent shake of her head. "You're the only single guy I know that could do this."

The downside to still being single at twenty-nine—most everyone else was already married.

I had nothing against Maya taking some pictures of me—it wouldn't be the first time—but doing a couples shoot with a girl I'd never met? Awkward wasn't a strong enough word to describe it. From what I remembered about her from Maya's endless word vomiting, Elsie was the quiet, reserved type. How had *she* agreed to do this?

I opened my mouth to say as much when my mom leaned forward, fixing me with a stern glare.

"Jameson, you need to help your cousin. She helped you find a better physical therapy clinic to work at. The least you can do is help her do well on this assignment so she has better opportunities too."

Ugh.

Well, when she put it that way.

I looked Maya in the eye, too tired after the long day to fight against them both. "Fine, Maya. I'll do it."

Elsie

Sweat was already dripping down my spine.

The autumn sun was bright in the sky, slowly sinking toward the horizon, taunting me with its heat as if it had a personal vendetta against me.

Why today of all days, sun? You couldn't do me a favor and hide behind some clouds, or, you know, be chilly like you're supposed to be this time of year?

Had I known it was going to be this hot and miserable, I never would've agreed to this photoshoot. It was nerve-wracking enough as it was.

At the thought, more sweat slid down my back.

Oh no.

I pinched the fabric of my black blouse and yanked it away from me, attempting to fan myself, though it did nothing to cool me down. I mentally kicked myself for wearing black, thinking it would hide my nervous sweat the best. Turns out it only made me sweat more. I glared at the offending sun, wishing the giant ball of fire would turn its gaze away from me.

My dirty blonde hair hung in loose waves, falling just past my shoulders, and was far too heavy on the back of my neck. I toyed with the elastic around my wrist, desperately wanting to throw my hair into a ponytail.

I can't do this. Why did I agree to this?

The question circled my mind like an incessant bug as I wiped my wet palms against my light wash jeans and rubbed at my forehead, hoping it would relieve my heat-induced headache. The amount of sweat pooling at my temples only made me grimace.

This guy is going to think I'm a sweaty freak.

I pulled the phone from my back pocket and opened the text thread with Maya, fingers hovering over the screen. I had to cancel. I couldn't do this. I couldn't meet a guy for the first time when I felt like I just jumped into a lake of sweat, let alone take lovey-dovey photos with him.

A lone cloud slid over the sun, blessing me with a moment of relief from its glare. My fingers tapped out a frantic message.

Sorry, Maya, I can't do this. I know this photoshoot was for your assignment, but I can't be photographed with a strange man when I'm a sweaty mess—

"That better not be a text bailing on me," a voice said over my shoulder, and I yelped, flinching so hard I nearly dropped my phone.

"Maya," I breathed, putting a hand over my heart as I turned to my best friend, who had her arms crossed and her foot tapping against the dirt. She wore a cute denim jumpsuit, her platinum hair pulled into a sleek topknot.

"I know that look, Elsie, and you're not getting out of this. Besides, he'll be here any minute." Maya stomped down the path into the trees. "Come on, I picked this amazing spot at the end of the orchard. It's a field of sunflowers."

With shuffling steps, I followed, ignoring the sand and dirt kicking up and coating the back of my sweaty ankles. Sweat was everywhere, in all the little nooks and crannies that sweat didn't belong—like little bugs multiplying until they were out of control.

Yep, that's what I had. An infestation of sweat. That was a thing, right?

Lifting my arms away from my body, I winced.

Oh crap. Do I have pit stains now? I probably look like I went swimming in Niagara Falls. Sweaty and dirty. What a great first impression.

"Hurry up, Els," Maya called over her shoulder. "Your mystery man will be here any minute."

I could have sworn my sweat glands heard her words and instantly doubled their efforts to drown me and my clothes.

"*My* mystery man?" I squeaked. "No, no, no. This was all your idea. He's no man of mine."

Maya barked out a laugh. "Calm down. I'm joking. Mostly." She turned to me, her eyes roving over my frazzled appearance. "You'll be fine, and you look great. It's just a photoshoot. It's not like you're required to marry the guy."

At the word "marry," my stomach jumped up into my throat, and I fought down a gag. The word was no longer in my vocabulary. It died a swift death four years ago.

"Just remember what we talked about," I reminded her. "We'll look coupley in the photos, and I'll let him hold me in awkward poses, but *no kissing.*"

"Yeah, yeah," she replied, waving a dismissive hand. Then she added, "I do appreciate you doing this though." She fiddled with her camera settings. "The assignment was to create a unique photoshoot, and all the other students came up with the lamest ideas. They're totally missing the point. Sure, some of them might have been in unique locations, but they all lacked *heart.* All their ideas have been done before, like the engagement session underwater or a couple playing with puppies. But when have you ever seen two *strangers* doing a couples shoot?"

Maya winked at me before fanning herself with a hand. "I'm calling this The Heart Shot." She paused, staring at me, waiting for me to react. "Get it?" She held up her camera. "Like, camera shot? Lovey-dovey photo shoot? *Heart shot?*"

Her cheesy smile was full of pride, as if it was the cleverest thing. Maybe she did have something special here, but why did *I* have to be the one suckered into it? I crossed my arms and fixed her with a glare.

"Oh, put Ms. Grouch away. Just get through this and you never have to see the guy again if you don't want to." She pointed to the thickest area of the sunflowers a few feet away, then looped the camera around her neck and rubbed her hands together like an excited child. "Go stand in there out of the sun. He should be here any minute."

Rolling my eyes, I pushed through stalks taller than my head, sighing as the shade enveloped my body, cutting off the sun's brutal rays. The petals of the sunflowers tickled at my face, but I pushed farther, wishing I could keep running and escape this nightmare all together. People chatting and children shouting in the distance met my ears, smothering my senses along with the overwhelming scent of dirt.

It was late in the season for sunflowers, but Raspberry Farms always pressed their luck by planting as late as possible, so people could enjoy the sunflowers and the fall foliage at the same time. It was a lost cause when we had a cold fall, but worth the risk when it was unseasonably warm, like this year.

"Els?" Maya called, much farther away than I expected. Exactly how far into the sunflowers had I gone? "Els, come back!"

Instead of doing as she asked, my feet had a mind entirely their own as they propelled me farther into the flowers. Maybe if I moved far enough away, Maya would forget about me and the pictures, and I wouldn't have to endure this guy's hands on my sweaty, damp clothes. The thought fueled my desperation to get away, and my footsteps quickened, my gasps loud in my ears.

"Elsie!"

At the sound of my name a cry erupted from my throat, and I broke into a run. My heart was a war horse stampeding in my chest, and I couldn't catch my breath. The rough stalks of the sunflowers bit into my palms as I pushed my way through the field.

Why was I panicking? Why couldn't I get my feet to stop or my racing heart to slow?

All at once, the frantic, screaming thoughts in my head stopped as I collided with something hard and fell backward into the dirt.

"Whoa," a voice said, but my eyes were glued shut.

My arm ached from the impact, and my bottom sang from my ungraceful tumble into the ground.

"Are you okay?" the voice asked, though it was muffled, like I was underwater.

A warm hand wrapped around my upper arm and gently pulled me to my feet, but my eyes still wouldn't open.

"Hey," the voice tried again. This time I had enough awareness to recognize that it was a man. Those warm hands had yet to let go of my arms.

I pried my eyes open, the movement as difficult as getting sand off wet feet, and gasped, stumbling backward once again.

"Whoa," the guy repeated, his grip tightening. "Are you okay? Did you hit your head?"

The stranger had the most stunning hazel eyes I had ever seen, with dimples for days and perfectly tousled dark hair. He wore a simple dark-green henley shirt and blue jeans that clung to his muscular build.

"Um…I'm…err," I stuttered, my eyes glued on his face, mind unable to form words. "Sunflower?"

"You're…Sunflower?" he asked, cocking his head as the corners of his full lips twitched. "Is that your name?"

"Um…"

"There you are!" Maya burst through the stalks behind us and came to a halt. Her gaze roved over what must have been a very interesting scene. A random man holding me upright, my freshly dirt-stained jeans, and carefully curled hair all over the place. I probably looked like I had a fight with the ground and lost.

Maya crossed her arms with a sly smile. "I see you've already met."

"What?" I tore myself from the guy's grip, backing away like a cornered animal. "You…you're…"

"Is she always this eloquent?" the man asked Maya with a smirk.

"Only when she's flustered. Jameson, this is Elsie Feran, the other half to this photoshoot."

When Maya told me the guy was attractive…the word did not do him justice. This guy could've been a model. Crap, he probably *was* a model. And here I was in my frumpy—albeit carefully chosen—outfit, with sweat-slicked skin and dirt smeared all over me from my fall.

I was a walking disaster, and this stranger had a front row seat.

"What took you so long?" Maya asked him.

He took a step back, putting more space between us, and I gulped down precious air.

"The lot was full so I had to park on the other side of the field." He ran his hand through his perfect hair exactly like a model would, and my knees may have wobbled.

Agh! Get a grip, Elsie! He's just a boy! I gave him another once-over. *Err, a man. Definitely* not *a boy.*

Maya pulled off her backpack, rummaged through it, and handed me a small, pink towel. "Here, you have a bit of dirt on your cheek."

Ears burning, I snatched it and turned away from them, wishing I could disappear. My hands strangled the non-existent life from the towel as I tried to keep my breathing calm.

This'll be fun, Maya had said.

Yeah, *so* fun.

Another moment passed when a sudden warmth radiated into my back, a large shadow falling over me.

"Here, let me." Those same callused fingers brushed my hands as Jameson took the towel. A blink later, he pressed the soft fabric to first my chin, then my cheek with the lightest of touches.

Were his eyes giving me third degree burns, or was my face spontaneously combusting?

Finally, his hand dropped, that dimple piercing his cheek as he said, "There, all better."

"Great!" Maya said, far too loudly, clapping her hands together. "Come on, the light is perfect here." She pushed a little further into the flowers, where the earth hadn't been dented by my body, and stopped in a spot where the flowers were a little sparser. "This is it." Her eyes glowed with excitement.

Jameson looked at me. "Shall we?"

I gestured for him to go first, not trusting myself to speak. When his back turned, I yanked on my shirt, trying desperately to dry the sweat beneath before he was forced to put his hands on me.

I had never done a couples photoshoot before, thanks to my deadbeat ex who never wanted any photos of us together, but I had seen enough pictures on social media to understand the gist of the poses we'd be doing. We had to convince Maya's photography professor that we could act like we were in love on camera, even though we had never met before.

This was the very definition of insanity.

"Okay, we'll start with something simple. Els, let's have you stand over there, and then Jameson will come up from behind and hug you," Maya said, pointing to where a large sunflower drooped a few feet away.

"Um, don't you think we should g-get to know

each other first?" I stuttered, pressing my clammy palms against my jeans.

Maya looked at me as though I had lost my mind. "Fine. Elsie, what's your favorite color?"

I crossed my arms. That wasn't what I meant.

"Well?" She tapped her foot on the ground.

"Black."

Maya snorted. "Just like your soul. Jameson? How about you?"

"Chartreuse." He didn't miss a beat, and Maya burst out laughing while my own mouth fell open. Then he turned his dimples on me and winked, adding softly, "Kidding. It's green like the flecks in your eyes."

A smothering heat overtook my face. *Like my eyes?* Did that mean...he liked them? My eyes were brown with a hint of green specks, but most people never even noticed.

No, Elsie. Stop overthinking it. That's not what he meant. He's a stranger, and he will remain as such. I forced my face into a blank expression, and killed the strange flutter in my stomach. There would be none of *that*.

"Perfect," Maya said, missing his words and my internal scolding. She clapped her hands. "Now that that's settled. Elsie, chop chop." With a wave of her hand, she directed me to the drooping flower.

Jameson winked once more before swaggering over to his spot.

With heavy legs and drenched armpits, I stalked to the flower and crossed my arms, waiting with my back to a stranger.

"You better wipe Ms. Grouch from your face by the time Jameson touches you," Maya called, her camera already clicking away.

What could she possibly be photographing? Jameson was still feet away and—

Strong, warm arms suddenly wrapped around my waist from behind and all my senses narrowed to the feel of his hands on my stomach, and then to his nose as he pressed it against my neck.

Whoa.

My breath hitched, and I was immensely grateful that Jameson was only human and not some mythical being with enhanced senses like in the fantasy books I loved to lose myself in, otherwise he would have been able to hear my heart skip a beat at his sudden closeness.

No, Elsie. You feel nothing. It's not real.

I squeezed my eyes shut, praying he couldn't feel the dampness of my shirt. Would he think I was disgusting? Would he stop touching me?

You didn't want him touching you anyway, I reminded myself. *This is all fake.*

"This okay?" he murmured in my ear.

Was it? I wasn't sure. I nodded automatically, but there were too many conflicting emotions happening here. The click of the camera shutter was a bomb clock ticking down in my mind. What happened when it stopped? My body stiffened.

"Relax," Jameson whispered, his lips barely brushing against my skin. Goosebumps erupted beneath his touch.

I squeezed my eyes closed again. "I'm sorry I'm sweaty," I whispered back, my throat tight. *Why did I say that?*

"Don't worry about it," he replied, his grip tightening on my waist. "It's hot."

We both froze. A beat of silence passed.

Then Jameson coughed. "I mean, it's hot out here. N-not that you're hot—I mean, you are, but that's not—" He sighed, frustrated with his own words.

The first twitches of a smile moved my lips, and I bit the inside of my cheek to keep it at bay. Maya's camera clicked faster.

Jameson's breath tickled my neck. "I just meant that it's hot outside. I'm sweaty, too. It's okay."

His reassurance smoothed the ragged edges of my insecurity like aloe on a sunburn, and I could finally take a deep breath, my muscles relaxing a bit.

He took one hand from my waist and gently moved my hair over my shoulder, tucking it behind my ear. The sensation was so unexpected that I couldn't help turning my head toward him and closing my eyes.

Maya's camera went crazy.

Stop it, body. Stop reacting to his touch.

"Y'all are too cute," Maya called. "Jameson, take

Elsie's hand and turn her around like you're spinning her in a dance."

There wasn't an ounce of hesitation in his body or a drop of sweat on his palm as he took hold of mine and slowly turned me around, letting Maya capture every angle. Though he claimed he was sweaty, I saw no sign of it and couldn't help but wonder if he hid his disgust behind that dimpled smile.

The spin finished and, as if hearing my swirling thoughts, Jameson pulled me against him, his hands sliding around to my back. My hands naturally went to his chest, so, *naturally,* I noticed the ridiculous amount of muscle hidden beneath his shirt. He looked down at me, his hazel eyes flickering in the shafts of sunlight peeking through the flowers, those infernal dimples making another appearance.

"Hi," he whispered. His breath smelled like mint.

I swallowed hard. "Um, hi."

Jameson chuckled. "It's just pictures. There's no reason to be nervous."

"I'm not nervous," I snapped, a little too loud.

He took it in a stride, and his smile widened.

"I see Maya was telling the truth."

I arched a brow. "What's that supposed to mean?"

His hands tightened before he cradled my head against his shoulder. I hated how good this felt. I hated that part of me wanted to stay like this. I reminded myself it was only because it had been at least four years since I was shown any type of physical affection.

That's all this was: a result of loneliness.

Right?

I glared at Maya from this new position, though all I could see was the giant camera lens covering her face. This was all her fault.

"Smile, Elsie!" Maya sing-songed, and my scowl deepened.

"Don't worry," Jameson reassured me. "She didn't say anything bad, unless you disagree with her assessment that you're a grumpy firecracker."

I snorted, pulling back far enough to look at him. "Maya has an uncanny ability of nailing personality types."

"Look longingly into her eyes!" Maya ordered Jameson, sounding far too happy.

Jameson tilted my face up with the tip of his finger under my chin. "So, you don't disagree?" he asked, before his hand moved to cup my cheek.

I froze at the touch, at the shiver it sent through me. My cheeks were probably fifty shades of red, but I couldn't move, couldn't break his stare. His thumb traced a line over my cheek.

I was vaguely aware of Maya moving closer, getting shots from different angles, but my sole attention was on Jameson and the hold he had on my body.

"No," I finally answered. "I don't disagree. I know I'm a grump."

Jameson's dimples deepened as he smirked. "Hey,

Maya," he said without breaking eye contact with me. "What's my personality?"

The click of the camera paused. "If there was a magic potion that combined the rays from the sun and the happiness women feel when they drink their first pumpkin spice latte of the season, I think you would have consumed seven of them."

I burst out laughing.

The camera resumed clicking.

Jameson chuckled along with me, his hazel eyes bright. "How very specific."

"Do you disagree?" I echoed his earlier question.

His weight shifted before he took one of my hands in his and dipped me backward, as though we were in the middle of a dance. He held me there, the sunflowers behind him framing his face.

"Not at all."

The breath fled my lungs as he pulled me up, twisting me around so that I was wrapped in his arms again.

"Isn't it...exhausting being so happy all the time?" I blurted.

His brows rose. "I think it's *more* exhausting being constantly grumpy. Life is much more enjoyable when you look for rainbows instead of storm clouds."

"Hey, that's grumpy *firecracker*," I reminded him.

Jameson laughed. "Silly me, how could I forget."

It was far too easy to get lost in his smile and hazel eyes. Far too easy to fall into him and enjoy his embrace. I needed to stop that line of thinking immediately because I shouldn't be enjoying it. This shouldn't be so easy and natural. Sometime in the last twenty minutes, the awkwardness fell away, and now it was only me and Jameson and the click of Maya's camera. His eyes kept capturing mine, and I couldn't find it in myself to look away.

At least, until my friend's voice cut through the swoony fog over my mind.

"All right," Maya declared. "Let's see you kiss."

4

Jameson

Elsie went still in my arms, her face turning redder than a beet.

"What?!" she shrieked, giving me a hard shove that caused me to stumble backward. Whatever chemistry had built between us was instantly gone. An annoying flash of hurt flickered through me, but I shoved it away. I wasn't about to be upset that she didn't want to kiss a guy she had just met.

Even if her lips were inviting, and the brief glimpse of her smile she'd given was mesmerizing. Even if she was *stunning*, with those caramel-colored eyes with the tiniest specks of jade in them, wavy dark-blonde hair, and curves in all the right places. Sure, she was a little quirky, but her awkwardness only added to her charm.

"I said no kissing, Maya," she growled.

Maya rolled her eyes. "On the cheek, Els. Calm down. Jameson," she said, looking at me, "lean in slowly, and then hold a kiss on her cheek."

Despite her request, I wasn't about to do that if it wasn't something Elsie wanted. The last thing I wanted to do was make her uncomfortable.

I took a step closer and whispered, "I don't have to do that. Say no, and we'll do something else."

Elsie swallowed hard, her eyes locked on mine. For a moment, I wished I could read her mind. What was she thinking? My fingers twitched, begging to skim across her cheek, to memorize the feel of her skin. I was quick to shove *those* thoughts away. I had only just met her, after all.

Even so, I'd never had an instant connection with someone. Did she feel it, too, or was it only me?

Finally, her eyes dropped to the ground, her shoulders loosening.

"It's okay," Elsie whispered back.

A slow smile spread across my face, warmth spreading along my limbs. It was an effort of self-control to lean forward as slowly as possible when all I wanted to know was how soft her skin would be against my lips. The heat of the day, the sweat pooling on my lower back, and any sign of her nerves faded away, my concentration solely focused on her skin mere centimeters from mine.

I closed my eyes as I pressed my lips against her cheek in a gentle caress. My fingers tightened on her waist, and I dared to pull her closer, our chests almost touching.

What was happening to me? I wasn't *that* guy.

I wasn't the love-at-first-sight guy. I wasn't the guy that instantly dove in. I tried to stay level-headed, not wanting to get too involved with someone unless I could see a future. I needed a warmup, like before a workout. But something about Elsie had me losing my inhibitions, my restraints disappearing entirely.

The click of the camera was white noise in the background as the softness of her skin brushed against my lips, and I inhaled the scent of jasmine in her hair.

Seconds ticked by and, inch by inch, she melted into me, her muscles relaxing beneath my touch. I wasn't sure how long we stayed pressed together, but it wasn't nearly long enough when the camera went silent.

"That was great! Y'all are so cute together," Maya commented. Elsie's cheeks reddened and she pulled out of my arms. She tucked her hair behind an ear, fixing her gaze on the ground.

My arms were slow to lower, my hands twitching to pull her back into my embrace, but I summoned the gentleman my mom had raised me to be and stepped back a respectful distance.

"Did you get what you need?" I asked Maya, trying to distract myself.

"And then some," she said, winking. I swallowed the strange sting in my throat.

What did that mean?

Elsie wrung her hands in front of her and dragged the toe of her sneaker through the dirt. I didn't know her well enough yet to know if she was embarrassed by how close we had been, or if she was fighting the same thoughts as me and equally confused by them.

A beeping filled the air, and Maya muttered something unintelligible. "Crap, my camera battery is almost dead. I left the spare in the car." She glanced at the sky, where the sun was quickly dropping toward the horizon. "We still have a good amount of light left, so let me run and get it. I'll be right back!"

Without waiting for a response, Maya took off through the sunflower field. An awkward silence descended between me and Elsie, and she kicked at the dirt again.

"How long have you known Maya?" I asked, shoving my hands in my pockets.

"Best friends since middle school," she replied. "What about you?"

"Maya's my cousin," I responded, chuckling when her eyes widened. "Never mentioned me, huh?"

She bit her lip and shook her head. "Not by name. She's mentioned her cousins once or twice before, but she never said you were..." Elsie trailed off, gesturing at me.

"I was what?"

Her cheeks flushed again. "Um, nothing. Forget I said that."

"Hmm, I don't know if I can forget that very vague statement."

Elsie expertly switched topics, forcing me away from whatever she wasn't saying. "I'm surprised I've never run into you before. It's not like Meridel is a big town."

The smirk slid off my face. "I live on the outskirts of town, and aside from work, I haven't left my house much over the years."

"Why's that?"

The question was innocent, but I hated the memories it brought up. "I had a lot going on." Two could play at the avoiding game.

Her caramel eyes studied me but she didn't push. "So, is that how she got you to agree to this? She pulled the family card?"

"Worse. She got my mom involved."

Elsie's laugh shimmered in the air, giving me that feeling I had during the first snowfall of the season. It's beauty made my breath catch in my throat.

Get a hold of yourself, Jameson. She's just a girl. Maya's best friend. Don't make it weird.

"That makes sense," she said after a moment. "Who in their right mind agrees to a couples photoshoot with someone they've never met?" She gestured around us before fidgeting with her hands. "She must've been desperate if she pulled your mom into her meddling."

The way she said the words made it sound less like *who would've agreed to such a thing* and more like she was asking who would agree to do such a thing with *her*.

The thought made me want to reassure her, even

though I didn't know anything about her. "It was no big deal," I said, and her eyes met mine. "I had nothing to lose. Besides, you're a natural on camera."

My compliment made her pause, cocking her head. "What if I had turned out to be a freak?"

The corner of my mouth twitched. "I see no freaks here."

"Wait a little bit longer. One is bound to show up eventually."

A quiet laugh bubbled out of me, and I took a step closer to Elsie. "I have a hunch that's not possible."

A blush tinted her cheeks. "You don't know anything about me, Jameson."

"Maybe we should change that."

The words were out of my mouth before I could stop them, but I didn't regret them, not even a little bit. I'd always been a straightforward guy, not mincing words, and often saying whatever was on my mind.

I wasn't going to lie and say that I didn't want to see Elsie again.

If it weren't for the faint rustle and Maya's characteristic muttering in the distance, telling me she was almost back, I would've asked Elsie on a date right then and there.

I felt like an eager puppy waiting for a treat, wanting to know what Elsie would say next, when Maya interrupted her.

"Got the battery!" Maya declared, pushing through the tall stalks of flowers. "There's a small hill that way, and the light is perfect," she added, pointing in the distance. "Let's head over there and get a few more pictures."

Without waiting for a response, she pushed through the sunflowers, leaving us to follow.

I glanced at Elsie. What had she been about to say? I wanted to put that smile she fought so hard to hide back on her face—to hear that laugh one more time. I internally cringed. What spell had this girl cast over me to make me lose my mind so completely?

I gestured after Maya. "Ladies first."

She ducked her head and shuffled past me, her hand brushing the dirt on her backside which I was determined not to look at. By the time we made it to the hill, the sun was almost below the horizon, casting just enough light to set the grass, the flowers, and Elsie ablaze. If I thought her eyes were stunning before, it had nothing on how they glowed now.

Maya gave me a meaningful look, nodding at her friend, which I took to mean *get moving, meathead.* Whether my cousin would have ever used the term meat-head was beside the point.

It felt like the most natural thing in the world—walking up to Elsie and wrapping my arms around her waist, tugging her into me. And her hands sliding up my chest before circling the back of my neck was equally as natural. I was vaguely aware of Maya's camera clicking again, but it was lost in the background as every brush of her fingers against my skin set me on fire. The way her breath caught every time I adjusted my hold on her told me the feeling was mutual.

"See?" I said, smiling next to her ear. We were slow dancing to music only we could hear. "You're a natural."

Elsie shook her head, her cheek brushing against mine. "You make it easy," she admitted.

I adjusted my grip on her hand and spun her in a slow circle, then pulled her against my chest. "Likewise, Elsie."

Being with Elsie was like I was drowning inside of something I couldn't drink enough of. I barely held back a snort at my own thoughts. I wasn't sure that even made sense—but then again, neither did this connection between us.

Without any prompting from Maya, Elsie slid her hands around my waist, holding my back as she rested her head against my chest. The camera shutter filled the silence, the earlier awkwardness of this shoot fading into something much more comfortable—and heated. Who knew a hug could be so sexy?

Her hands settled on my low back, causing little fires to erupt, even through the fabric of my shirt. Elsie leaned her head back to look at me, eyes flashing with an emotion I couldn't quite name. It was pure instinct to brush her hair behind her ear and cup her cheek with my palm. Somewhere during the photoshoot, her resistance to me had dissipated, her earlier hesitation of being so close to me vanished, and her toes shuffled forward, pressing our bodies together, as if she couldn't get close enough.

Is all of this in my head? I wondered. *Am I only*

seeing what I want to—what I hope for?

Maybe my loneliness was making me delusional.

Then Elsie tilted her cheek into my hand, her eyes fluttering closed.

Nope, nothing delusional about that.

The thought of kissing her entered my mind for only a split second before I shut it down. We might have had a quick spark, but even I knew that only meeting an hour ago then trying to kiss her was too fast.

I settled for a light peck on her forehead, letting the click of Maya's camera drown out my desire for more.

5

Elsie

The sun settled beneath the horizon, erasing our light, and forcing the photoshoot to end. After *three* hours, not the promised *one*, Maya's camera finally went silent, and Jameson and I reluctantly separated. Or maybe the reluctance was only on my part.

How this had made *me*, the one adamant about not dating and remaining single forever, want to stay in his arms, I had no idea.

Maya handed me a bottle of water and I chugged it eagerly, desperate for something to do with my hands. For three hours, she hadn't run out of ways to make us pose, and I was certain I'd be blushing when she showed the pictures to me. Like when I had to straddle Jameson's lap and "stare longingly into his eyes." The memory of his hands on my waist, and the way his dimple had pierced his cheek, was permanently burned into my brain.

My favorite pose, which I would deny if anyone asked, might have been jumping on Jameson's back and feeling the hard muscle beneath his skin. Normally, I would've been self-conscious about having that much physical contact with someone; knowing that he had felt the squish of fat on my legs while he held my thighs to keep me on his back, but I was too lost in the feel of his... not squish.

The guy was ripped. Did people even say *ripped* anymore?

How had Maya never mentioned that her cousin looked like *that* and probably lived a double life as an underwear model? A niggling kernel of self-doubt crept into my head. Did she keep her very attractive cousin a secret because she didn't think I was good enough for him? I didn't *think* she'd have such thoughts about me, but my mind wasn't exactly kind, implanting doubts and insecurity like it was its only job.

"Do you have everything you need, Maya? My cheeks are going to fall off my face from smiling and I'm starving," I asked.

The photoshoot had gone longer than anticipated, and the rumble of my stomach reminded me we'd posed right through dinner.

Maya was silent for another moment, looking at the screen on her camera with intense concentration. Finally, appearing pleased, she lowered it and let it dangle from the loop around her neck. "That was perfect, you guys. I couldn't have asked for better photos." She rubbed her hands together. "I can't wait to edit them. Sorry for torturing you for so long."

I scowled. "Nice of you to apologize *after* the torture."

Jameson's low chuckle had my stomach clenching in a way that had nothing to do with hunger.

"Hardy-har. Come on, let's go get some burgers. My treat as a thank you."

The blood drained from my face. Did she mean…all three of us?

"Jameson, want to meet us at Get In My Belly?"

My stomach simultaneously leaped for joy and sank to the ground. Yep, she meant all three of us. Pretending to be in love with a stranger was awkward enough. Now I'd have to sit there and try to eat *and* talk with him? That was a little too close to a date for my liking.

Jameson's face lit up at the mention of my favorite burger place in the next town over, but when he glanced at me, his lips pressed into a line. His gaze rendered me immobile, plastering my feet to the ground until he took a step back, creating more space between us, as if I had the words *get away from me* tattooed on my forehead.

"Actually, I have somewhere else I need to be. Rain check?"

Maya didn't miss a beat. "A rain check will be accepted just this once."

He chuckled, giving her a shake of his head. "Ladies,

it was a pleasure," he said, bending in a mock bow. "It was very nice to meet you, Elsie," he added, those hazel eyes piercing mine.

I could only nod, my tongue thick and heavy in my mouth.

Then Jameson was gone.

"Happy? You scared him off," Maya scolded, turning on me.

I scoffed, crossing my arms. "I did no such thing."

"Please. Your basically screamed 'don't you dare come with us.'"

With a roll of my eyes, I headed through the sunflowers toward the car. "No, I didn't. More importantly, why didn't you tell me that the man you got for the photoshoot was your *cousin*?"

Maya stilled before giving me a sheepish smile. "Oh, that came up, did it?"

"Oh, that came up, did it?" I mocked in a whiny voice. "First of all, why didn't you tell me? And second, why have you been hiding him the entire time we've known each other?"

She flinched. "I wasn't hiding him, Els. He's had a really hard few years—or ten—and I didn't want to make things more stressful for him by forcing him to socialize with my friends. Plus, you were with Ben, so I don't see how it matters."

I scowled. "Surely, it would have come up at some point in the last decade that you not only had a cousin who looked like *that*, but who lived in Meridel too."

Maya rolled her eyes, her smile strained. "Well, he lives on the outer edge of town, and the clinic he had been working at was thirty minutes away. With everything going on in his life, he wasn't in Meridel proper often. I promise I didn't hide him on purpose."

She paused, tucking her camera into her bag. "His sister, Emma, and I grew close after my mom stopped... being a mom. Jameson was the annoying big brother I never had. He barely tolerates me." I remembered hearing about Emma every once in a while, but I had never met her, either.

"Besides, the last time I tried to fix him up it...didn't go well. But you guys..." Maya trailed off, giving me a meaningful look.

"So, instead, you set *me* up with him?"

"Jameson is a great guy, Elsie. Why are your walls up before you've even had a full conversation with him?"

"I'm not talking about this." I picked up speed, beelining for my car.

"If this is about your parents—"

"Maya, stop." I screeched to a halt, swinging to face her. Any earlier happiness, contentment, or even my ravenous hunger disappeared in the wake of her words. Any faint trickles of admission that she might be right vanished at the pain and anger the memory of my parents brought up.

Maya's face softened. "Els, it's been years. I know it

was hard on you, but—"

"I said stop," I whispered, my eyes burning with unshed tears.

My best friend didn't relent. "I know you're lonely, Elsie, and you're not the type of person who is meant to be alone forever. Jameson is a good guy, and your chemistry was insane. Just give him a shot."

I shook my head, killing her words in my mind before they could take root like a bunch of weeds.

"I'm taking a rain check, too. I'll see you later," was my only reply as I made it to the other side of the field, and all but ran to my beat-up Civic.

"Elsie," she called, but I didn't stop.

"I'm going to give him your number!" she threatened.

My eyes and throat burned with tears I tried so hard to suppress, keeping my retort in my mouth.

You can cry in the car.

Right now, I didn't care if Jameson had my number. All that mattered was getting away from here, from the words Maya had said, and from the memories they dredged up.

Maya yelled something else, but my grief drowned out the words.

I shoved it deep, deep down inside, back to where it never should've surfaced from.

And by the time I got in the car, I was numb once again.

6

Jameson

"I'm only giving this to you because I love you both and want you two to be happy," Maya explained over the phone after she'd sent me an unknown number in our text thread. "Elsie's too stubborn and seemingly incapable of getting over her reservations about dating."

I squeezed the phone between my ear and shoulder as I finished putting my clothes into the washing machine.

"And you think I'm the one to make her happy?"

"I have no doubts, Jam-Jam. If you saw what I saw yesterday, you wouldn't doubt it either."

I sighed into the phone, plopping down on the couch. My dog, Luna, all seventy-five pounds of her, curled onto my lap like she thought she was a two-pound Yorkie. A vanilla-tobacco scented candle burned on the mantle, though it didn't do much against the smell of Luna. I made a mental note to give her a bath later before forcing my attention back to my cousin.

"Don't you think your friend would have an issue with you giving her phone number away to strange men?"

"I told her before she left the sunflower field that I was going to and she didn't say anything."

"So naturally you took that as a yes." I rolled my eyes so hard it made me dizzy.

Surely if Elsie had wanted me to have her phone number, she would have given it to me herself. Maya was going to make me look like a creepy stalker.

And yet, the idea of having Elsie's phone number made me...giddy.

"It wasn't a *no*."

"That logic will definitely hold up in a court of law."

A snort came through the phone. "Sometimes Elsie needs a loving push." She cleared her throat suggestively. "Much like you."

"Maya..."

"Just don't do anything stupid," she ordered.

"What do you think I'm going to do with it?" I retorted. "Prank call her?"

"You better not, or so help me, Jam-Jam."

I rolled my eyes again, both at her false threat and that incessant nickname.

"I would think my cousin would know that I'm not a heartless guy that uses women."

She exhaled, the phone crackling from the force of

it. "Yeah, I know. She's just…it's been a hard few years for her. Elsie's determined to stay single for the rest of her life, but that's terrible because she's so amazing. Someone needs to cherish her."

"And you think I'm that person?" I deadpanned.

"I don't know," she replied honestly. "But I think you both deserve the chance to find out."

A beat of silence filled the space as her words settled.

"Besides, you didn't see the chemistry between you two. It was…quite intense," she said.

I tried not to groan, digging my fingers into Luna's fur and giving her a neck scratch instead. "We were posing for the camera."

Maya laughed. "Okay, Jam-Jam. Keep telling yourself that."

It was my turn to sigh. "You do realize that I was pretending for the sake of your stupid photoshoot. Whatever you think you saw was fake. I really wish you'd stop meddling with my love life."

I pictured Maya putting her hands on her hips and scowling at me as she said, "I know what fake looks like, Jameson. That wasn't it."

"You're delusional."

"Mmhmm. Well, we'll see if you stick to that tune once you call her."

The thought of calling Elsie, of seeing her again, made my stomach squeeze. This was ridiculous. I only just met her and didn't know anything about her. Besides, she'd made it clear that she didn't want to spend unnecessary time with me. Her face had been quite obvious when Maya had suggested going to Get In My Belly.

"What makes you think I'm going to call her, Maya?"

I swear I could hear her smile through the phone. "Deny it all you want, but I saw the way you two looked at each other. I felt like I needed a cold shower after that shoot."

"Maybe you were just overheated from the sun."

She growled. "You stupid man, just call her. You can thank me later."

"I'm promising nothing," I bit out.

I must not have kept my voice neutral enough because Maya let out a maniacal laugh before crooning, "Bye Jam-Jam."

7

Elsie

A gentle breeze blew through my living room window, filling the house with my favorite smell: fall. Some people thought the smell of damp ground, falling leaves, and that distinct smell of cold air was musty and gross, but I loved it. It was a sign of the seasons turning, of endings and beginnings, and it was the best time of year. I only wished I could have been outside, enjoying the weather, rather than stuck inside working. I was spread out at my kitchen peninsula, and it had been a long day of researching and writing the strangest blog post I'd ever been hired to write—an article I titled *Flatulence as a Method of Self-Defense*.

I truly didn't know whether to laugh or be greatly disturbed.

My phone buzzed on the counter next to me, and I

was so deep in thought on how to make this article *not weird* that I didn't think twice before picking it up and shoving it between my ear and shoulder.

"Hello?"

"Is this Elsie?"

The male voice on the other end was unmistakable.

My body locked up and the phone fell from my shoulder and clattered onto the counter.

"Crap," I muttered, my fingers stiff as I struggled to grab it again.

I took a deep breath, piecing myself together, and put my ear back on the phone. "Um, yes?"

"Hey, it's Jameson. Maya gave me your number."

I pinched the bridge of my nose. Apparently, that hadn't been an empty threat. *Darn you, Maya.*

"Oh, um. Hi." I smacked my forehead. *Real eloquent, Elsie.*

"Sorry to call you out of the blue, but I wanted to ask you something." The smile was evident in his voice.

"Erm...okay?" Wow, I was really slaying this whole talking thing. I shifted on my seat so I could bang my forehead on the edge of the counter.

"I was wondering if I could take you out for coffee." He cleared his throat. "Or dessert. Whichever you prefer."

Intense dread, like the moment before sticking your hand into a vat of spiders, crawled over me.

He wanted to take me out? But...why? Sure, the photoshoot had been more fun than I had expected, and yes, there had most definitely been a spark between us, but couldn't he leave it at that? A fun memory?

Surely my awkward self, with the Niagara Falls pits and the dirt on my butt from falling right in front of him, hadn't made *that* good of an impression.

"Um, I don't think that's such a great idea." The words were automatic, void of feeling, the smart part of my brain taking over.

A beat of silence. "You don't?"

I shook my head, then smacked myself again when I remembered he couldn't see me. I was certain my forehead would have a red mark the size of Texas after this call.

"Are you dating someone?" he asked, his voice betraying his confusion. "Maya said you weren't."

"N-no," I stuttered. "I...don't date."

I expected him to give up, like any normal man sensing emotional baggage would, but he pressed further. "Then it won't be a date. It'll just be two acquaintances getting to know each other better. Over coffee. Or sweets. Whichever strikes your fancy."

"Strikes my fancy?"

He laughed. "It sounded cooler in my head."

I strangled the giggle that wanted to burst from my mouth.

"Come on, I don't bite," he prodded when I remained silent.

Would it be so bad, Elsie? You know you had a good time at the photoshoot with him. It wouldn't be the worst thing to see him again, and get to know him. Would it? At the very least, you could get free food out of it.

I wished my internal romantic, who I called Smitten Elsie, would shut up but since she wouldn't, Smart Elsie would have to do the job. "I'm sorry, Jameson. You seem like a nice guy but I can't. It was nice to hear from you, though."

And then, like the coward I was, I hung up.

"Please tell me you didn't," Maya begged through the phone. "Elsie! Why would you turn him down?"

"Maya, you know I'm not interested in dating. I can't believe you gave Jameson my number! You shouldn't have done that." My hands balled into fists in my lap as I tried not to yell into the phone on the counter.

"Oh, can it with that crap. I know you're lonely. I know you better than anyone, so trust me when I say I hand-picked the perfect guy for you. Why would you walk away from that?"

I scowled at her through the phone. "I'm not answering that when you already know why."

Maya huffed. "You are impossible. Jameson is literally your perfect match. I've done a lot of couples shoots, Els. I've never seen anything like that." She paused, and the sound of a mouse clicking filled the background.

"Here, I'm sending you a few of the pictures so you can see what I'm talking about."

My phone buzzed a second later. "Maya…"

"Just look at them before you say anything else."

I sighed before opening up our text thread. My breath caught in my throat at the first one. As much as I despised admitting it, Maya wasn't lying.

The first picture was Jameson with his hands on my waist, my own on his chest, as we stared into each other's eyes. It was a seemingly harmless pose, except for the way my body melted toward him. But what really caught my eye was the way he looked at me. It wasn't uncomfortable like looking at a stranger should have been, or even polite, simply being pleasant because Maya asked him to.

No.

Jameson's eyes crinkled in the corners, his mouth pulled into a half-smile, as if he genuinely enjoyed being there, holding me—like maybe he'd felt the spark between us that I had.

I swiped to the second photo. This time my back was to him, and his arms were wrapped around my front, nose nestled into my neck. My own expression had me pausing this time. There was a bright smile on my face, one I hadn't seen myself make in quite some time. My eyes were closed, in the middle of laughing.

I was clearly enjoying having his arms around me.

And then I got to the third photo and let out a gasp. Maya laughed through the phone.

"Aha. You see," she said smugly.

Jameson was dipping me backward under a drooping sunflower. His one hand held me tight around the waist, and he had interlaced his fingers through mine with the other. I would be lying if I said the look on his face wasn't joy personified.

I swiped the photos away, closing the thread. "Okay, fine. We have chemistry. But that's all it is, Maya."

She scoffed. "Prove me wrong then. Meet him for coffee."

"Maya—"

"It's just coffee. If you don't feel anything for him afterward, then fine. Part ways and that'll be that, but at least give him a chance."

I rubbed at my temple, a headache forming from this conversation.

Come on, what's the harm, Elsie? Smitten Elsie crooned. *He sure was handsome, and you know you loved the way his arms felt around you.*

I swallowed hard at the memory, refusing to admit that my inner romantic was right.

"I'll think about it," I sighed. "But that's all I'm committing to."

An evil giggle came through the phone. "That's my girl."

8

Jameson

I was fully aware of how ridiculous it was that Elsie's rejection made me feel like I had been kicked where the sun didn't shine, but there was no other way to describe it.

I wasn't the type of guy who became a lovesick puppy over a girl. I'd always been the cool, calm, confident kind. I wasn't afraid to talk about feelings, but I didn't go out of my way to express them, or dwell on them.

The fact that she never called or texted me after I called her, when I really hoped she would, got under my skin and itched. I found myself repeatedly checking my phone, thinking I heard the text tone, but my screen remained blank.

It was absurd because I barely knew her. We spent three hours taking cutesy photos together, and even when we did talk it wasn't a super deep conversation.

And yet, I couldn't get her out of my head. Couldn't stop thinking about her soft skin, or how she fit in my arms like a missing puzzle piece.

Sure, she was a little quirky, maybe a tad clumsy, too, but I found it...endearing.

Never mind the fact that she was stunning. Her wavy, honey-colored hair that was perfect for running my fingers through, those caramel eyes with flecks of green that I swore saw straight through me, and curves I wanted to run my hands over.

There was no denying I was attracted to her, but attraction only went so far. There needed to be a connection, a spark, chemistry, *something*. And even in that brief time of taking photos, I felt all of it. She could deny it if she wanted, but I knew she felt it, too. It was in those small smiles, the way her fingers lingered a moment too long on my skin, and how she blushed when she was in my arms.

I stared at my phone where it sat face down on my kitchen counter, resisting the urge to check it again. I finally caved a few minutes later. As usual, the screen only showed the picture of Luna wearing a pumpkin costume. My lips spread into a small smile.

I gave a little whistle and Luna, my golden retriever, bounded over to me, tongue lolling out of her mouth. Her tail wagged a happy beat as I petted her head and scratched her ears.

Was Elsie a dog person? I hoped so.

Whoa. Where did that thought come from? Slow down there, Jameson.

I sighed, turning my phone back over right as it vibrated in my hand. My heart jumped into my throat and promptly plummeted to my feet as I saw Maya's name on the screen instead of Elsie's.

MAYA

Hey Jam-Jam. Any word from our girl?

ME

OUR girl?

MAYA

;)

Elsie is amazing, but sometimes she needs a nudge for her to get over her fears so...

ME

Sigh what meddling are you going to attempt this time?

MAYA

[GIF of a sneaky smile]

We're currently getting coffee at The Roasted Bean. ;)

ME

And you're telling me this because?

MAYA

Did you know they have cold brew?

I know it's your favorite.

ME

Are you trying to bribe me into showing up there?

Shouldn't you be paying attention to your friend?

MAYA

eye roll emoji

She's working while I sit here looking pretty.

I'm trying to help you, Jam-Jam. Now's your chance to come woo her.

ME

I wasn't aware that millennials still used the term "woo"

MAYA

[unamused GIF]

Are you going to come surprise her or not?

My fingers hovered over the screen, uncertain. Though Maya had good intentions, I didn't want to be *that* guy who showed up wherever Elsie went. I didn't want her to think I was desperate, or a stalker.

MAYA

She won't think you're a stalker.

My brows rose at my cousin's ability to read my mind from miles away.

MAYA

And even if she did, she'll get over it once she gets to know you.

ME

Your confidence in this plan is astounding.

MAYA

Get your butt over to The Roasted Bean right now.

You can thank me later.

ME

Did you ever think I might be working?

Normal adults do have jobs you know.

My cousin was constantly changing jobs and working odd hours while she pushed toward making photography a career. It was easy for her to forget that most adults didn't operate that way. We couldn't do whatever we wanted at the drop of a hat.

MAYA

I happen to know that you aren't at the clinic on Wednesday afternoon.

So, get your butt over here.

Dang it. This had my mom's name all over it. She was the only one who could've told Maya my schedule. What was with the meddling women in my family?

I sighed, hanging my head, and my phone buzzed again.

MAYA

Get moving, cousin. Time's wasting.

ME

You're insufferable.

MAYA

See you soon. :)

I chuckled, placing my phone back on the counter. I ran to the bathroom, socks sliding against the hardwood floors, and quickly fixed my hair before giving my neck a quick spritz of cologne.

Did Elsie like cologne? Would she like *mine?*

I shook my head at the thought. I was being ridiculous. I wasn't trying to impress her; I only wanted to get to know her.

An idea formed in my mind. Elsie would probably

shoot me down if our last conversation was any indication, but it was worth a shot. If I didn't take the risk, there was no chance at all, and that thought had my feet moving toward the door.

Double checking that Luna had food and water, I gave her a quick belly rub before I slipped out of my house, climbed in my truck, and drove into town to find the woman that had stolen all the rational thoughts from my head.

9

Elsie

Quiet jazz music filtered through the speakers at my favorite local coffee shop. Maya sat across from me, engrossed in her phone, as I stared at my laptop trying to muster the motivation to finish that love-at-first-sight-meet-cute piece I'd been working on for a couple of weeks. No matter how hard I tried, I couldn't bring myself to put my hands to the keyboard and type up the article.

It was also hard to focus when my mind kept spinning back to the fact that I hadn't taken Maya's advice to call Jameson. Every time I thought about contacting him all I saw was a relationship that would end in disaster. We'd develop feelings for each other, maybe even fall in love, then Jameson would pull off the mask I expected from everyone, and everything would fall apart. I would be broken; maybe even worse than before. I couldn't put myself at risk like that. Not again.

If there was one thing I had learned, it was that I must keep myself safe, no matter the cost.

I slurped the remaining cold brew through my straw and begged my brain to focus. There were only a few other people in the coffee shop—a guy studying while jamming to whatever filtered through his humongous headphones, and a girl in the far corner clacking away on her tablet. The occasional ring of the bell over the door had me glancing up every few minutes.

As crafty as Maya was, I don't know why it surprised me so much when I heard a familiar voice next to me.

"Fancy meeting you here."

I closed my eyes, stomach sinking to the floor. My heart took off like it was running toward Chick-Fil-A on the first day of peppermint chip shakes.

Ugh. *That cold brew might have been a bad idea.*

Cracking an eye open, I glanced up at Jameson standing next to me and sighed.

"Jameson!" Maya crooned, and my suspicion grew. "What a pleasant surprise. Here." She paused, kicking out a chair for him. It groaned against the wood floor. "Have a seat."

I fixed my best friend with the most intense glare I could muster.

I'm going to get you for this, Maya.

"Hey, Elsie," he said to me, a half-smile curling his

lips. I was so annoyed at Maya that I was unable to wipe the scowl from my face. He chuckled, sliding into the seat across from me without waiting for a response.

Jameson was dressed in light wash jeans and a green quarter-zip pullover that hugged the muscles on his arms just right, and made his hazel eyes pop.

Stop ogling his muscles, Elsie. You need to get rid of him, Smart Elsie snapped in my head.

"What are you doing here?" I asked, unable to keep the bite from my tone.

Jameson flicked his eyes to Maya, who abruptly stood, chair squealing behind her.

She snatched her coffee up. "Well! Look at the time. I better get going."

I really should have noticed the to-go cup sooner. The Roasted Bean always put iced coffee in big mason jars unless you were taking it to go. Maya never intended on staying long.

"Bye Els! I'll see you later!" In all the time I'd known her, I had never seen my best friend run out of a building so fast.

Jameson's amused gaze flitted to me. "This was all her idea," he admitted, putting his hands up in surrender. "She told me you both were here and bribed me with coffee."

"Of course, she did," I muttered.

He glanced at the door. "However, she didn't say she would immediately leave if I came." Those hazel eyes pierced right through me. "I can go," he offered, both a statement and a question.

I *should* tell him to go. For multiple reasons. The practical side of me knew I needed to get work done, and there would absolutely be no brain-ing going on with him only a few feet away, staring at me. But besides that, I shouldn't encourage him to stay when nothing would ever happen between us. It didn't matter what kind of connection we had. I was sticking to my guns—I would not entertain the idea of dating him.

I didn't answer right away, and his sunshine personality must have taken that to mean he could stay. His lips quirked into a grin. "Can I buy you a drink?"

I pointed to my empty glass that once held a beautiful, vanilla cold brew. "Already had one."

He didn't miss a beat. "Would you like another? Or maybe a scone? A donut?"

Though he appeared calm and confident on the exterior, his rambling gave away his nerves, and I wanted to kick myself for finding it so endearing.

Instead of accepting his offer, I blurted, "Why are you here, Jameson?"

His smile slowly faded. "Like I said on the phone, I'd like to get to know you, Elsie. Even if that only means friendship."

Yeah, right. Like we could ever be just *friends.*

"And if I don't know what I want?" I didn't know where *that* question came from.

"Then I'll be here until you figure it out. If you let me."

My stomach flipped. This was madness, complete and utter foolishness. I tried to picture my mom's sobbing face, or my dad's angry sneer the night they split, or the way Ben went from sweet in public to cruel the moment we were alone. I tried to remember all the reasons why I didn't date, why I couldn't take a chance on Jameson, or anyone. But when I closed my eyes, all I saw was that ridiculous dimple. It was like a dart poking through the balloon of my reservations.

Dang you, you stupid dimple dart.

I exhaled through my nose, hating myself for even considering it. It shouldn't have been such a complicated thing. Getting to know each other as friends *should* be easy. Who didn't want more friends? But as I studied his soft smile, the way his eyes glimmered in the dim light of the coffee shop, I held back a sigh. I could see it already—there would be no *friends*.

I would fall for him. Hard.

I opened my mouth to shut him down, but instead I said, "I'll take a caramel latte with a pump of vanilla. Decaf." The last thing I needed after a giant cold brew was more caffeine, especially when Jameson already made my heart pound an irregular rhythm.

His responding smile was that of watching a child opening a box of puppies on Christmas morning.

"I'll be right back."

By the time he returned with a mug for me and a cold

brew for himself, I had barely managed to talk myself out of panicking and running for the door. When I looked at Jameson, all I saw was a big, flashing neon X. A sign that meant I should run and not look back. A sign that said I would get hurt if I kept pursuing this.

And yet, I couldn't move, couldn't leave.

Jameson's knees knocked against mine as he took a seat once again, and he smiled in apology, that dimple creasing his cheek.

Don't look at the dimple, Els. Be strong.

The mug was borderline scalding as I wrapped my fingers around it. "Thank you," I said, pulling it toward me, taking a big whiff of one of the best scents in the world: caramel coffee.

I peeked into his cup.

Of course, he drinks it black.

When I glanced back up at him, his brow was arched. "Something fascinating about my coffee?"

I gave a quick shake of my head. "Nope." He continued staring, skepticism all over his face, so I added, "It's just…of course you drink black coffee."

His mouth spread into a bemused smile. "What's wrong with black coffee?"

"How can you drink it without any sugar?" I stared longingly at my own drink. Sugar and milk with a dash of coffee was exactly how I liked it.

"It puts hair on your chest," he deadpanned.

"Is that a concern you have?"

His lips twitched. "Can't say it is."

A beat passed before I burst out laughing, and he sat back, arms crossed, clearly pleased with his ability to make me laugh. Then Jameson leaned forward again, resting his elbows on the table, expression turning serious. "So, I wanted to ask you something."

I gulped down my coffee, trying not to choke as it burned its way down my throat.

"Mmhmm," I hummed. The hot drink and my nerves were tied for first place on which was the cause of the acid swirling in my stomach.

He put his hands up, placating. "Just hear me out before you say anything, all right?"

Uh-oh. That can't be good.

"I would like to take you out on a date. Well, *three* dates, if you'll let me." His eyes went round, cutting straight to my heart like a pair of big puppy-dog eyes. "Maya didn't elaborate, but she told me you never date. I don't know why, and you don't have to tell me unless you want to, but I'd love to take you out if you'll give me a chance."

Three dates? That was worse than one. I glanced at the door out of the corner of my eye. Could I make a run for it?

I sighed through my nose. Why was I being so ridiculous about this? Going on a date with Jameson would only show him that we're no good for each other. He'd see all the things Ben had hated about me and run for the hills.

When I didn't immediately say anything, his eyes lit with something akin to hope.

"Go on three dates with me and, if there's nothing between us, if you don't want to continue, then we'll part ways, no harm done." His fingers twitched on the table as if he were resisting the urge to touch my hand.

Three dates. With Jameson.

I needed to say no. This was a terrible idea.

Maya, why did you do this to me?

I tried to open my mouth to decline, but my lips were glued together as a little, dangerous thought slithered in my head. Would it really be so bad? I knew that Maya had my best interests in mind, and wouldn't set me up with a guy who would be bad for me. And honestly, it wouldn't take much to be better than my ex.

Three dates, having some fun, and not being alone for once *might* be okay. Maybe we'd find out the chemistry between us was nothing more than that. Maybe Jameson was dreadfully boring.

The idea was growing on me, though I loathed to admit it.

Smart Elsie immediately started naming stipulations in my head, sensing my answer wasn't a definitive no.

If you do this, you have to keep your walls up, Elsie. Keep him at a distance at all times. Be like a stone—like concrete—completely unaffected by his charms.

I wanted to roll my eyes at that inner voice begging me not to do this. Next, Smitten Elsie joined the party in my mind.

Would it really be so bad, Elsie? You've been alone for so long. What's the harm in having some fun with a man for once?

Rubbing at my temple, I banished their argument from my mind, risking another glance at Jameson. It would be nice to get Maya off my back about dating, and the people pleaser in me didn't want to disappoint my best friend. *And* Smitten Elsie was right—I had been alone for so long. Though I liked to think I was better off that way, I *was* tired of being lonely.

Could I do this? Could I go on a few dates with this ridiculously attractive man and keep my heart closed off? Could I say yes but still protect myself?

Somewhere in asking myself those questions, my mouth made the decision for me.

"Okay," I conceded. "Three dates. That's it."

Jameson's face lit up like Times Square; the sheer joy in his perfect, white smile had my own lips curving up.

"When do we start?" I asked, taking another sip of my coffee.

"How about tonight?"

This time I did choke, spewing latte all over Jameson.

Jameson

"You're going to be nice, right?"

I fixed Aunt Jo with a stern look. She was over thirty years my senior, but she was such a mischievous punk that I felt more like a father reprimanding a teenager than her nephew.

She rolled her eyes, pulling her silver hair up into a bun on the top of her head. "Oh, Jamie. I'm always nice."

My responding snort was both disbelieving and unattractive.

Aunt Jo pursed her lips. "Maybe don't do that in front of the girl though."

"Thanks for *that* helpful dating advice."

"Anything for you, dear," Aunt Jo sing-songed, disappearing into the back room.

Tonight was my first date with Elsie, and I'd be lying

if I said I wasn't nervous.

Outside, my family's pumpkin patch, Beck's Pumpkins, buzzed with people. Parents and children ran around, picking pumpkins, others wandered into the shop to purchase cider and pastries, and out in the distance, the hayride rolled over the uneven ground, ushering kids over to the corn maze.

My grandparents had started the patch decades ago as an extension of their farm, not only to bring in extra income, but to offer the small town of Meridel something fun to do in the fall. There wasn't anything overtly fancy about it—it was your standard patch with cider, pumpkins, and a corn maze—but it was my family's pride and joy. Aunt Jo ran it even better than her parents had. She was the only reason it was still in business at all.

Why had I chosen this as the location of my first date with Elsie? I honestly couldn't say.

In my head, it seemed like a good idea. I hoped the familiarity would ease my nerves a little bit, and I hoped the simplicity would put Elsie more at ease. We could wander the grounds, enjoy some cider and donuts, then get lost in the maze. There wouldn't be the pressure of trying to force conversation over dinner, or attempting to stomach a full meal when we were both on edge.

I thought this would be a good compromise, but after Aunt Jo's comments and knowing her streak for being nosy, I wondered if I made a mistake inviting Elsie here.

My stomach did a little spasm as I checked my watch. It had only been a few hours since I left her at the coffee shop, but it felt like days. Knowing Elsie would be here any minute had my pulse racing, pounding in my ears. I thought about waiting out by the parking lot and greeting her there, but I had a feeling she was the type who would need a minute to settle herself once she arrived. I wanted these dates to go well so badly that I would do whatever it took to keep her happy.

"When's she getting here?" Aunt Jo said, emerging through the colorful beads hanging in the doorway that separated the store from the back room.

"Any minute."

Aunt Jo marched up to me, adjusting the collar of my flannel. "Just be yourself, Jamie. There's no way she'll be able to resist you." She winked before handing me a big bag of donuts. "Besides, no girl can say no to my apple cider donuts."

I chuckled, taking the bag. "She might be the first," I admitted with a wince.

"What makes you say that?"

"Maya made it sound like Elsie has a lot of emotional baggage, which makes her resistant to dating."

Aunt Jo pursed her lips. "Maya also talks a lot." I barely suppressed a snort this time. "Even if that's true, the girl agreed to meet you here."

"Hesitantly."

"Hesitantly is still better than a flat-out rejection.

Maybe you're the man to help her unpack that baggage and put it away for good." She patted my cheek. "You're a good man, Jameson. Give yourself some credit."

Her words soothed me like cold sweet tea on a hot day. "You think so?"

Aunt Jo's cheeks crinkled as she smiled. "If anyone can do it, it's you."

I wrapped her into a hug. "Thanks for the vote of confidence, Aunt Jo."

"You always have my vote, Jamie." When I let go, she spun me around, giving me a swat. "Now, go get your girl."

Elsie

The late fall warmth finally receded, leaving a pleasant chill behind.

Late September was the best time of year. The leaves changed from green to bright hues of red, yellow, and orange, painting the horizon in vibrant color. The air was finally cool enough to break out the cozy sweaters, but still warm enough that digging out the giant, winter puffer coat was unnecessary.

I pulled into the parking lot of Beck's Pumpkins, gliding my car into a spot on the end before banging the back of my head against the headrest with a *thunk*. I couldn't believe I was here—on a first date with Jameson. Me, the girl with the strict no dating policy.

I took a moment to breathe, trying to calm my racing pulse.

It's not a big deal, Elsie. It's just a couple hours with a very attractive man, and then it'll be over. No harm done. You can do this.

After that pathetic attempt at a pep talk, I climbed out of the car and made my way toward the long field of pumpkins, the heels of my boots sinking into the hay beneath my feet.

I refused to admit I thought a date at a pumpkin patch was romantic, even if Smitten Elsie currently swooned in my mind.

Jameson had texted me the details for our date with about one thousand exclamation points not long after I left The Roasted Bean. I wasn't sure if he was trying to get the point across that he was excited, or if he was like an old man that couldn't quite figure out how texting worked.

Kids ran back and forth through the patch, trying to pick up pumpkins nearly twice their size. There was a couple being photographed at the end of the field, and I thanked my lucky stars that Maya wasn't here to embarrass me further. I could do that enough on my own.

The sign at the entrance boasted hayrides, a corn maze, and fresh apple cider donuts—all of which I had no complaints about. My only gripe was that I was here on a date when I absolutely shouldn't be.

But still, I couldn't remember the last time I'd been to a place like this, and I was determined to *try* to enjoy it.

Despite the sun sinking toward the horizon, the

patch was chaos with people and kids milling all over the place. I glanced around, wondering where Jameson was, but I didn't see him anywhere.

"Boo," a voice said behind me, and I jumped, struggling to suppress the smile twitching at my lips. My stomach flipped, and I internally scolded myself. *None of that, Elsie. This is just a casual date and then it will be over.*

"Boo who?" I replied, turning to face him.

Be still, my heart.

He wore a white t-shirt and a red flannel that emphasized his muscles, making him look like a sexy lumberjack. Was my life turning into a Hallmark Movie?

Jameson's dimples deepened. "Don't be sad. I brought treats." He held out a bag of cinnamon sugar-coated apple donuts.

I smirked at his lame joke, taking the bag, adamantly ignoring the sensation that went up my arm as our fingers brushed. "Ah, sugary treats. The way to every girl's heart."

Tilting his head, he asked, "But is it the way to your's?"

Smitten Elsie shouted in pure glee in my mind. "It's a start."

"I'll keep trying then." Jameson nudged me with his elbow, shooting me a smirk of his own. His hazel eyes shimmered in the light of the setting sun, and I was suddenly far too warm, like I was standing next to a bonfire and not this handsome man.

"I thought we could pick out pumpkins first," he offered, pointing to where countless orange balls were nestled on the ground. "I set up a small carving station on the side of the shop."

A table *he* set up? Did the owners take kindly to random people setting up tables to carve pumpkins? That seemed like a bad idea.

It doesn't matter! Get moving, missy! Smitten Elsie was going wild.

"It's been a long time since I've carved a pumpkin," I admitted.

"That's okay. I brought a book of little designs you tape onto the pumpkin. I can show you the rest."

Out of excuses, I could only nod and follow his lead, wondering which was worse:

Agreeing to this date with Jameson...

Or having to touch pumpkin guts.

Jameson

My fingers burned from the effort it took to keep from taking Elsie's hand as we wandered through the pumpkins, trying to find the perfect one.

Thankfully, the crowd in the patch had dwindled, most of the younger kids leaving for the night, and only a few couples lingering here and there. Soon the sun would fully set, and the patch would be completely silent. It was my favorite time to be here. When the symphony of nature filled the air and the stars winked into the sky one by one. Carving pumpkins was only a ruse to pass more time until the light of day was gone. Until the night revealed the patch's true magic.

Then we could go out to the corn maze, and she would have to stick close to me to make it out of there in the dark.

I wanted her to need me, to press close and grip my arm for safety. I had been out of the dating scene for a long time, but my inner romantic wasted no time making an appearance once more.

"How about this one?" Elsie asked, kneeling to pick up a small pumpkin and tipping it over to look at the price. "It's less expensive than the others."

The way she bit her lip made me wonder if Elsie was worried about money.

I shook my head, brushing my fingers over her hands as I took the pumpkin and set it back on the ground. I smiled at her. "I think that's too small. Besides, I already took care of the cost, so don't worry about that. Pick a bigger one."

Her lips pursed as she glared at me, and it was clear she wanted to argue. Maya's term *grumpy firecracker* came to mind again. Eventually, Elsie let out a huff and grabbed the next closest pumpkin. It was only *slightly* bigger than the last one. The back was flattened, but the front would work for carving, even if it was a little small.

Wanting to wipe the scowl from her face, I said, "It's perfect," took the pumpkin from her hands, and headed toward the table.

I was particularly proud of the station I set up next to the shop. At first, Aunt Jo was hesitant because she didn't want little kids getting into the carving supplies, but I agreed to tuck the table out of sight and put a "Reserved for Private Event" sign on it to turn people away. That seemed to satisfy my aunt.

I pointed at the booklet sitting on the end. "Designs are in there. Pick whichever one speaks to you."

She arched her brow. "Not what *strikes my fancy?*"

I huffed a laugh. "Definitely sounded cooler in my head."

A rare, full smile spread across her face, so infectious I couldn't help but grin back. It slid from her face a moment later, as though she remembered she wasn't supposed to enjoy our date. Returning her attention to the booklet, Elsie flipped through several pages before she landed on a design of a snowman.

"Let's do this one."

I set the paper towel I had been using to wipe the dirt off the pumpkin down, and made quick work of sawing the stem off the top. When I saw which design she chose, I had to cover my mouth to keep from laughing. Any other person would have chosen something spooky or fall-themed, since that's what was expected when carving pumpkins. But no. Elsie, this beautiful woman, chose a snowman.

"Perfect," I said through a laugh, and her cheeks reddened further.

Elsie stared at the page, her shoulders creeping up to her ears. "I can choose something else." She started to flip through the designs again, but I put my hand on top of hers.

People could say what they wanted about characters

in movies and books feeling a shock when they touched their love interest, saying it was fake all they wanted. The fact of the matter was, when I touched Elsie, sparks absolutely ran through my fingers, up my arms, and into my heart.

"Do the snowman, Elsie. It'll be great."

A moment passed before she finally agreed, ripping the snowman out of the book and handing it to me. I taped down all four corners and gave her a permanent marker.

"Use this to put a little dot in all the holes on the stencil. It'll tell us where to carve," I explained, and she completed the task in less than a minute.

"Now we carve?"

I picked the pumpkin up, pointing to where I had cut the top off.

"Guts first, then we carve."

Her nose scrunched at the idea of pulling out the squishy innards, and it might have been the cutest thing I had ever seen.

"I'll hold it for you while you scoop out the inside." I handed her a giant spoon. "You want it to be nice and smooth, with no seeds or stringy bits."

Elsie hesitated. "Maybe you should do this part."

"Scared of slimy pumpkin guts?"

A glint flashed in her eyes, accepting my challenge.

"I'm not scared," she said, crossing her arms awkwardly with the spoon still in hand.

I held out the pumpkin in further challenge.

When she still made no move to start scraping, I set it on the table and moved behind her.

"May I?" I gestured at her hands. Elsie's throat bobbed before she gave a single nod. I wasted no time taking one hand in mine, and resting the other on her side.

"Just like this," I whispered into her ear, relishing the shiver that shuddered through her as I guided her hand through the pumpkin innards. It wasn't the most pleasant feeling in the world, and the squelching sound left a lot to be desired, but it was all drowned out by having my skin on hers, of holding her in my arms.

I wasn't sure if she leaned back into me or if I imagined it. My heart stuttered a strange rhythm as I held onto her while she scraped out the pumpkin. Thanks to its small size, it was disemboweled far too quickly, which meant it was time to let go of her. It was an act of self-control, every ounce I had within me, to release my hold on her.

"Now it's time to carve," I declared, prying my fingers away.

Her eyes were hooded as though my touch had sent her brain into a fog.

Likewise.

Showing her how to stick the sharp tool into the pumpkin, then carve out the snowman went too fast after that with no further excuses to touch her.

Elsie's concentration was so focused on slicing through the thick flesh that it left little room for conversation. Instead, we fell into comfortable silence. It was easy to be around her. I didn't have to think about it—or overthink it for that matter. It was natural, like breathing. None of the disastrous dates I had been on in the past month were like this. I had had to fight tooth and nail for any ounce of conversation, while trying to come up with a valid excuse to escape the date as soon as possible.

But not with Elsie. With her, I found myself not wanting the night to end.

The last piece of the pumpkin fell away, leaving a hole the shape of a snowman. It wasn't perfect, with lots of jagged edges and a spot where she had cut a little too far, but it was cute. It had *Elsie* written all over it, and *that* made it perfect.

"All done," she said. Her nose scrunched as she studied her work. "It's terrible," she laughed, noticing the snowman looked more like a wavy oval than anything else.

I brushed her hair over her shoulder, stepping closer. "No, it's great. Way better than most of the kids here do."

"Wow. Better than a child. What a compliment."

My body shook with laughter.

"Are we done then?" she asked, cutting my laughter with a knife, sobering me.

"Do you want to be done?" I studied her face, trying to understand her. Maybe Elsie didn't feel what I felt. Maybe there was no spark for her, though I had a hard time imagining such a thing could be possible.

Elsie didn't respond as her brown eyes flicked back

and forth between mine, likely trying to figure me out, too. Finally, she gave a slight shake of her head. The movement had her curls slipping over her shoulder, the scent of her floral shampoo lingering in the air.

The fact that Elsie admitted she didn't want our date to be over loosened tightness in my shoulders, and the donuts I ate before she arrived stopped churning in my stomach. A wide smile spread across my lips, and I nodded toward the hayride in the distance.

"Come on. The night's not over yet."

13

Elsie

As Jameson led me back through the patch toward a wagon attached to a massive tractor in the distance, a chill settled beneath my jacket in the fading sunlight. The faint scent of fried donuts lingered in the air, and my stomach rumbled quietly. I had been too nervous to eat before our date, and the few donuts Jameson had given me when I arrived hadn't been enough. The lack of food made my hands tingle and my brain was fuzzy.

My hands were slightly sticky from the slimy pumpkin innards, and I kept wiping them against my jeans, hoping it would get rid of the residue in case Jameson decided to hold my hand.

Why are you thinking about him holding your hand, Elsie? No touchy, no kissy. Don't get attached, remember?

I sighed at Smart Elsie's reminder. Clearly, I needed

to eat something so my mind would work right. I couldn't afford to have jumbled thoughts around him—err, *more* jumbled thoughts.

Jameson looked at me, one brow raising as he studied my face. "How do we feel about a hayride?" He gestured to the wagon ahead. "It'll take us to the corn maze."

The idea of getting lost in a maze with Jameson made my mouth dry up like the Sahara Desert, although Smitten Elsie whooped for joy. The conflicting emotions made me hesitate a moment too long, so Jameson cleared his throat and put more distance between us.

"Or we could get some cider first and then head toward the wagon," he offered, shoving his hands into his pockets. "I could use a drink after all that carving."

"You didn't do any of the carving," I teased, wanting to erase the sudden stiffness in his shoulders. While I didn't particularly care for the scraping guts part, having Jameson's arms guiding me while I did so was a nice distraction.

So worth it, Smitten Elsie concurred.

The carving had taken the better part of an hour, and with the sun almost below the horizon, I figured that meant our date was over. Smitten Elsie was a little too happy that Jameson seemed to be prolonging the night.

"Watching you work was exhausting," he teased in return. He smirked bringing the butterflies in my stomach back to life.

"Cider sounds great," I said, unable to keep a small

smile from my face.

Jameson's shoulders loosened a fraction, and he nodded toward the little shop. We walked in a strangely comfortable silence; it was somehow not awkward the way first date silence should have been. The red door loomed in front of us, and I fully expected him to drop the door on me—like Ben always had—but he paused, holding it open with a smile. I ignored the stutter of my heart, determined not to swoon over something so simple. I murmured a thank you and walked inside, instantly overwhelmed by the mingling scents of apple pie and cinnamon sugar.

It was a quaint store with three aisles stocked full of baked goods ranging from pumpkin and apple pies to little apple donuts and other seasonal pastries. I made a mental note to grab a carton of donuts before I left.

The shop was empty aside from a lady wearing denim overalls with her silver hair tied up in a bun. She stood at the register in the corner, a little notepad and pen in hand as she scribbled something down. There was a fridge on the right full of jugs of cider and other beverages.

Jameson's hand skimmed across my low back, sending a shiver through me. I hoped he missed it; I didn't want him to get the wrong impression, especially since I couldn't stop flinching every time we touched. It was electric—his touch.

He grabbed a cup and filled it before handing me the steaming apple goodness. Once he had filled his own, I crossed the store to pay for mine. The old lady beamed at me, her nose scrunching when I tried to hand her a few dollar bills.

She shook her head, that smile still plastered on her face. "It's on the house, my dear."

"Oh no, I can't take it for free."

Jameson's fingers touched my arm, lowering the money to my side. "Thanks Aunt Jo, we appreciate it." His hand returned to my lower back as he herded me outside.

Aunt?

I threw a confused look over my shoulder, but the lady only smiled as if I were God's gift to the Earth. I wanted to turn back, to leave the money on the counter, but Jameson's chuckle stopped me.

"She'll only be offended if you keep trying to pay her."

I arched my brow, reluctantly putting the cash back in my pocket once we were outside. "Why? She put work into that, so why wouldn't I pay her?"

"Because she's my family," he replied simply.

His dimples made a spectacular reappearance as he pointed to himself. "Jameson Beck." Then he pointed at the sign over the entrance. "As in Beck's Pumpkins. My grandparents built this place. Aunt Jo is my dad's sister, and she runs the patch now."

Oh.

Well, that explained the look she'd given me.

"Do you bring a lot of girls here, then?" The words were out of my mouth before I could filter them. I didn't want to know the answer, didn't want to know how many girls Jameson had brought here on dates—or how common that made me.

Jameson smirked, as if he knew the direction of my thoughts. "Nope, you're the first."

With his unexpected confession, my entire body flushed with heat.

Ooh! You're the first girl he's brought to the family patch! Smitten Elsie squealed, and I mentally shushed her.

He cleared his throat. "I don't date much, so you can imagine my aunt's excitement when I showed up with you."

"But why is it so exciting that you brought me? It's just a first date." I laughed uncomfortably. "It's not like we're serious or anything."

A strange emotion crossed his face, too quick for me to decipher. "You know how family is."

I nodded, holding back a wince. I knew how family was *supposed* to be, but I couldn't say mine was like that. I wasn't about to tell Jameson that, though. He didn't want or need to know about my family issues.

We continued across the field, a weighted silence falling between us. Thanks to the loss of daylight, the pumpkin patch was deserted aside from us, leaving the hayride utterly empty. Holding out his hand, Jameson helped me climb the steps into the wagon before following and sitting next to me.

His thigh brushed against mine, and heat shot up my leg. I didn't know why my body reacted so strongly to a simple, accidental touch, but there was no way I'd be able to keep a clear mind if it continued. Needing more distance between us, I scooted a few inches away.

The bored teenager driving the tractor barely looked away from his phone as he shifted into gear, and we jerked forward.

"I can't remember the last time I went to a pumpkin patch," I admitted, avoiding his gaze, which seared a hole in my face.

He clasped his hands together between his legs, resting his elbows on his knees. "I've been coming here my whole life. As a kid, my mom made me work here whenever I wasn't in school."

"Sounds like a fun way to pass the time."

The teenage boy whistled an off-key tune as the wagon bumped over uneven ground, and the last of my cider sloshed inside the cup. It was a struggle to keep from leaning into Jameson's side to stay steady.

He chuckled. "Maybe now, when I can appreciate it all. As a kid, I absolutely hated it." Jameson sobered after a moment. "Though it's been a while since I've been back." His eyes roved over the countless vines and pumpkins on either side of the hayride.

"How come?" I leaned closer, hanging on every word.

Jameson shrugged, not meeting my eyes. "Life's been...busy. Not much time to visit."

I nodded, letting the conversation drop. I knew avoidance when I saw it. I was the Queen of Avoidance. If avoidance had a town, I'd be the mayor.

If he didn't want to share, I wouldn't push or pry, even if my curiosity spurred me to ask what he meant.

Curiosity killed the cat, Elsie.

I shifted on the hay bale, my backside going numb despite the hard pieces of straw poking through my jeans. The wagon bumped along, the corn maze looming ahead in the dark. I exhaled a shaky breath, and Jameson turned to me.

"Whoa!" the wagon driver shouted as the tractor dipped into a deep hole.

The wagon slid to the side, and I jolted forward off the seat, my hands smacking onto the rough wood floor before warm hands circled my waist, pulling me backward. I stiffened as I landed on something much softer than the hay bale. It took a second for my brain to catch up with the fact that I was now perched in Jameson's lap, his hands grasping my waist.

His eyes twinkled. Yes, twinkled. *Dang him.*

"You all right?"

His face was inches from mine, but I refused to look at his lips. *No Elsie, don't you dare.*

"Um, yep. Great," I squeaked, sliding off his lap, my tailbone protesting as I slammed onto the hard hay.

Phantom versions of his hands remained on my sides, burning through my layers.

"How are your hands? The floor is pretty rough."

I looked at my palms, struggling to see in the dim light of dusk. They were red from the force of the impact, but thankfully, I had been spared from any slivers making a home in my skin.

"They made it out unscathed," I replied.

Jameson ran his fingers over my palms, checking for himself. I was so engrossed in his skin on mine that I missed how close we had become. The woodsy scent of whatever cologne he wore permeated my senses, making me lightheaded in the best way.

He's going to have to stop wearing that cologne or you'll never make it out of this alive, Smart Elsie chided.

Jameson's hazel eyes met mine, and I didn't miss the way they flicked to my lips for the briefest moment. Scared of what would happen to my ability to remain unattached if he tried to kiss me, I jumped to my feet.

"Shall we?"

Jameson huffed a laugh before climbing off the wagon. He helped me down, and I fervently ignored the electricity that shot through my hand, my legs wobbling as my boots sunk into the soft ground.

Whether he thought I was clumsy or amusing, I couldn't tell, nor did he say. He only gave me a lazy smile, like he knew what that simple touch had done to my brain.

Jameson gestured at the corn maze behind me. "After you."

I gave a tight-lipped smile that I hoped didn't betray my nerves before stalking toward the entrance in a way that was very unbecoming on a first date, much like a linebacker on a football team, thanks to sitting on the unyielding hay.

Welp. Here we go. Time to get lost in a maze with a man I will not fall for.

14

Elsie

The top of the corn stalks loomed over my head, and if it weren't for the light of the moon I wouldn't have been able to see my hand in front of my face. Jameson kept his distance, though I could feel his amusement as he watched me walk back and forth, trying to determine which way to go. It had only been a few minutes, but the entrance was long gone, and I was hopelessly lost. Me and directions did not mix.

And then a thought hit me.

"Wait," I blurted, coming to a stop. "If your family owns this place, does that mean you know the way out of the maze?"

He arched a brow, smirking. "That would be cheating."

I crossed my arms. "Should I take that as a yes?"

Jameson ran a hand through his dark hair, chuckling.

"Unfortunately, I do not. My aunt is determined to make each year of the maze unique. It's never had the same layout twice." He paused, studying the stalks around us. "Besides, even if I did, it's too cute watching you try to figure out where to go."

Heat bloomed over my cheeks.

He called me cute.

I shook my head, not allowing his words to sprout roots. It didn't matter if Jameson thought I was cute. Not when this was going to end after three dates. I only agreed to this to get Maya off my back and abate my loneliness for a while.

I swallowed, putting my hands on my hips. "Yes, well, I'm directionally challenged, so unless you want to live in this maze for the rest of your life, you should probably take over."

Challenge flashed in his eyes. "You trust me to get you out of here?"

I quelled the butterflies trying to take flight in my stomach. "*Trust* is probably not the right word."

Jameson took a step toward me. "Then what is?" Another step. His warm breath pooled in the air between us.

"S-self-preservation." I stumbled over the word, desperate to keep him from getting closer—not because I didn't like it, but because I *did*. My palms were clammy and my heart was dancing a strange rhythm in my chest.

Jameson threw back his head and laughed. It was low and sexy and had my insides constricting.

"That's fair," he mused, taking a step down the path to the left, nodding his head for me to follow. The scent of dried corn stalks, like decaying grass, was everywhere, and hay crunched beneath my boots. I *tried* to focus on those things rather than the jolt that went through me each time his hand bumped into mine.

Several minutes passed as he led me through the maze. Or, at least, I assumed he was leading me through. For all I knew, he was as lost as I was.

The moon hung in the sky, taunting me as Jameson walked down shadowy paths that challenged my ability to see in the dark. So, of course, my foot snagged on a stalk that had fallen over. With a cry, I flew forward, squeezing my eyes shut and bracing for impact. It took a moment for my brain to register warm arms cradling me instead of the cold ground.

My eyes flew open, and I gasped when I found Jameson's face inches from my own. He had somehow managed to not only catch me but twisted us in a way so he landed on the ground instead of me.

And that put me right on top of him.

It had been a softer landing, but not by much. Jameson was a bed of warm, hard muscle. His hazel eyes glowed in the moonlight, flickering with amusement.

"You're a little clumsy," he whispered, his breath tickling my nose.

I swallowed hard. "Clumsy is my middle name."

"That's okay." He brushed my hair behind my ear.

"Gives me more excuses to be near you." His fingers trailed a line of fire across my cheek.

He's going to kiss you, Elsie. Move. Get up. Something!

The voice in my head was loud, but the desire flaring in me was louder.

I couldn't move—didn't *want* to—as calloused fingers skimmed the back of my neck, pulling me closer, his breath hot on my lips.

"There you are," a voice called, shattering the moment like glass.

Like a teenager caught making out with a boy, I flung myself off of him. My face burned like I had just face-planted into an oven. Jameson's exhale was full of frustration, and he slowly pulled himself off the hay-covered ground.

Aunt Jo stood a few feet away, hands on her hips, eyes darting between us with a smug smile on her face.

"We were, um, trying to get out of the maze," I stammered, unable to look at her.

Aunt Jo pointed a long finger behind us. "Exit is right there."

I glanced over my shoulder. Sure enough, the maze exit was a few feet away. How had I missed that?

You were too busy almost kissing the man, that's how!

"Did you need something?" Jameson asked, rubbing at his neck. He seemed less flustered by being caught almost kissing and more...annoyed.

"I did," she smirked. "But it can wait until this is done." Her hand flopped between us.

Jameson looked at me, and I squirmed beneath his gaze. Finally, he sighed and answered, "Let me walk Elsie to her car, and then I'll meet you at the shop."

To say my stomach sank was an understatement, the sensation so irritating that I wished I could kick myself in the butt. Why was I reacting this way? I shouldn't want to stay; I shouldn't want to continue whatever almost happened between us. My mind was at war with itself, both wanting to stay with him and wanting to distance myself as much as possible.

"Oh, pish posh," his aunt said, waving her hand again. "She can help move the crates of apples into the fridge, too." Without a backward glance, Aunt Jo exited the maze.

Jameson tunneled his fingers through his hair. "I'm sorry. You really don't have to help. I'll walk you to your car."

I considered leaving for a moment, and Smart Elsie and Smitten Elsie had a little angel versus devil argument on my shoulders.

Come on, Elsie, go help his sweet aunt, and spend more time with the hunk!

Oh, quiet you! She doesn't need to get any more confused about all this. She needs to limit her time with Jameson. Or have you forgotten what we've gone through?

Smitten Elsie would not be deterred. *Oh, there's no reason why Elsie can't do a little hugging and kissing with him.*

Smart Elsie facepalmed.

Shoving their unhelpful voices away, I looked at Aunt Jo across the pumpkin patch. While it would have been smart to quit before something serious happened, his aunt *had* invited me to help, and I didn't want to disappoint her.

Hello, people-pleaser. Smart Elsie crooned.

Hush, you. Just let her enjoy the rest of her time with the hunk.

Wow, I need to see a therapist, I thought to myself.

Jameson's eyes locked on me, likely studying every ridiculous expression crossing my face as Smart and Smitten Elsie battled in my mind. The deep hazel was mesmerizing, and my foot stepped forward of its own accord, bringing me closer to him.

The corners of his lips twitched as he glanced at my feet then back at my face.

"I'd like to help," I finally said, kicking Smart Elsie away for a moment.

His face lit up with surprise, followed by a sly smile. "Aunt Jo is relentless. Are you sure you want to put your-self through that?"

Smart Elsie would have said no, and walked away right then. Smart Elsie would have nipped these dates in the bud and never seen Jameson again. Smart Elsie would have protected her heart at all costs.

But Smart Elsie was currently smothered by Smitten Elsie.

So I gave a small smile and nodded. "Let's go help your aunt."

15

Jameson

I couldn't get Elsie's face out of my mind—the one that told me she wanted to kiss me as much as I wanted to kiss her. If it weren't for the fact that she was clumsy, giving me a reason to be close enough in the first place, I never would have tried. Not on a first date. But when she started to fall, my body simply reacted. And when she was *right there* on top of me, her face inches from mine, all I could think of was pressing my lips to hers.

Until Aunt Jo interrupted and ruined the moment.

Resisting the crackling lightning between us that beckoned me closer, I led her across the patch, praying she wouldn't change her mind and make a beeline for her car. By the time we got there, a closed sign swung in the window of the empty shop, and the parking lot was vacant aside from my truck and Elsie's little black Civic.

The metal knob was ice cold as I opened the door, the bell tinkling overhead before we were suffocated by the sweet scent of cider and donuts.

"Back here!" my aunt yelled.

We followed her voice, squeezing through the narrow aisles, which forced Elsie and me closer together, our shoulders bumping into each other. A pink tint colored her cheeks, and it was so cute that it might have become my new favorite color.

"Don't be shy," Aunt Jo said, emerging from the doorway of the walk-in refrigerator along the back wall. "Grab a crate from the shelves and get moving!" Despite her age, she bounced on her feet as she carried heavy wooden crates of apples into the fridge.

A throbbing started at my temples, and I rubbed at them to ease the ache. I wasn't embarrassed by my aunt—not at all—but I didn't want Elsie to be scared away, especially by Aunt Jo's overzealousness. I waved at the shelf where a dozen wooden boxes waited to go into their overnight resting place.

"Some places don't refrigerate their apples overnight as it's not necessary, but you'll never convince Aunt Jo of that," I explained when Elsie turned her confused eyes on me. "You don't have to lift these heavy crates," I added, moving to pick one up. "I'll just be a minute and then we can leave."

With a raised brow, completely ignoring me, she walked to the closest shelf and put her arms around a crate, as if to prove she was stronger than she looked. However, the moment she tried to lift it, the apples shifted and it toppled to the side. I jolted forward, putting my hands over hers to hold it steady. Heat shot straight up my arms and spread through my chest. Her skin on mine was like sticking my finger in an outlet—electric and shocking—except instead of painful, it was exhilarating.

"You okay?" I asked, losing myself in the jade flecks in her eyes.

A small squeak came out of her, and I choked back a laugh. She cleared her throat. "Mmhmm. Fine. Heavier than I thought."

"Can I help you?" I asked, not wanting to make her feel small by taking the crate away from her. If she wanted my help, I would give it, but I wouldn't force it upon her.

"I'm not weak," she whispered.

"I would never dare to think so."

Small puffs of air escaped her mouth, and she glanced at my lips. I was vaguely aware of Aunt Jo humming somewhere in the shop, but my focus narrowed on Elsie and me, inches apart, her floral scent making me dizzy. I leaned toward her, her soft lips beckoning me forward.

"I'm glad you're here, deary," Aunt Jo declared to Elsie as she came around the corner. Elsie took a giant step back, relinquishing the crate into my hands. A groan worked its way up my throat at yet another interruption, but I swallowed it down. "I haven't seen my nephew smile like that in ages."

"Aunt Jo," I sighed, face growing hot. It wasn't a lie, but she didn't have to say it out loud.

Elsie bit her lip, holding back a smile. I forced myself to put one foot in front of the other, walking the crate into the fridge before coming back for the others. Their low voices filled the shop, but I couldn't quite hear which embarrassing stories my aunt was telling Elsie. Probably about the time I had pooped my pants on a Ferris wheel as a kid.

To my horror, when I came back around the shelf, Aunt Jo was saying, "You take care of him, dear. He's had a rough time with—"

"Aunt Jo," I interrupted, crossing my arms. I didn't need her sharing anything about how hard the past decade had been. I didn't need her scaring Elsie away before I had the chance to get to know her. "Stop interrogating the poor woman."

She waved a hand and retorted, "What kind of an aunt do you think I am?"

"The meddling kind."

Exaggerated outrage twisted her brows low over her eyes, but I spoke before she could utter a word.

"Apples are in the fridge. I'm going to walk Elsie to her car before you start pulling out my baby pictures," I said, my hand hovering over Elsie's lower back.

Aunt Jo studied me through narrowed eyes before sighing. "Fine. It was a pleasure to meet you, Elsie, dear. I do hope to see you again soon."

Elsie gave my aunt a sweet smile and nodded before heading toward the door. "It was a pleasure to meet you too, Aunt Jo."

Elsie calling her *aunt*, even if everyone called her that, made my heart squeeze in my chest. A smug smile lit Aunt Jo's face as she met my gaze briefly before disappearing once more into the back room.

I blew out a breath. "Shall we?" My fingers skimmed her low back, and she shivered.

"Sorry for my aunt," I apologized as soon as the door shut behind us. "She's a little temperamental sometimes."

"She's sweet," Elsie replied, pressing her lips into a firm line.

The stars were bright overhead as we walked to the parking lot, the brisk night air biting through my flannel.

I needed to say goodbye and let her drive away, but my shoes were glued to the ground. All I could do was stand there, staring into those caramel-colored eyes as we stopped next to her car. That strange pull lingered between us, like two magnets being drawn together, and I dared a step closer. Elsie fidgeted with her keys as she leaned against the door.

"Thank you for coming tonight," I said, voice quiet as I took another step. "And thank you for being so kind to my crazy aunt."

"I meant what I said, Jameson. She's a sweetheart."

My body went still at the sound of my name on her lips, and a smile spread across my face. I dared another step closer.

"I had fun tonight," I said, my voice dropping lower. I lifted a hand out of my pocket and lightly gripped one of hers, my thumb tracing a line across her skin as I added, "With you."

Her eyes moved from where our fingers touched, up my chest until they landed on my face. A breath shuddered out of her as she nodded, and I didn't miss the way she licked her lips. If I closed the distance between us, would she let me kiss her? Would she kiss me back, or would she shove me away and leave? I wished I could read her better, wished I knew her reasons for why she was so against dating.

Rocks shifted and crunched beneath my feet as I closed the last bit of space, and when she didn't pull back, I took that as an invitation.

My lips *barely* skimmed hers when Aunt Jo yelled across the field.

"Jameson, I need your help with this blasted register!"

Elsie sucked in a breath, pulling back, the connection broken.

Dang it, Aunt Jo. Your timing could not be worse.

Elsie's eyes shimmered in the moonlight, and that beautiful pink color had returned to her cheeks. I forced my feet backward, my movements awkward and stiff, like a toy soldier.

"I'll see you soon?"

Elsie nodded. Taking one last risk, I placed a lingering

kiss on her cheek, like I had during the photoshoot. Her breath released in a shaky exhale. For all her attempts to make me think she wasn't interested, to keep me at a distance, her body sure said otherwise.

"Drive safe, Elsie," I murmured against her skin.

"Goodnight, Jameson."

It took all of my self-control to turn and jog to the shop, when all I wanted was to stay by Elsie's side and finish what I imagined would wreck me for all future kisses.

When I got inside, my aunt was leaning against the counter, a wry smile twisting her lips.

"Well, now. I think I need a cold shower after watching the two of you dance around each other all night."

I huffed a laugh, scratching at the back of my head. "First of all, gross. Second, you're delusional, Aunt Jo."

"Anybody in their right mind would have felt the pull between you two."

"And yet, you interrupted us multiple times."

"Yearning makes the heart grow fonder," she retorted, crossing her arms.

"I don't think that's how the saying goes."

"Eh. It's close enough."

"Be that as it may, Aunt Jo, Elsie has some serious reservations about dating me, and I didn't want anything to put more distance between us." I blew out a breath, staring at the ceiling. "I really like this girl."

She straightened. "You do?"

I winced, nodding. It wasn't a bad thing that I liked

Elsie. It *was* a bad thing, however, that she had so many walls up. That I might not get a chance to tunnel beneath them to uncover the real Elsie, and that she might push me away before things could go anywhere.

Aunt Jo studied me for a second. "I don't remember the last time I saw you this smitten, Jamie. Heaven knows that girl is clearly smitten with *you*."

My stomach did a weird somersault. "What?"

Her grin stretched further. "I think it's safe to say that girl likes you as much as you like her. Though, she sure made a valiant effort in trying to hide it." Aunt Jo's smile defied physical boundaries as it stretched even wider. "She's a keeper, Jamie. I can already tell."

Could she be right? Did Elsie like me too? Maya had said Elsie didn't date, and Elsie herself had been very adamant about that fact. But *not wanting to date* and *developing feelings* were two separate things. That would explain why she hadn't pulled away the few times I tried to kiss her.

Aunt Jo cleared her throat, breaking me out of my thoughts. "Anyway. I can't get this register door open. I need you to work your magic on it."

"And by magic you mean pushing the right buttons?"

She nodded. "Yes. Exactly. Magic."

I chuckled. Though Aunt Jo ran Beck's Pumpkins, her age and her resistance to learning the latest technology always gave her issues when it came to upgrading things, like the register. I stepped up and hit the two buttons—

yes, just two—and the door dinged and slid open.

"Ah ha! Magic." Aunt Jo clapped. "Now, get out of here and get some rest. Be sure to text Elsie something sweet before you go to bed!"

I laughed. "I know how to talk to a woman, Aunt Jo. But thanks for the tip."

The amusement slid from her face, and she looked me dead in the eye. "Don't let that one get away, Jamie." She pointed a finger in my face. "She's something special."

"Don't worry, Aunt Jo, I don't plan to."

16

Elsie

Numb everywhere but where his hot lips had touched my cheek, I climbed in my car, turned the key in the ignition and banged the back of my head against the headrest. That light brush of his lips couldn't even be considered a kiss, but my insides were melting like an ice cream cone on a hot summer day.

Oh boy. You're in trouble.

This was not good. I couldn't afford to feel like this from an almost kiss. I shouldn't feel this way *at all.* Jameson was smooth, I'd give him that, and there was definitely a connection between us, but how long would it last?

My old Civic groaned as I shifted into gear, and pulled away from Beck's Pumpkins, two words repeating in my mind.

Well, crap.

I drove in a daze, making it home through sheer muscle memory. I hated driving at night, but I didn't even notice the blinding oncoming headlights, or how the twists and turns of the road were barely visible in the dark without streetlights to illuminate the way.

By the time I pulled into my driveway, any lingering warmth from Jameson had faded into the crisp night, and a shiver wracked my body as I struggled to pull myself out of the car. For a moment I just stared at my house. It was a cute little two-bedroom bungalow that I saved for three years to buy. It needed some TLC, but it was mine, and it was home.

But, as much as I loved it, I couldn't help but feel the weight of the darkness, the emptiness, as I unlocked the front door and went inside. My stomach curled in on itself as I flicked the light on to reveal the small living room, void of anyone but my cat, Rhys, who gave me a hearty meow, then went back to sleep on the cat tree.

I sighed, hanging my purse on a hook by the door.

Maya was right.

I *was* lonely.

As much as I knew protecting myself and staying single was worth it, that knowledge did nothing to soothe the ache in my heart at being alone each night, or waking up to a chilly home and facing another day by myself. Sure, I had the house and a big bed all to myself, but if I was honest with myself, I'd take the reassurance of another person in the same space, of knowing I could wake up to someone next to me.

I flicked another lamp on, heading into the kitchen to get some water. For a moment, I pictured Jameson sitting on my couch, his smile lighting up the room and my heart. I slammed the cupboard closed, banishing that mental image. I couldn't let myself go down that road. Chugging down some water, I studied my little house once more, careful not to imagine a certain man again.

It was cute, a cozy little place, perfect for me.

Maybe, if I said the words enough I would convince myself.

I rubbed at my stupid heart, wishing the ache would stop. It hadn't gotten the message that this was for the best. Being alone might hurt now, but it was nothing compared to what it would feel like if I allowed myself to fall in love only to lose it, or to find out Jameson wasn't who I thought he was.

Kicking my boots off, I plopped down on the couch right as my phone buzzed. My heart gave an annoying flutter when Jameson's name flashed across the screen.

JAMESON

Did you make it home?

Be cool, Elsie. Give a simple answer and be done with it. Smart Elsie had finally overtaken Smitten Elsie, and wasted no time in making sure I smothered anything

I felt over his text. My fingers hovered over the screen, and it took forever to formulate a simple response.

ME

I did, thanks for checking.

The three dots appeared on the screen before another message came through.

JAMESON

I hope my aunt didn't scare you too much. I really did have a great time tonight.

He had a good time with *me*? Me, the clumsy, awkward person who couldn't even walk through a corn maze without tripping, or sit on a hayride without taking an ungraceful tumble?

Back when Ben and I had dated, he never said such things. In fact, he always made it seem like spending time with me was a chore.

But Jameson…enjoyed it?

ME

Nothing I couldn't handle. *muscle emoji*

Crap. Was that too flirty?

JAMESON

Good :) I'm looking forward to our next date.

My breath caught in my throat. Somehow, I had

already forgotten I still had to go on two more dates with him. And based on the slight fluttering in my stomach over a simple text conversation, I'd really have to work to keep my walls up.

I would not, could not, let myself fall for Jameson Beck.

I typed a quick reply.

ME

When might that be?

JAMESON

Soon :)

ME

That's not very helpful :)

Crap. Why did I send that smiley? That was definitely *flirty.*

JAMESON

Aunt Jo always says to keep 'em guessing. :)

ME

Well, you hit the nail on the head.

JAMESON

It'll be soon, I promise. I'm excited to see you again.

Ooooh. He likes you, Smitten Elsie crooned in my head. Smart Elsie scoffed.

Yes, the thought that I was legitimately nuts crossed

my mind. But *everyone's* heart and mind battled against each other, didn't they? The only difference was I had given them names.

How did I even respond to his text? I didn't feel like I could say "me too" since I was still figuring out what the heck I felt to begin with, but I also didn't want to encourage him. Despite agreeing to the three dates, there would be no future for us.

I had to convince myself as much as I had to convince him.

So, instead of writing something nice back to him, I effectively ended the conversation.

ME

Heading to bed. Night!

And like the gem he was proving to be, he didn't miss a beat and replied:

JAMESON

Sweet dreams, Elsie.

I quickly silenced the pitter patter of my heart, ran into my bedroom, crawled beneath the blankets, and waited for sleep to find me.

17

Elsie

"**S**o, how did it go with the hunk?" Maya asked the next day over lunch at Chick-Fil-A, the best restaurant on planet Earth. The day this glorious chicken place opened in the town ten minutes east of Meridel would be forever marked as one of my favorites.

The restaurant was bursting at the seams, with a long line nearly out the door, kids running and screaming in the play area, while we gorged ourselves on chicken sandwiches and waffle fries. Though it was crowded and noisy, I didn't pay any attention. It was only me and Maya at our little table in the world of Yum.

Yep, my own personal Chick-Fil-A world was called Yum. I wasn't ashamed.

"*Hunk*? Really, Maya?" I said around a mouthful of fries.

She shrugged, the smile remaining on her face. "What? He is. You can't deny it."

I rolled my eyes. "Gross. He's your cousin, Maya."

Maya laughed. "I'm not saying he's a hunk to *me*, weirdo. But I know someone like *you* would appreciate how attractive he is."

"Well, Mr. Hunk has a name."

"Oooh, defensive. It must have gone well then."

"It was fine," I mumbled through a bite of my spicy chicken sandwich.

"Just fine?" A piece of waffle fry flew from her mouth. "Ew."

Maya waved it off with a laugh. "You have to give me more than that."

I shrugged. "He took me to the family pumpkin patch."

Maya gasped, her eyes bulging. "He brought you to Beck's Pumpkins? Was Aunt Jo there?"

My face must have said it all because she burst out laughing. "She can be a bit much, can't she?"

I cringed. "She was sweet."

"If you think a wolf in sheep's clothing is sweet. Though, she really helped Jameson when his dad died. She'd do anything for him." Then she put her hand to her heart. "He brought you to a place that's important to him. How romantic." She took another bite. "Did he kiss you?"

The question made me suck in a breath, and a piece

of chicken lodged itself into my throat, sealing off my airway. I wheezed and coughed, but it wouldn't move.

"Whoa, you okay?"

I couldn't stop coughing, couldn't get air into my lungs.

You know that saying *my life flashed before my eyes*? Yeah, no. It didn't. The only thing flashing before me was Jameson's face, though I couldn't tell if it was real or a figment of my air-starved brain.

My head grew dizzy from the lack of oxygen, and I barely noticed someone's arms winding around me, shoving their fist into my abdomen until the piece of chicken launched itself from my throat and across the table, bonking Maya on her forehead. She squealed, but all my attention went to the warm hand sliding across my back, patting a few times. A low voice spoke in my ears.

"Breathe in through your nose, relax your muscles. Breathe." My body responded automatically, and precious air streamed into my lungs. Tears streamed down my cheeks. "Breathe," the voice repeated, and my coughing finally slowed.

I avoided looking around at all the people whose gazes pierced into me like little needles, and kept my eyes squeezed shut as the room, ever so slowly, returned to a normal volume.

"Better?" the voice said, and it was only then that I realized I recognized it—recognized the warmth of the hand resting between my shoulder blades.

I turned to my savior with watery eyes. "Jameson?" I croaked.

So maybe my brain *hadn't* imagined him appearing while I was trying not to die.

"Hey, Elsie." He smiled. "Are you all right?"

I managed a nod, hoarsely saying, "Other than the almost death by spicy chicken sandwich, and the mortifying fact that you witnessed it, I'm just great."

Jameson let out a low chuckle that had my insides curling tighter before he slid into the booth next to me. "Who would've saved you if I wasn't here?"

I spared a glance at Maya, who watched us through wide eyes with her chin propped on a hand, hanging on every word. When she noticed me looking, she grabbed her purse and tray with inhuman speed and yelled, "Well, look at the time!" She flaunted a watchless wrist. "I'm glad you're not dead from that sandwich, Els. I have to go now. Hi Jam-Jam! Bye Jam-Jam!"

Jam-Jam?

"Talk to you later!"

"What?" I whisper-yelled, watching her scramble out of the booth. "You're leaving *again*?"

You and your ridiculous meddling, Maya.

"Byeeee!"

Then she was gone, leaving me alone with the man I had almost kissed the night before. The man who saved me from a killer chicken sandwich.

And he was sitting *very* close to me.

"W-what are you doing here?" I asked, trying to nonchalantly scoot further away.

"Same as you," he chuckled. "Getting lunch."

"But why here?" I narrowed my eyes. "Did you know I'd be here?"

Jameson lifted his arms in surrender. "My work isn't far from here. Besides, this is the best place to eat. I swear I did not know you'd be here, nor did Maya tell me, but I would have *definitely* come sooner had I known."

I fervently tried to ignore the flip flop of my stomach as I avoided his gaze and stared at my half-eaten food.

"Do you want me to leave?" Jameson asked, his fingers twiddling on the table.

Did I? Did I want this guy, who made me both squirm and melt, to leave? Who saved me from evil chicken sandwiches and helped me escape corn mazes? A guy who apparently shared my love for Chick-Fil-A?

I *should*. To protect my heart, that would be the smart thing. But the thought of finishing my lunch alone was almost too much to bear. Nothing could ever happen between me and Jameson, but there was nothing saying we couldn't be friends and spend time together. Right?

"No, you can stay," I finally said, hoping I didn't regret that decision.

The light of his answering smile gave the sun a run for its money.

With a nod toward the registers, he said, "I'll be right back."

Several minutes later, after struggling to finish my lunch, Jameson returned with a tray full of food—way more than one person should be able to eat. There were two containers of chicken nuggets, two large fries, and even a side of mac and cheese. And to top it off, every sauce available was neatly stacked on the side.

"I know you already ate, but I bought extra in case you were still hungry."

And then he plopped a large cookies n' cream shake in front of me.

"You seem like a cookies girl."

Though I'd never admit it out loud, I was swooning *hard*.

"Thanks," I said, wrapping my hands around the cup and suppressing a grin. "It's actually my favorite."

Jameson smiled, pleased with himself for guessing correctly. He dug into his chicken nuggets, dunking them into every single sauce, while I slurped away, daring to grab a waffle fry and dip it into my shake.

His brow arched as he watched me dip another one.

"Listen, I know it's weird, okay? But it's the perfect combination of salty and sweet, and it's sheer bliss in your mouth. Don't knock it 'til you try it." Without thinking, I reached across the table and shoved the shake-laden fry into his mouth. He didn't fight it, and it wasn't until his soft lips closed around my fingers that I realized what I had done.

I just hand-fed Jameson.

His warm lips grazed my fingers, sending a jolt through me that lit up my insides. My cheeks burned, and I couldn't meet his gaze as I yanked my hand away, covering it, and holding it beneath the table.

"Okay," he said after swallowing, completely oblivious to my internal freakout. "I see the appeal."

It took a second for my tongue to unglue itself from the roof of my mouth so I could squeak, "See? Not everything that sounds weird is *actually* weird."

Jameson laughed, his hazel eyes bright. "Touché."

Had they cranked up the heat in Chick-Fil-A or had my clothes caught on fire? Either way, I was overheating from the look Jameson gave me. I took another sip of my shake, trying to cool myself down. He continued munching away at his food. In that moment, I realized I liked that we were comfortable enough to let silence reign rather than pushing to keep talking.

That was one thing my ex always hated—silence. When we were together, I felt constantly compelled to keep conversation flowing. When I inevitably failed, he'd pop in an ear bud and turn on some sports show or finance podcast, saying it was my fault that I wasn't keeping him entertained.

"This doesn't count as a date, by the way," Jameson explained after he had demolished his chicken nuggets.

It was my turn to arch my brow. "Then what do you call it?"

Jameson gave a coy smile. "When I take you on a

date, you'll know it's a date. This is just…a spontaneous lunch. Unplanned."

My stomach tightened at the implication of his words. "So, you're saying I still have to go on two more dates with you in addition to this Chick-Fil-A demolishing session?"

"Is that really so bad?"

It very well could be.

I shook my head. "Just remember, I only agreed to three. Nothing more."

Jameson sobered, setting down the fry that had been halfway to his mouth. "That might be what you agreed to, but we'll see if you still feel that way by the end."

My toes curled in my boots at his confidence.

"Yes, we will," I murmured before slurping down the last of the shake. Desperate for a subject change, I said, "What's up with Maya's nickname for you?"

Jameson grimaced. "I went through a phase as a teen where I loved playing guitar. I'd jam out in the garage, playing for her and my sister. They started calling me Jam-Jam and, unfortunately, it stuck."

I bit my lip to hold back a laugh. "Do you still play?"

"Not really. I think my guitar is somewhere in the basement, collecting dust."

"That's a shame."

Jameson's eyes flashed. "Why is that?"

"Most girls love being serenaded."

"Is that the ticket to winning you over? Because I'd happily dig it out for you."

I shook my head. "Don't waste your time."

His face fell, and I immediately regretted my words. But why? Why did I suddenly care if I hurt his feelings? It was better that he saw my grumpy side now, so he knew not to get further involved with me.

"So," he said, clearing his throat. "What do you do when you're not eating Chick-Fil-A?"

"Besides running into you?"

He huffed a laugh. "Yes, when I'm nowhere to be found and you're not filling your mouth with a killer chicken sandwich—pun intended by the way—what might one find you doing?"

I wiped my fingers with a napkin, erasing all signs of the greasy, heavenly fries.

"I'm a freelance writer."

"No kidding," he said, leaning forward as if it were the most interesting thing in the world. "How long have you been doing that?"

My gaze went to the ceiling as I considered my answer. It took two years after breaking up with Ben for anything I wrote to gain credibility, for any newspaper publications or people searching for ghostwriters to be interested in my work. Eventually I landed a few bigger gigs ghostwriting novels, which allowed me to finally quit selling mini-donuts to pay the bills and save up to buy my house. Miraculously, I still loved donuts, though I didn't know how after spending years smelling fried sugary dough seven days a week, but even so, I never wished to return to those years again.

"I've been writing forever, but only seriously pursued it the last four years or so."

He rested his chin on his hands. "What do you write?"

"Mostly newspaper or magazine articles. Sometimes I help people write blogs, and occasionally I get hired as a ghostwriter to help with someone's book."

"Do you ever write anything for you?"

I froze. "For me?"

He nodded. "You do a lot of writing for other people, but do you ever write things that bring *you* joy? What would you write if you didn't have to worry about money?"

His question was a punch to the gut. All I ever dreamed of was being able to write and publish fiction novels, anything from epic fantasies to romantic comedies, or even a thriller or two. I loved books, no matter the genre.

"If I didn't need the money to pay bills, then I would write fiction."

Jameson's eyes widened, his dimple making an appearance. "What kind?"

I gave a small chuckle. "Any kind, really. I've started a handful of books over the years when I've had the time, and finished one or two of them, but the publishing world is difficult to break into when you're unknown. And I have bills to pay." I ended with a shrug.

"That's amazing, though."

I squirmed in the booth. Why would he think that's amazing? Most people didn't understand how hard writing truly was, and tended to judge writers for not having a "real" job. If only people understood just how much writers had to battle anxiety, self-doubt, and imposter syndrome, all while trying to be creative...and it was even worse when you had to write on behalf of someone else. It took *people-pleasing* to a whole other level.

Don't get me wrong—I loved writing. But sometimes it was a lot, and I wished I could simply do it for me and have it be enough.

But that wasn't how the world worked.

"Have you ever tried to publish your work?"

"Um," I hesitated. "I've thought about it, but never pursued it. The novels I completed are rough." I winced at the thought of those files, which I hadn't touched since I ended things with Ben.

"Well, maybe you should—"

"Is there anything else y'all need?" a Chick-Fil-A employee asked, appearing out of nowhere, gesturing at our now empty tray.

Jameson gave the girl a smile and shook his head. "We're good, thank you."

"My pleasure," she said before disappearing the way she had come.

His attention returned to me, excitement lighting up

his eyes. "I was saying—"

"Actually, I need to get going," I interrupted, grabbing my purse and throwing it over my shoulder. I didn't need him to tell me what I should or shouldn't do with writing, or to fill my heart with hopes and dreams I'd worked hard to quell. What I did now paid the bills, and that was that. There wasn't room for anything else.

Jameson's face fell. "Oh. All right."

"Thanks for the shake and fries."

It took a moment, but his dimple reappeared. "I'll see you again soon?"

I gave a small nod. As I slid out of the booth to leave, his fingers latched onto my wrist like they had last night at my car, and my stomach swooped. Why did his touch make my body react like this? He was just a man. There were no attachments, no feelings, no romance. This was, and would remain, purely platonic. But, no matter how much I told myself that, it didn't stop goosebumps from sliding over my skin, or the little fires that followed.

"I didn't mean to scare you off, Elsie. I just wanted to get to know you."

I studied his face. How did he see right through me? How could he possibly know my fears and insecurities had risen to the surface with his questions? How could he possibly know that I was terrified?

He didn't know about my past, and I wasn't about to share *that* baggage.

My parents had always appeared to love each other,

and I looked up to them when I was a kid, but when I turned eighteen, a switch flipped. The masks came off and the yelling started. I didn't know if they had always been fighting, or if they simply stopped bothering to hide it once I was old enough to understand. Them walking away from each other after nearly thirty years of marriage left a deep gouge in my heart that I didn't think anything could ever fill. It erased any hope in my heart that real love existed.

And don't even get me started on my ex. Ben never saw me—he never *cared* to see me. He was more annoyed by all my *issues* than he was interested in learning why I was the way I was.

But Jameson wanted to get to know me, despite my attempts to ward him away. Why? Why wasn't he running for the hills?

"You didn't," I lied. "I have errands to run and… things." I struggled to come up with an excuse because the truth was, he did scare me.

He scared me so much.

"Good," he said, thumb stroking my hand. "Then I look forward to next time."

My tongue weighed a thousand pounds in my mouth, and I could only nod before pulling out of his grip and fleeing Chick-Fil-A like the chicken that I was.

18

Jameson

I was fully convinced my dog could sense stress. The moment I got home I collapsed on the couch after a long day of work, and Luna wasted no time plopping onto my lap and running her slimy tongue all over my face. Switching to a new clinic and meeting new patients had made this week difficult, to say the least. I kept reminding myself to be grateful for the job, but my knees ached from being on my feet for hours, and my hands throbbed from endless massaging.

Luna's fur between my fingers calmed me as I mindlessly flipped through channels on the TV. It had been several days since I had heard from Elsie after our spontaneous chicken lunch, and I was starting to feel the time apart like a nagging caffeine headache. I had wanted to text her throughout the week, but I was so exhausted after each workday, I could barely scrounge up dinner, let alone think of a single word to say to her.

Luna let out a squeaky yawn before staring me down with those chocolate brown eyes. If she were capable of speech, I knew she would be saying, "What are you waiting for, Human? Text her!"

Well, who was I to argue with a dog?

Pulling the phone out of my pocket, I typed up the most basic message ever.

ME

Hey, what are you up to?

It took a few minutes before a response pinged on my phone.

ELSIE

Every adult's favorite past time.

Grocery shopping.

ME

My sincerest condolences.

ELSIE

Condolences accepted.

I couldn't hold back a grin. I loved her quick wit, the effortless way we bantered back and forth. It was both refreshing and drove me crazy because I wanted to be *there* bantering instead of tapping it through a screen.

An idea sprouted roots in my mind, and approximately two seconds later, I threw myself off the couch and shoved my feet into boots before tromping out through the leaves in the yard to get to my truck. Was I heading to Wally's Market, the only grocery story in Meridel, just for a chance to see her?

Yes, I absolutely was.

Did that make me creepy? Maybe a little. But I also needed more milk, so I had a legitimate reason to go to the store. At least, that's what I told myself.

The neighbor across the street was screaming into his phone in the driveway as I drove out of our cul-de-sac. I had only met the guy a couple times. He had a habit of getting angry at Luna for pooping in his yard, and then at me when I was a millisecond too slow cleaning it up. I felt sorry for whatever woman ended up with that sorry excuse for a man. If he treated me and my dog in such a way, I could only imagine how he'd treat a woman.

I tried to be neighborly and wave at him, but he only scowled at me before turning away.

Whatever, dude.

The seven minutes it took to drive into town were too long. My thumbs tapped an anxious rhythm on the steering wheel until I finally arrived at Wally's, parked in the small lot, and walked inside the store.

The scent of produce slammed into me, and I forced my steps to slow, not wanting to appear too eager. I wanted to see those brown eyes, see her smile, hear her laugh.

What was happening to me?

Wally's Market was empty, other than the cashier who was enjoying singing along to the fifties ragtime music playing over the speakers. With casual footsteps, I walked up and down a few aisles, trying to find Elsie. When I came up empty, part of me deflated at the thought of missing her.

I skirted around the outside aisle where all the meat, dairy, and produce were. My boots squeaked on the tile floor as I came to an abrupt stop. Elsie was in the cheese section, a different block of cheese in each hand as she stared at them with the cutest scrunched-nose expression. I bit my lip to hold back a chuckle and approached her slowly, afraid I'd scare her away like a skittish animal.

At the sound my shoes made, she looked up, then did a double take.

And then she dropped both blocks of cheese.

"Jameson?" she asked, her face turning red. "What are you doing here?"

I bent to pick up the cheese and awkwardly held them out to her. "Your text reminded me I needed to do some shopping of my own," I said, realizing how stupid that was since I didn't have a cart or basket.

Elsie's eyes narrowed further as she took the cheese from me before glancing over my shoulder. I should have thought to grab a cart.

"Do you eat invisible food or something?" she

deadpanned.

My cheeks warmed. How did I play this off? *When I heard there was a chance you'd be here, I was so desperate to see you that I drove all the way here. I promise I'm not a creep, though.*

Yeah, *that* would go over well.

I huffed a nervous laugh, shoving my hands into my jacket pockets. "No, I just found what I was looking for," I said, then winced at my lame attempt at flirting.

Elsie cocked her head, the corners of her lips twitching. *Come on, smile.*

Another second passed, and any amusement I thought I saw slid away, replaced by a wall of wariness. What had happened to make her respond in such a way? I wanted to erase it, to help her forget whatever it was that made her so distrusting, so hesitant to open her heart.

Elsie cleared her throat, and it was then that I realized I had been awkwardly staring at her without saying anything. "And what were you looking for?"

I gave a sheepish smile. "Uh…" I racked my brain for any answer other than *you, of course,* but the only thing my mind could come up with was, "Cheese?"

The corners of her lips twitched again, and I made a show of turning to the cheese display and studying them intently. The text on each label blurred before my eyes, and I couldn't make out which was which. When did they change cheese labels to another language? I swore the letters did a little jig, taunting me for being an idiot.

How could one person scramble my brain so much? I waited a solid thirty seconds, hoping that was long enough to make me seem like a serious cheese shopper, before glancing at her out of the corner of my eye.

"Need any help?" I nodded at the blocks in her own hands.

She stared at the cheese for a moment too long before looking at me, her nose scrunching again. "Help with picking out cheese?"

I gave a vigorous nod, as if cheese selection was a life-or-death decision. I stepped closer, forcing my eyes to focus and read the label.

"Mmm, gouda," I hummed, tapping the one in her left hand. "Great snacking cheese with crackers. Also melts well on meat. If you cook chicken breast, then put gouda and jalapenos on top, it's delicious."

I was rambling. About cheese.

I met her gaze, expecting to see alarm at my obvious insanity. Instead, the edges of her lips curled ever so slightly.

"And this one?" she asked, holding the other block out.

I took it from her just so I could brush my fingers against hers, a shiver running through me with the mere touch.

Oh boy, I needed help. I had clearly been single for too long.

It had been close to eight years since I had been in

any type of serious relationship, and it was evident I was a little rusty. Outside of the almost kisses with Elsie, I couldn't remember the last time I'd received any sort of physical affection that wasn't from a family member.

My eyes finally focused on the cheese label. It was a wedge of parmesan.

Gouda and parmesan? I peeked in the basket hanging off her arm. There was a roll of refrigerated cinnamon rolls, a loaf of bread, and a giant jug of orange juice. Not exactly the most versatile ingredients.

I coughed, handing the cheese back to her. "Parmesan is a delicious nutty and salty cheese that goes well on just about anything. Salads, soups, pasta…" I trailed off when she bit her lip, fighting a smile.

"Is that so?" Was her tone flirtatious, or was I imagining it?

"Mmm, yep."

Mmm yep? Where did the cool, confident, smooth Jameson go?

Then Elsie smiled, *full on smiled*, and I realized smooth Jameson had dissolved into a puddle on the floor.

A quiet chuckle escaped her lips, and she set the gouda back on the refrigerated shelf.

"Parmesan it is then."

"Good—" My voice cracked, like a teenager instead of the fully grown adult that I was, and I coughed, clearing my throat. "Good choice. Need any more help?" I offered, desperate for even a few more seconds with her.

"Are you some sort of food guru or master chef?"

"My mom taught me how to cook, but I'm no expert," I answered honestly. "But if it lets me hang around you, I'll be whatever you need." A lovely pink tint rose in her cheeks, and she tucked her hair behind an ear. "Unless you'd rather I leave," I added, hoping with everything in me that she wanted me to stay.

Elsie hesitated again, and my stomach dropped. Would she tell me to leave? Would she say she didn't want to see me outside of our dates? I thought our spontaneous lunch at Chick-Fil-A had been a lot of fun—besides the choking part—but I didn't know if she felt the same. Maybe she really wanted nothing to do with me at all. The thought of that cut deeper than I cared to admit.

"No, you can stay," she said at last, heading down the nearest aisle, the swish of her hair sending a wave of jasmine shampoo into my nose, and my knees weakened.

Relief swept over me, like walking into an air-conditioned house after spending all day in the hundred-degree heat, as I watched her scan the shelves. With her back to me, I took a moment to study her. She wore a long, blue sweater over a pair of black leggings that did wonders for her legs. I couldn't stop my thoughts from drifting to sitting on the couch with my arms around her, running my hands up those legs—

Stop it, Jameson. Get a grip.

I swallowed hard, shaking the thought from my mind. It took me a minute to get my feet unglued from the floor before I followed her, staying a respectable distance away.

"Anything I can help you find?" I asked, desperate for any interaction with this woman to silence the pummeling thoughts in my head.

She smirked at me over her shoulder. "Do you secretly work here or something?" Elsie gave me a once-over, studying me from head to toe, and I couldn't help standing a little straighter, hoping I appeared confident and unaffected by her stare.

Blast it all. I *was* a confident guy, but something about not knowing what Elsie was thinking had me second guessing everything.

"You don't strike me as a grocer," she remarked as she finished perusing me. Something akin to approval flashed in her eyes.

I chuckled. "Not quite a grocer, no, but I know my way around Wally's Market."

Her eyebrows rose, and any playfulness disappeared from her countenance. "Is this where you bring all your dates?"

I scoffed. "If by dates you mean where I get food to feed me and my dog, then yes."

Her eyes widened, her mouth opening in an *o* of surprise. "Really?"

"Is that so hard to believe?"

Elsie hesitated, grabbing a jar of peanut butter off the shelf, though I didn't think she even paid attention to what she put in her basket. "You seem like the kind of guy to have a wealth of women wanting to date you, so yes, it's surprising."

Now it was my turn to gape. "I'm not some kind of a player, Elsie. I don't date around, and I don't mess around. Things have been…" I trailed off, not wanting to get into my past in the middle of a grocery store.

"Things have been what?"

I swallowed hard as I scratched at the back of my head.

"Difficult," I said through a sigh, looking over her shoulder instead of in her eyes.

I was not ashamed of the past ten years in any way. My mom had been my priority over everything. It was unfortunate that the girl I was dating back then couldn't handle that. It was her issue, not mine, but it still put a bad taste in my mouth about dating, even after everything had settled and I had the time and desire to try again.

At least until I met Elsie. Now, all I thought about was her.

"Difficult how?" The basket swung from her hand next to her.

I smirked. "Is this really a conversation you want to have *here*?"

She glanced around. "I suppose not." Elsie turned on her heel and marched toward the checkout. "So then let's go somewhere and talk."

My stomach squeezed in delight. I gave a mock gasp, and she stopped dead in her tracks to look at me.

"Elsie Feran, did you just ask me on a date?"

Her cheeks turned bright red. "I—what? No—" she stuttered.

I laughed, closing the distance between us, and took a chance by swinging my arm around her shoulders as we made for the cashier. "Don't worry, Elsie. I'm teasing. I'd love to go somewhere and talk."

19

Jameson

Thirty minutes later, after driving home to put her food away, Elsie met me at Dina's, a popular little diner in town. Dina herself sat us at a two-person table near the front window, and I couldn't help but wonder if that was her way of meddling—getting us front and center for everyone who passed by to see. The diner was packed, and I didn't miss the way everyone kept looking at us. Meridel was small enough for people to be in everyone else's business.

I secretly loved that these people felt like family. That's one reason why I never felt compelled to leave, even after my mom moved out of my house. Meridel was home.

"What are you getting?" Elsie asked, peering over the top of her menu. My stomach did somersaults under the scrutiny of her brown eyes.

"I think I'm going to get the chili and cornbread." It was a crowd favorite at Dina's, and with the late autumn heat finally fading, leaving a brisk chill behind, I was ready for some hot soup.

Alhough, Elsie set me constantly aflame, so that might have been a bad call.

She nodded, returning her eyes to her menu.

A moment later the waitress came by, and I gave my order, handing her the menu.

"And for you?" she asked Elsie.

Elsie bit her lip. "Um, I'll just do a Caesar salad."

I arched a brow. "You don't want anything else?"

She hesitated, scanning the menu once more. I couldn't help but wonder if money was a concern for her, based on her comment over the cost of that pumpkin on our first date, and the way she hesitated now. Her grocery basket had been fairly empty, too, now that I thought about it.

"Just the salad for me," she reaffirmed.

Elsie handed the waitress her menu and I quickly added, "Actually, make that two bowls of chili, please."

The waitress nodded and disappeared before Elsie could object.

I didn't know what came over me, or if she even liked chili, but the thought of her only eating anchovy-covered lettuce because that's all she could afford made me sad. I knew from experience what it felt like to be hungry, and to have to settle for a mediocre meal because of money.

Besides, my mom had raised me to be a gentleman, and I wasn't about to make Elsie pay for her own meal when we were on a…non-date.

"Why did you do that?" she demanded, leaning forward, a deep crease in her forehead as she glared at me.

I had always been a blunt person, unafraid to say what I was thinking or feeling, so I asked, "Did you only order a salad because you're worried about the cost?"

Her brows lowered over her eyes, the tips of her ears turning red as she fixed her gaze on the table, folding her hands together.

"I don't need you to take care of me, Jameson."

I took her avoidance as confirmation.

"I know," I replied. "But it doesn't mean I don't want to."

Her eyes snapped to mine. "Why?"

Why, indeed.

I wasn't about to voice that I couldn't get her out of my head, that I cared more than I should. That was a surefire way of scaring her away for good.

So, instead, I settled for, "Everyone needs to eat. Everyone deserves a solid meal."

Elsie's knuckles were white from how hard she squeezed her hands together. It was instinct to reach out and cover them with my own.

"Elsie, it's fine. I was going to pay for your meal anyway."

She slipped her hands from beneath mine, and the air was suddenly too cold, too empty without her touch.

"I can pay for my own food, Jameson."

"Just because you can, doesn't mean you should."

She shook her head. "I can take care of myself."

"But when's the last time someone took care of you?"

Her entire body stilled as she met my gaze, and I supposed that was answer enough.

I leaned forward, wishing the table wasn't in my way so I could take her hands in mine. "I'm sorry that someone forced you to learn to care for yourself, but you don't have to do that with me, Elsie."

"You don't even know me," she bit out. I couldn't tell if she was angry or flustered, unable to understand my motives.

"Maybe I don't know you well *yet,* but everyone deserves to be taken care of." She opened her mouth to object, but I interrupted. "Who made you think other-wise?"

Her eyes filled with tears, and I immediately wanted to rake the words back into my mouth.

"I'm sorry, I shouldn't have asked that."

Elsie squirmed in her chair. "It's fine...I just..." She let out a long, slow breath. "My pare—" She paused, her words catching. "My ex often ordered for me like that, and I guess it was triggering."

Understanding swooped in like an eagle snatching a fish. "I'm sorry, Elsie. I didn't know."

She shrugged, sniffling. "My dad was the one to set us up, thinking that my ex, Ben, would give me stability after I graduated college. Little did he know that Ben was worse than no one at all. Ever since…" Elsie sighed, and I sensed there was more that she wasn't telling me. "I don't want to have to rely on anyone but myself. I can make my own decisions, pay for my own meals. I don't *need* anyone else."

I was quiet for a moment, trying to find the right words to say. I wanted her to know that I would never treat her poorly on purpose, nor did I think she *needed* me. The only reason I ordered for her was to ensure that her stomach was full by the time we left Dina's.

The waitress appeared with two bowls of chili, a basket of cornbread, and the tiniest Caesar salad I had ever seen.

"Enjoy," the waitress said before disappearing again.

Elsie didn't even look at the salad, and instead picked up her spoon and played with the chili, eyeing the bowl like she was conflicted over whether to eat it or not.

"Elsie, I'm sorry if I reminded you of your ex by ordering for you. I promise I never intended to insinuate that you couldn't order, or pay for your own meal. I just wanted you to *eat* without worry. I'm happy to pay for you."

Her lips pressed together, and it looked like she wanted to argue, but her stomach gurgled loudly, and she gave in, spooning some chili into her mouth. A small groan of pleasure slipped through her lips, and my entire body went on alert.

"Good?" I asked before taking a bite of my own.

"Mmhmm," she hummed. After a few more bites, she changed the subject. "Enough about my past. I barely know anything about you. Tell me why *things have been difficult*." She put air quotes around the words.

As much as I didn't want to open that can of worms, Elsie had shared a small bit of hers, and the least I could do was reciprocate. I took a sip of water and cleared my throat.

"Ten years ago, when I was in college, my mom was diagnosed with breast cancer. At the time it was just the three of us—my mom, me, and my sister—and it fell on Emma and me to take care of her."

I paused, swallowing down the sudden emotion in my throat. My dad had died when I was little, and it had been…overwhelming trying to take care of her when I was barely an adult myself. It had been years, and thankfully my mom was in remission now, but the fear I'd experienced, and not having a dad to share the load with…it was more than anyone should have to bear.

"We couldn't afford the medical bills of keeping her in the hospital, so I dropped out of college and moved back home to take care of her."

Elsie's gaze softened. "That must've been really hard."

"It was the hardest thing I've ever gone through," I admitted. "But it made me into the man I am today."

Elsie fidgeted with her napkin as she started to ask, "Is your mom…"

"She's alive. When the treatments weren't working as well as they hoped, my mom agreed to try a new experimental drug. While it helped to cure her cancer, it made her bones brittle and body weak. She's unable to live by herself."

"Does she still live with you then?" Her question harbored no judgment or disdain one might expect from learning a man in his late-twenties lived with his mother.

"No, last year she was—in her own words—tired of me moping around. She moved into an assisted living home twenty minutes away. She told me she wanted me to have my life back, and she somehow understood I couldn't move forward until I knew that she was taken care of."

"That must have been a difficult decision—for both of you."

I nodded. It was one of the most difficult decisions I had ever made—putting my mother's care in someone else's hands. I went from my entire life revolving around caring for my mom, to waking up to only my job and Luna.

"And dating?" she asked after a moment.

I couldn't hold back a wince. "I dated a girl about two years after my mom got sick. Everything was great at first, but she eventually grew to resent how much my mother needed me, and walked away without ever looking back."

"I'm sorry."

I shrugged, unbothered. Sitting across from Elsie now, I was glad things with that girl had ended. "It's in the past. My mom is alive and I'm moving on, like she wanted."

"But no dates." It wasn't a question.

I smirked. "Not until recently, and none worth remembering. Except you."

Elsie blushed but asked, "Why?"

"My sister was able to take care of my mom in the evenings while she was still in high school, then put off going to college so I could finish school. Once I got a job at a clinic, the hours were long and grueling, and I just... didn't have the time. Or the mental energy."

"So, why now?"

I took another sip of water before answering. "Maya found me a better clinic to work at. Higher pay and less hours, and with my mom taken care of, I feel like I'm in a better place to pursue dating."

Elsie nodded, nibbling on a piece of cornbread, her chili devoured.

"Okay," she finally said.

"Okay?"

"I don't think you're a player."

My mouth flopped open. "I wasn't aware that you did."

She gestured to me. "I mean, look at you. I'm sure women are all over you."

Was that a...compliment?

"I'm not sure whether to say thank you or be offended by that." Elsie's answering laugh had my heart constricting in my chest.

"Sorry," she giggled, but the amusement in her eyes said she wasn't. "Confident, attractive guys are usually a magnet for women. I just assumed that went for you, too."

Elsie thought I was attractive? My chest swelled at the thought.

"Well, thank you for that...sort of compliment, but I am neither a player nor do I have a constant stream of women wanting my attention."

She nodded, avoiding my eyes. "That's good."

"Besides," I continued. "Even if I was a so-called babe-magnet—"

"I don't remember using the term 'babe-magnet.'"

"—there's only one woman that has *my* eye anyway."

I settled my gaze on her, hoping she understood my meaning. From the first moment we met in the sunflower field, she had done something to me. I wasn't a player like she had assumed, and I didn't have a mass of women following me around, but even if I did, they would all pale in comparison to her.

She ducked her head, cheeks reddening, and I desperately wanted to reach across the table and hold her hand, or brush my thumb across her cheek, or... literally anything.

Instead of responding, she shoveled the rest of the cornbread in her mouth, pushing the bowl away when she finished.

"I should probably get home. I have an article I need to finish."

Why did the idea of her leaving, going home to somewhere I wasn't, have my stomach sinking to the floor? She wasn't mine. We weren't even officially dating, although everything inside me wanted to change that.

I couldn't help but think we would be good together.

We'd only been on one official date so far, and her walls were so high they might as well have been Jericho. But I would willingly march around her for days and days, screaming and shouting until those walls fell, if that's what it took.

I wanted her to stay, to offer to keep her company while she worked, or even have her bring it over to my place and I'd make her some dessert...but I didn't want to scare her away.

So, instead of saying any of the swirling, jumbled mess of thoughts in my head, I gave a slow nod, hoping my feelings weren't written all over my face.

"I'll take care of the check. I'll see you soon?"

She stilled, her coat halfway on. "You tell me."

A small smile bent my lips. "Yes, I'll see you soon. We have two more dates."

Elsie cocked her head. "This didn't count?"

Pushing out of my chair, I stepped around the table

and helped her the rest of the way into her coat. My fingers grazed hers and something electric crackled between us. She glanced over her shoulder, her lips only inches from mine. All it would take was a shifting of my weight to kiss her.

As much as I wanted to, I didn't want the first time to be surrounded by people at Dina's. I cleared my throat and stepped back, putting my hands in my pockets so I wouldn't pull her into my arms.

"Oh no." I smiled, taking a step back. "This wasn't a date. This was just…hanging out."

Elsie fidgeted with her coat buttons, avoiding my gaze. Her fingers trembled, and she struggled to get the wooden buttons through the proper holes. Unable to resist, I stilled her hands with my own, buttoning her up one by one, before I put a finger to her chin and tilted her head up to look at me.

"You don't have to be afraid of me, Elsie."

Her throat bobbed as she swallowed. "I think it's better if I am."

I opened my mouth to ask why, but she pulled away from me, and a sudden cold smothered me in her absence.

"Thanks for dinner, Jameson."

Before I could say anything else, she tucked her hands into her coat pockets and hurried into the chilly autumn evening, taking my heart and all rational thoughts with her.

20

Elsie

Rain poured from the sky the next day, giving the air that typical crisp but musty fall scent. Meridel's only gas station was packed with people as I waited in a long line of cars for my turn to fill up. Twenty minutes—and a mental note not to visit Gas & Things at lunch time—later, I finally made it to a pump. By then, almost everyone had come and gone, so I didn't feel bad about running inside to grab a quick snack before filling up my car.

The scent of gas station coffee and fresh donuts lingered in the air, making my stomach rumble. I snagged two donuts from the case—a chocolate glazed one and a cinnamon sugar bear claw—paid, then headed back to my car. I was too busy stuffing my face to pay much attention to my surroundings, at least until a shadow moved into my peripheral.

My first thought was of those news reports from years ago warning of women getting kidnapped at the pump. So, of course, what was my natural defensive response?

I spun around like a ninja and chucked the donut at the person's head.

I also may or may not have screamed, "WA-CHAW!" like a kid practicing karate, though I'd plead the fifth if I was ever asked to confirm or deny doing so.

The donut flew through the air, smacking into the kidnapper's cheek before breaking into a bunch of pitiful pieces on the ground.

I probably should have been embarrassed that my first response to a kidnapper was a flying donut to the face instead of running for my life, but all thoughts fell out of my head as I turned to find Jameson with a cheek now covered in cinnamon sugar.

"Nice to see you too, Elsie," Jameson laughed. "Sorry for startling you."

I put a hand to my chest. "I thought you were a kidnapper."

He arched a brow. "Do you often fear getting snatched in broad daylight while eating a donut?"

I crossed my arms and snapped back, "It never hurts to be prepared."

"Oh yes, your donut definitely would have stopped somebody trying to steal you away."

The gas nozzle made a *thunk* as it finished filling,

causing me to flinch. It then got stuck in my car as I tried to pull it out. I gave it a few good yanks before it finally sprung free, and I stumbled backward. An amused smile twisted Jameson's lips as he watched me.

I really needed to stop doing embarrassing things around him or my face would perpetually feel on fire for the rest of my life. When I finally got the pump situated, and the gas cap on my car closed, I turned to him with hands on my hips.

"So, you're not trying to steal me?"

His response was quick. "Maybe just your heart."

The words were unexpected and caused a violent return of the butterflies in my stomach. I shook my head, trying in vain to shake his words loose from my brain. Jameson was a smooth talker, that much was clear, but I couldn't let him get to me.

Nope. There would be no stealing of hearts here. Only broken donuts on the ground. I glanced at it again, thinking about running inside for another one. Anything to distract me from the man smirking at me while my thoughts spun in circles.

I had to remind myself, over and over, that it wasn't worth the risk. No matter how lonely I was—or how much my heart ached for someone like Jameson to see me, to want me.

A memory flashed behind my eyes of happy smiles transforming into angry, sneering faces, screaming voices, and hatred. I squeezed my eyes tight, trying to shut out the painful reminder of why there could be no future for Jameson and me.

"Hey, you okay?" Jameson asked, taking a step closer.

This guy was too observant—the complete opposite of Ben.

I could have eaten shrimp, blown up like a balloon, coughing, unable to breathe, and Ben would still have had his eyes glued to his phone, utterly oblivious.

But Jameson...he missed nothing.

Part of me liked it, and part of me didn't. He was more likely to see all the things I've worked for years to keep hidden—all my faults, insecurities, and pain.

Everyone wanted to feel seen—to have someone see all of them and still accept them—but that didn't make it any less terrifying when someone finally did.

"I'm fine," I finally said through clenched teeth. "What are you doing here?"

"I was heading back to work but had to stop for gas. It was a lucky coincidence that I saw a familiar blonde girl emerge from Gas & Things with a donut in her mouth." He winked and I ducked my head, embarrassed that he had caught me donut-handed.

"Right. Well, I better get going." I pointed at my car with a thumb, needing to get away from this guy who was absolutely on the road to stealing my heart. "Sorry about the flying donut."

He opened his mouth like he wanted to say something

but seemed to think better of it as he nodded instead.

"I'll talk to you soon." He turned to leave. "Oh, and Els?" I paused the awkward crouch thing I was doing to get into my car, glancing at him over my shoulder. "You can hit me with a donut any time."

The next two weeks were a blur of Jameson.

Every morning, I woke up to a good morning text, followed by, "what are you doing tonight?" or, "have any plans this evening?" He kept saying he wanted to see me but was adamant that it wasn't an *official* date.

My resolve to keep my distance crumbled a little more each day, and I ended up spending almost every evening with him. We ran errands around Meridel, had dinner at Dina's several times, and sat at The Roasted Bean, talking for hours. He had helped me rake the leaves in my yard, though I was careful not to let him come inside, and then destroyed the pile after we had gotten into a tickle fight and fell into the leaves. Smart Elsie would tell you that she hated it, but Smitten Elsie wanted to repeat that day over and over again.

Every moment ran together in my mind as though my entire brain was now made up of Jameson; a warm, fluttery feeling of *"I like this man."*

Which was the absolute most dangerous thought I could have.

Why was he so irresistible? It wasn't like we were going on extravagant dates or anything. It was simply… enjoying each other's company. It was *so simple*, yet it was *everything*.

Every time I saw Jameson, he was all smiles and genuinely invested in everything I had to say, even when it was obvious work had been long and challenging that day. Each time I saw him, he was quick to remind me that our time together didn't count as a date. Though, after two weeks of these non-dates, he still hadn't asked me out for the second official date.

Was he drawing it out so that he could spend more time with me before I ended things? Or was it worse than that and he was simply trying to figure out if he even wanted a second date at all?

I didn't know and so, as usual, my brain continued to overthink it all.

But I did know that my stomach squeezed each time I saw his smiling face and that infernal dimple. I got lost in those hazel eyes.

Our time together had even inspired me to finally finish that article I'd been fighting against for weeks.

He hadn't tried to kiss me again since our first date, and for some inexplicable reason, it annoyed me. But then I got even more annoyed at myself because I shouldn't *want* him to kiss me. I should be putting an end to our nightly non-dates, not encouraging more. And yet…I couldn't bring myself to stop.

Bad Elsie. I was headed straight for Heartbreak Town—population me. I needed to get myself firmly back in Safe Town.

And that meant pulling back from Jameson.

So why did that make me feel so terrible?

Because I was a glutton for punishment, I plopped down at my favorite coffee shop, laptop open, with a large, iced mocha in hand. My phone sat on the table, my text thread with Jameson staring up at me as I debated asking if he was free.

Jameson had several busy work days this week, so we hadn't been able to get together for a few days. Not being able to see him made it feel like I couldn't get a full breath into my lungs—like I was missing a crucial piece of my day. I was tired of sitting in my house by myself with only my cat again.

Yes. I was the crazy single cat lady, and I never thought twice about it, until Jameson came into my life.

Or should I blame Maya? She was the reason why I met him in the first place.

Throwing caution to the wind, I tapped my fingers across the screen.

ME

Hey, whatcha up to?

The three wiggling dots flashed immediately on the screen.

JAMESON

Wishing I was with you.

Ugh. Why does he have to say things that make me swoon?

ME

It's your lucky day then.

I'm at The Roasted Bean if you're interested.

JAMESON

Interested isn't a strong enough word. Be there in 10. :)

Smart Elsie mentally kicked me again. I was doing a terrible job at keeping my heart out of the picture. And yet...all I could think about was seeing Jameson's dimpled face, hearing his laugh, and watching the way his eyes lit up when I inevitably embarrassed myself. My fingers simply acted on their own. I couldn't be held accountable for that, right?

I sipped my coffee, relishing the sugary drink as I stared at the dark screen of my laptop, my fingers twitching over the keys. Every time the little bell above the door dinged, I sat up straighter, searching for those familiar eyes, but it wasn't him. Desperate for a distraction, I turned my laptop on and searched for the file for one of my novels I hadn't touched in years. It took a minute to find the folder, but when I did, I gasped.

In the folder titled "Silly Things," there were not one or two books I had fully written years ago, but *five*. Five books, rough and unedited, sat on my laptop. I couldn't even remember writing them all.

Two romance novels, one fantasy, and two mysteries.

Wincing as if the file was going to physically slap me when I opened it, I double-clicked on one of the untitled romances.

"Fancy seeing you here," a voice crooned. I let out a squeal, slammed my laptop shut, and almost knocked over my iced coffee.

I put a hand to my chest, breathing hard, like I had just run a marathon while dragging an elephant behind me. Jameson's smirking face came into focus. "You scared me," I breathed.

"I can see that." His dimple was on full display as he nodded to my laptop. "Whatcha got there?"

"Nothing," I said, resting a hand on top to keep him from opening it.

He arched a brow. "That reaction said otherwise. I think you almost gave that granny over there a heart attack."

I peeked over my shoulder at the older lady in the corner. She glared daggers at me, her hand resting over her heart.

Well then. You try hiding the romance book you don't remember writing from the guy you're trying not to fall for, lady.

"Can I get you anything?" Jameson asked with a chuckle, pointing at the counter.

"I think I'm covered," I replied, pointing at my giant coffee in front of me. He gave me a smile that had my knees wobbling despite the fact that I was sitting down, and went to order.

By the time he came back, I had clicked out of my romance novel, vowing to never open it again...at least not in public.

A chocolate glazed donut appeared on the table in front of me.

"It wouldn't be a Saturday morning without a proper donut," Jameson explained, taking a seat across from me.

"I'm surprised you were free this morning," I said with a smile, looking for any way to distract myself from the warm fuzzies in my stomach. Saturdays were usually the day that "adults" did work around the house—things they had been neglecting all week.

Me? I still ignored all the things I needed to do on Saturday, especially when the sun was shining, illuminating the vibrant colored trees, and infusing warmth into my bones despite the chill in the air outside. Some things were more important than projects around the house.

I tried to wait a socially acceptable amount of time before stuffing the donut in my face.

Jameson reached his hand across the table and swiped his thumb across the back of my hand. "I wouldn't miss a chance to see you."

Well, that's certainly not helping to distract me.

"I figured after the busy week you had, you would've had other things to do today."

He brushed my hand again. "Those things can wait." Even though I was the one to invite him here, he tilted his head and asked, "Do you regret that I'm here?"

No, and that's what scares me.

But I couldn't tell him *that,* so I gave a small shake of my head instead.

His smile lit up the dark parts of me. "Good, because I was dying to see you."

I bit my lip. "Then why haven't you asked me on our second *real* date yet?"

His mouth quirked to the side. "I wasn't going to rush through the dates so that I only had a short time to get to know you, Elsie. Our time together the last couple weeks may have been *non-dates,* but they're every bit as important to me as the actual dates."

Swoon!

"Besides, I was planning our second date for tonight."

"Tonight?" Sweat instantly pooled in my palms and I begged the Niagara Falls pits to stay out of the sweat party my body was suddenly having.

His dimple deepened. "Yes, tonight." At my hesitation he leaned forward. "I'd like to cook dinner for you at my place."

His place?

Though we had spent many of our evenings together, neither one of us had ventured into the dangerous territory of being inside the other's house. It seemed like a line we shouldn't cross if I wanted to keep an expiration date on this thing between us. Being in his house was another layer of intimacy that would make it even harder to say goodbye at the end of this.

Smitten Elsie held an invisible hand over my mouth so I couldn't say no.

You know you want to go, she crooned in my mind.

It didn't matter if she was right. This had disaster written all over it.

And yet I nodded, barely squeaking out, "Okay."

I wished I could frame the smile that spread across Jameson's face and keep it in my wallet to take out on hard days.

"Great! Are you allergic to anything?"

"Um, shrimp."

"Got it. No shrimp. Anything else?"

I shook my head, struggling to form words.

"Cool. I'll text you my address. Six o'clock?"

That was a little over six hours from now. His eyes blazed a path across my face as he waited for a response. My mind warred with itself, between the desire to enjoy Jameson's company and the need to protect my heart.

It was only dinner, right? What could possibly happen that would derail my plans of remaining unattached?

After another minute of awkward silence, I finally answered, "Six sounds great."

21

Elsie

Fate was a cruel thing.

I had just turned down Walnut Circle, searching for Jameson's house number, when realization slammed into me like a train.

Jameson lived in a *very* nice neighborhood.

But not just any nice neighborhood. No, it was one I had spent a lot of time in once upon a time. It wasn't until I got to the end of the road, arriving in the cul-de-sac where Jameson's house sat that I realized how truly terrible this was.

My foot crashed into the brake, stopping dead in the center of the circle, frozen.

Jameson's house was the second in from the right.

While Ben's was two houses down on the left end.

Yep. Jameson was neighbors with my ex-almost-fiancé.

Crap crap crap crap crap.

It had been four years since I had last seen Ben, and I didn't really feel like breaking that streak now. I slammed on the gas, pulling into Jameson's driveway as fast as I could, cringing when the tires squealed on the road. I jammed the gear shift into park and turned the car off, hoping that somehow made my car invisible just in case Ben happened to be looking out the window and recognized my car.

I hated that my ex was already ruining this date, forcing his way inside my head, when we hadn't been together in years.

Thankfully, the sun had mostly set, hiding me in darkness, as I ninja walked my way between the trees lining the walkway to Jameson's front door. I realized there was a possibility that my mind was making a mountain out of a molehill, and there was actually a very slim chance that, at this very moment, Ben would exit his house and see me creeping through the dark, but none of that helped to calm my racing heart.

I sighed, pressing my back against the rough bark of a tree, peeking around the trunk like I was a spy. There weren't any lights on in Ben's house. Maybe he wasn't home. Taking a bracing breath, I sprinted up the front steps and knocked on Jameson's door. My paranoia and need to avoid my ex were so strong that when he opened it, I shoved my way past him muttering, "Let me in, let me in."

I reached for the door, needing it closed, needing a second to breathe without the possibility of Ben seeing me. Jameson eyed me like I had suddenly grown a second head. I leaned against the door, breathing hard, sweat sliding down my spine.

All in all, it was not my finest moment.

"Well, it's good to see you too, Elsie," Jameson chuckled.

"Sorry, I—"

And then giant paws slammed into my stomach, and I yelped.

"Whoa, down, Luna!"

The fluffy Golden Retriever listened immediately, plopping into a seated position in front of me, tongue lolling out to the side.

Jameson put his hand on my waist, and leaned so his mouth was by my ear. "Sorry, she doesn't usually jump like that."

My heart hammered at his proximity. *Dang it, heart. Knock that off.* I needed to move, to put some distance between us, but the heat emanating from him was so welcoming, and his woodsy cologne made my brain spin like I'd had too many glasses of wine.

I cleared my throat, stepping out of Jameson's reach, barely able to meet his eyes, which flickered with amusement.

"I forgot you had a dog," I blurted. While I had always been more of a cat person, I couldn't deny his dog was cute. Jameson gave me a puzzled smile, probably wondering why I was acting so strange.

"Luna, go lay down." Luna's ears perked before she turned around and ran to a giant plush bed in the corner of the living room. "I rescued her from a shelter when my mom still lived here. I wanted someone to keep her company while I was at work." He paused, studying me as I crossed my arms. "Are you okay? You seem…" He gave me a once over. "On edge."

I gave an absurd giggle. "Oh, fine. I'm fine. Everything's fine." I had never related to that meme of the dog surrounded by fire so much in my life.

Jameson extended his hand, and because of the frazzled state of my mind, I thought he wanted a handshake. It was weird, but I went with it, placing my hand in his and giving it a firm shake.

Jameson laughed. "Thanks for the handshake, but I was offering to take your coat."

"Oh." I forced out a laugh that kind of sounded like a hyena cackling, and my cheeks turned to flames. Was it too late to leave and pretend none of this happened? Jameson probably thought I was an absolute lunatic.

Instead of releasing my hand, Jameson used it to pull me toward him, wrapping me in a hug. It was the first time anyone had ever used a handshake to lure me into a hug.

Was this the allure of those bro shake hugs?

If so, I could see the appeal.

Jameson's arms circled tighter around my waist, my face pressing into his chest. His cologne filled my nose, and his fingers were like little lightning bolts on my low back, despite the fabric between them.

I expected him to release me, keeping it quick so he could go back to whatever he was doing before I arrived, but he continued to hold me. One by one each of my muscles relaxed, his fingers trailing calming lines across my back.

After several moments, he whispered, "Better?"

He loosened his grip as I leaned back to look at him. How had he known I was falling apart and a simple hug would hold me together? How did he know that his soothing touch was what I needed? *I* didn't even know that's what I needed.

His hand released my waist to brush my hair out of my eyes, his fingertips skimming my cheek. Jameson really needed to stop setting me on fire. He glanced once, twice, at my lips and I knew if I didn't move that he would kiss me. It was written in the way he held me, in the way his fingers roved across my skin, in the way his dilated pupils betrayed his desire.

Almost every part of me wanted to lean in, to see what he tasted like, to experience what it would be like to kiss Jameson Beck. Every part except for Smart Elsie, who swooped in and took control, forcing me to pull out of his arms.

"So, what's for dinner?"

I wasn't sure if it was hurt or amusement, or a strange combination of the two that flickered across his face, but as quickly as it had appeared, it was gone, replaced by that dimple that pierced my heart like it pierced his cheek.

"I hope you're hungry," he said, helping me out of my coat, his fingers lingering a little too long against my neck, then my arms. "I made rosemary-garlic chicken with potatoes, veggies, and buttered rolls." At my gaping mouth, he added, "And chocolate cheesecake for dessert."

"Fancy. Do you have a secret degree in the culinary arts I should know about?"

He laughed and the sound was like seeing the sun after a severe storm—like I could finally breathe again because the danger had passed.

"Not quite. My mom loved to cook, and she spent many nights when I was a child teaching me what she knew, much to my chagrin."

The thought of a little version of Jameson helping his mom in the kitchen had a smile spreading over my face.

I followed him toward the kitchen, not bothering to hide my perusal of his house. It had bachelor pad vibes with lots of leather furniture, dark wood tones, and the general smell of cologne and that familiar woodsy scent hanging in the air. Luna lounged in the corner, content to watch our every move.

Despite the obvious lack of a woman's touch in the décor, I had to admit the house was cozy. I could envision myself napping on that couch, or watching a movie on his giant TV, cuddled in the huge thing that looked like a modern version of a bean bag chair. Or even—

No. I stopped that train of thought, smothering it with an imaginary pillow. I couldn't fantasize about being here with Jameson. There would be no cuddling or movies or napping. I would appreciate his house for the evening and that would be that. I would never come back here again.

I was firm in that decision until I walked into the kitchen of all kitchens.

If you took my Pinterest board full of dream kitchens and combined them all into one, you'd get this glorious room in Jameson's home.

It was a wide galley kitchen; the entire left wall was made of floor-to-ceiling cabinets painted in a subtle sage-green color with matte-gold hardware. On the back wall was a black stainless steel gas stove with an epic wooden hood hanging over it, and glass subway tiles for the backsplash. A giant farmhouse sink sat on the right, surrounded by floating shelves. Everything was tones of black, sage, and gold, and it was perfect.

On top of it all, it smelled like garlic and fresh bread, and I had to press my lips together to keep from drooling.

Jameson noticed my obvious gaping and chuckled. "Like the kitchen?"

"That's an understatement," I muttered.

"My mom helped pick out the finishes. She said if the rest of the house was going to feel manly, at least the kitchen could feel like a breath of fresh air."

"It's like my Pinterest dream kitchen," I admitted, and his resulting smile stabbed straight into my heart.

"I'm glad you like it."

Jameson went to the sink, washed his hands, then pulled a tray out of the oven. A fresh wave of garlic filled the air, and my stomach gurgled in response. I know he must have heard it but, like the gentleman he was, pretended not to.

"Anything I can help with?" I asked, watching him plate up the chicken and potatoes.

"Want to take the rolls out of the oven?"

I nodded, grabbing the striped oven mitts, that perfectly matched the décor, and pulled out the pan of bread.

"There's a basket on the counter there for the rolls," Jameson called over his shoulder, and I set to work plopping them inside, wrapping the delicious smelling carbs in the towel. I sighed. Carbs were the way to my heart. Sweet carbs. Bread carbs. Pasta carbs. It didn't matter. I was no respecter of carbs.

Jameson either talked to Maya to find out what I liked, which wouldn't have surprised me, or he was a very good guesser.

At this point, I wasn't quite sure which to put my money on.

Jameson finished scooping heaping portions onto the plates, which I greatly appreciated seeing as my stomach felt like it was eating itself, and I followed him to the table with the basket of bread. My eyes scanned the room, checking to make sure the curtains were closed, so Ben couldn't see inside. I shook my head, trying to shove my stupid ex from my mind.

The table was a small circle, perfect for the two of us. In the middle, two tall candles were lit with a little bundle of sunflowers between them. A bottle of sparkling wine sat chilling off to the side, and two smaller glasses of water sat next to the empty wine glasses. I felt like I was at a romantic restaurant instead of the middle of a man's home.

Don't get attached, Elsie. You'll be saying goodbye to him sooner than later.

Jameson set the plates down, then circled the table to pull my chair out for me.

Stop swooning! Maintain grumpiness!

Once I sat, he scooched the chair, his hands brushing against my shoulders. How could such a small, insignificant touch light my insides all the way to my toes?

After I was settled, he plopped into his own chair and filled my glass with a bubbly pink liquid.

"I hope you like it," Jameson said as he gestured for me to dig in.

"It's garlic, potatoes, and bread. What's not to like?"

His cheeks bulged with potatoes as he gave a closed-lip smile. It was way too adorable.

You're killing me, Jameson.

I popped the first bite into my mouth and audibly groaned, bringing a smug smile to his face. The rosemary was perfectly balanced with the garlic, and the potatoes were so tender they literally melted on my tongue. The bread was soft and light and deliciously carb-y, and I was in food heaven.

"Your mom taught you well," I mumbled around a mouth full of roll before I froze, remembering all the times Ben had scolded me for talking with my mouth full.

I waited for a reprimand, but Jameson smiled. "She's a good teacher."

When no scolding came, I swallowed, my shoulders loosening, feeling more at ease on a date for the first time...ever.

"Tell me more about your job," I said, needing a distraction. "Maya mentioned you recently changed jobs?"

Jameson wiped at his mouth, then took a drink. "Changed locations, yeah. I'm a physical therapist. I used to work twelve-hour shifts at the old place, but thanks to my cousin, I'm now at a new clinic with a much better work-life balance."

At the words "physical therapist" my eyes went straight to his strong hands, then to his forearms and thick biceps, wondering how good he must be at massaging.

"That's cool," I squeaked out, my mind lost in images of his hands on my neck, my shoulders...

I tugged at my sweater. Was it getting hot in here?

Of course, he didn't miss my gaze flicking to his hands, and I didn't miss the smirk on his face as a result.

I cleared my throat. "Do you like being a physical therapist?"

He nodded. "I do. I enjoy seeing the progress of my patients as they recover from whatever brought them to me."

Picturing him helping the elderly gain more mobility, recover from surgery, or even a little kid trying to strengthen their body after breaking bones…I hated what it did to my insides—how my stomach fluttered.

I needed to get a grip.

"What made you decide on that career path?" I asked after swallowing an enormous piece of bread.

"My mom," he answered after taking a sip of water. "When she got sick, all the doctors said she wouldn't make it. She lost a ton of weight and nearly all her strength. Eventually, she started going to a physical therapist, and when I saw her getting stronger with each visit, I knew that's what I wanted to do."

"Wow." It was the only word my brain would come up with. "What about your dad?" The words slipped out and based on the way his face fell, I knew I made a mistake.

Jameson's answer was soft as he cut a piece of chicken. "He died when I was a kid."

Maya's brief mention at Chick-Fil-A about his dad dying replayed in my mind. How had I forgotten that?

"I-I'm sorry," I stuttered, but he waved me off.

"It was a long time ago. I barely remember him."

I couldn't imagine how hard that must have been, watching his mother die a little more each day, and having to step up and be the primary caregiver, a job that would have gone to his father.

"I'm just grateful my mom is in remission and doing well, and my sister, Emma, is off at college now, living her dream," Jameson said, trying hard to put a smile on his face. I couldn't imagine facing all he went through, sacrificing so much, then turning it around and doing something good with it. Something that helped people.

Jameson was a *really* good guy.

Crap.

"Are you close with your sister?" I asked, suddenly wanting to know everything there was to know about Jameson Beck.

"Yeah, we had to lean on each other a lot through the years. Maya and Aunt Jo helped when they could, but we both had to put our dreams on hold to take care of Mom. She's at Iowa State now, finishing her meteorology degree."

"Meteorology?" I hadn't expected that.

Jameson huffed a laugh. "Emma has always been fascinated by the weather, especially growing up in Tornado Alley. When we were kids and there was bad weather, I always had to drag her back inside to safety. She wanted nothing more than to stand on the front porch, watching the lightning fork through the sky, and the clouds twist overhead." He shrugged. "I never understood her love of weather, but it makes her happy, and that's all I want for her."

A tornado twisted through my mind, obliterating my reservations about Jameson. I had never met a man that was not only thoughtful but genuinely wanted others to be happy.

"What about you?" he asked, interrupting my thoughts. "Do you have any siblings?"

"No, I'm an only child. My parents—"

At the mere mention of my parents, an alarm went off in my head, and my mouth slammed closed, teeth clacking together. I had almost shared the one thing I hated discussing more than anything else.

"No," I repeated, sitting back in my chair. "It's just me."

Jameson studied me for a moment, clearly noticing my odd behavior, but instead of pushing me to talk about it, he stood and nodded at my empty plate.

"Ready for dessert?"

Though I was stuffed, I would never turn down chocolate.

At my smile and nod, he went into the kitchen, returning a minute later with gargantuan pieces of choc-olate cheesecake with white chocolate drizzle on top. My eyes bulged when he set it in front of me.

"I wish I could take credit for this, but baking is the

one thing I could never do well. So, this is courtesy of Mabel's Cakes."

I couldn't help but smile at his honesty as I picked up my fork, excited to dig in. Mabel's Cakes was the best dessert shop in town.

"Thank you," I said, before popping a bite into my mouth.

It was better than heaven. Was that even possible? The bittersweet dark chocolate combined with the slightly sweet and tangy cheesecake, and the super sweet white chocolate on top…Was it possible to get drunk on sweets? Because after one bite, I was halfway there.

"Thith ith amathing!" I exclaimed through a mouthful of cake. Clearly, I was the epitome of a lady.

Jameson's dimple reappeared, his eyes doing that ridiculous twinkling thing again. I didn't know if he thought I was cute or gross for talking with my mouth full, but he wasn't kicking me out, so I took that as a good sign.

But then, right on cue, like a cockroach that wouldn't die, Ben's words slithered back into my mind.

Ladies don't talk with food in their mouth, Elsie. You're a lady. Act like one. Men aren't attracted to gross women.

At the memory of his words, I dropped my fork, and it clanked against the porcelain plate.

Jameson's brows rose. "Everything okay?"

Why couldn't my insecurities leave me alone? Why

did Ben's scathing remarks still haunt me four years later?

I shoved another bite of cake into my mouth, trying to silence my thoughts. "Wep, mmhmm. Gweat!" *Crap, I did it again.* Ben's words repeated on an endless loop. My eyes burned, and I lowered my gaze to the plate, as if the sage-green design around the edge was the most interesting thing in the world.

Don't cry, Elsie. Pretend everything is fine and cry later. Jameson doesn't need to see your tears.

A sudden warmth appeared at my side, and I turned to find Jameson on his knees next to me, his strong hands gently brushing my hair over my shoulder.

"Elsie," he whispered, his eyes full of concern. "What's wrong?"

I shook my head. If I tried to speak, I knew a sob would escape.

His fingers drew a scalding line across my cheek. "You don't have to hide from me," he said, eyes softening.

"I hide from everybody," I whispered back, blinking against the tears filling my eyes.

Tentatively, he ran a hand up my arm before resting it behind my neck.

"Then let me be your safe place."

His words settled into me, easing the ache in my heart that I had tried to bury for so long. Could such a thing exist? Could Jameson be a safe place for me to share my fears, my dreams, and all the in between?

Jameson leaned forward, cupping my cheek. I needed

to stop him; to pull away, but I didn't *want* to. My eyes closed as his lips brushed mine. He was hesitant at first, as if he expected me to pull back. When I didn't, he leaned into it, taking my face in both of his hands.

I was right about them—strong but gentle.

His lips were equal parts soft and unyielding, tasting of chocolate and garlic, which was, strangely, an amazing combination.

My arms went around his neck, fingers sliding into his hair, and he took advantage of the moment to turn me so he knelt between my legs. I gripped his hips with my knees, my nails scraping against his scalp, and he let out a soft groan against my mouth.

His hands moved to my waist, squeezing, squeezing...

A knock at the door echoed in the quiet room, and Luna leaped off her bed, barking. Jameson and I pulled apart, breathless.

"Luna! Quiet," he commanded, and she went silent, sitting in front of the door, tail wagging. Another knock sounded, louder and more impatient than the last.

He turned remorseful eyes on me. "I'm sorry."

"Don't worry about it."

Jameson didn't seem convinced by my response, but he pushed to his feet, adjusted his shirt and hair that had gotten rumpled beneath my hands, and went to answer the door. Whoever was there didn't wait for Jameson to open it all the way before he started yelling.

"Mr. Beck, I found yet another dog ball in my yard.

How many times have I asked you to keep your rabid dog off my lawn and away from my house?"

My blood turned to ice at the person's voice.

"You must be confusing me with someone else because all of Luna's toys are accounted for. Go waste someone else's time." Jameson tried to shut the door, but the stranger's hand thumped against it, keeping it open.

"I'd be careful how you speak to me, Mr. Beck."

Every piece of me that had been warm from Jameson's touch froze over.

I knew that voice. I knew the arrogant face and the sneer that had uttered it.

I shifted in my chair enough to see over Jameson's shoulder.

It was Ben.

It had been four years since I had last seen him, but he still looked the same. Same cocky smirk, same carefully arranged blonde hair, same standard stuffy suit. The only change was the slightest trace of wrinkles around his eyes.

Dang it. Why couldn't he have at least gotten ugly?

Like the coward I was, I clumsily slid out of my chair, intending to hide under the table. Of course my knee knocked the table leg, and the dishes rattled.

Silence. Then—

"Elsie?"

22

Jameson

"Elsie?" my neighbor, Benjamin, with a last name I couldn't remember, asked with his mouth agape. *I'm sorry, what?*

How did my terrible, nuisance of a neighbor know Elsie's name?

I glanced over my shoulder, and every protective instinct in my body went on alert. Elsie was crouched by the table, chest heaving, all the color drained from her face. It was clear she knew this guy, and based on her reaction, that was *not* a good thing.

"Elsie?" he asked again, his tone changing from surprise to slimy arrogance. A smirk tilted his lips, and my hands clenched into fists to keep from punching it off his face.

He attempted to take a step inside, but I slid in front

of him. "I don't recall inviting you in, Benjamin." My voice was cold, void of all the warmth it held for Elsie moments ago.

"What are you doing here, Elsie?" Benjamin completely ignored me, and my vision went red. If it were possible, smoke would have been leaking from my ears like I was in a cartoon. My neighbor eyed me with disgust before spitting, "And with him."

"I don't believe that's any of your business," I snapped, putting a hand on his chest, giving him a little shove. It took all my restraint to keep from hitting him harder, from *forcing* him to leave.

Elsie's shoulders drooped as she stood. Over the past couple weeks, she had slowly started to come out of the hard shell she hid behind. Her confidence had grown more in the time we spent together, and a light that hadn't been there before filled her eyes. But now...now she was shrinking, curling in on herself because of this pathetic excuse for a man. The spark that had been growing within her went out in his presence, and I hated it.

"Are you dating this guy, Elsie?"

"Once again, I don't see how that's any of your business." My patience was a thin string about to snap.

Benjamin sneered at me, and my nails bit into my palms to the point of pain. Who did this guy think he was?

"Go away," Elsie muttered, and Benjamin cocked his head.

"What was that?"

"I said go away, Ben." Elsie's voice was quiet, pleading. It reminded me of an injured animal. Her palms pressed into her sides, trembling, and her eyes glistened, fighting back tears.

Benjamin's brows lowered over his eyes. "You told me you didn't want *anyone,* Elsie. And now you're with *him*? You little—"

Okay, that's enough.

"You heard the lady," I snapped, giving him a hard shove. "Time to go." The guy's chest was bony, void of muscle, as I pushed him outside and slammed the door in his face, twisting the deadbolt for good measure.

For a moment, I could only stand there, glaring at the door, hands flexing at my sides. How dare he speak to Elsie like that? How dare *anyone* speak to her like that? My heart pounded beneath my skin, the need to yell at that awful man for belittling her made me feel prickly and hot.

I focused on my breathing, trying to calm myself. I didn't want Elsie to see my anger and be afraid of me, or for me to remind her of that puny man who had insulted her. After a solid thirty seconds, my muscles relaxed, my fury under control.

At last, I turned to face Elsie, who stood watching me. Her face was pale, her caramel eyes wide. She trembled from head to toe.

"Elsie..." I wanted nothing more than to pull her into my arms, to show her that I would never treat her in such a horrendous way. I wanted to make her feel on top of the world, not the size of a bug. I wanted to fuel that spark in her, not extinguish it.

I crossed the room, intending to wrap her in my arms until her trembling subsided, but she blinked, that hazy expression disappearing before she took off down the short hallway. A door closed a moment later, followed by the click of a lock echoing through the house.

I tried to be kind and give her some time alone in the bathroom. If she wanted to talk about what happened, she would have already emerged and walked straight into my arms, where I desperately wanted her to be right now. As much as I wanted to know what she was thinking, I wasn't about to force her. I would wait patiently...or die trying.

My brain ping-ponged back and forth between the encounter with Benjamin and the kiss that had happened moments before.

That kiss...

Mind-blowing. Earth-shattering. Knee-wobbling.

Though it had been years since I had kissed anyone, I had never experienced anything like that before. That whole romantic notion of seeing fireworks with a first kiss? No, this was more like an atomic bomb going off.

Or a volcano erupting.

It was powerful.

It was everything.

I wanted to do it again.

After twenty minutes, anxiety needled its way out of my skin. I had cleared the table, washed the dishes—by hand, so it took up more time—and tidied the living room, even though it was already clean. There was nothing left to do but sit on the couch, twiddling my thumbs. Luna had followed Elsie into the bathroom, eliminating the one thing that could offer a distraction.

The clock ticked on the mantel. Surely twenty minutes was enough time, right? I couldn't take the silence anymore, couldn't take knowing she was sad and alone when I had the power to change it. My feet thumped against the wood floor as I went down the hall to the bathroom, giving two soft knocks on the door.

"Elsie?" I asked. "Are you all right?"

Silence greeted me before I heard her sniffle, then a weak "yeah" filtered through the barrier between us. That sniffle was my undoing. I needed to help her, to hold her, *anything* to show her that she didn't deserve to be treated like that.

She was safe with me, and I needed her to believe it.

"Can I come in?"

A grunt followed by the lock clicking and the knob twisting had the door swinging open. Despite the seriousness of the moment, I had to bite my cheek to hold back a laugh at the sight of Luna, all seventy-five pounds of her, sprawled across Elsie's lap. Elsie's face was buried in Luna's soft coat, who looked up at me with big eyes that said, "Fix this."

I'm going to try, Luna girl.

I knelt and leaned against the wall, the tile hard and unforgiving beneath my knees. The bathroom was small, so it was a tight fit with the three of us taking up the entire floor.

My hand settled on her back, rubbing in circles. "Are you okay?"

Elsie's face was tear streaked, her eyes and nose red as she turned to look at me. The sight of her tears made my heart crack in two, and I fought the urge to chase down that loser and make sure he could never make her cry again. She shrugged, punctuating the movement with another sniffle.

"I'm here if you want to talk about it," I offered. "Or, if you don't want to talk about it, I'm still here." Fresh tears filled her eyes, prompting me to add, "I'm sorry about my neighbor. The way he spoke to you was unacceptable." I paused, glancing at her out of the corner of my eye. "You guys seemed to know each other."

Elsie huffed a breath, and gave Luna a kiss on the head, who then gave her a slimy tongue to the cheek in response. I wasn't sure what I wanted her response to be. There was history between them, that much was obvious, but to what extent?

Elsie blew out a long breath before giving a single nod. "Ben is my ex."

"Huh. Small world." What were the chances that Elsie's ex would be my neighbor? "How long were you guys together?"

She hesitated, running her fingers through Luna's fur. "Four years."

I let out a low whistle. "That's a long time."

"I broke up with him the night he was going to propose."

Her admission made me sad for her but also elated because it meant she was here with *me* now. If they had ended up getting married, she wouldn't be sitting on my bathroom floor right now, and I wouldn't have been able to kiss her thirty minutes ago.

"Hmm, well it seems you dodged a bullet there," I mused, wanting to say so much more, like how he was a horrible person who didn't deserve her, and that I was so happy she was in *my* house instead. But I held the words behind my lips, not wanting to overwhelm her anymore than she already was. A stray tear slipped down her cheek, and I wiped it away. Goosebumps pebbled on her skin.

"I'm sorry he spoke to you like that. I should've slammed the door in his face sooner."

She shrugged. "That was nothing new. That's just Ben."

"He's talked to you like that before?" My thumb traced a line across her face as she nodded, and my heart cracked further.

How could anyone treat Elsie that way? Not only was she beautiful, but she was whip smart, funny, and one of the kindest people I had ever met. Benjamin clearly took advantage of her sweet nature, forcing her into a box in which she didn't fit—nor was she meant to. Men like that—if you could even call them such—didn't deserve someone as amazing as Elsie.

It all made sense now—why she acted the way she did; why she was so hesitant to open up to me, to offer her heart. It was clear her ex made her believe things about herself that weren't true, and spoke to her in a way that had her cowering behind her walls. Elsie had learned to protect her heart at all costs. I couldn't even fault her for it.

"You deserve better than that."

Elsie closed her eyes, her head thumping against the wall. "He always made me feel small and never paid much attention to me. Our breakup was long overdue. The only reason I stayed so long was because..."

I waited, letting her sort through her thoughts. It was the first time Elsie was truly open with me, and I wasn't about to rush her.

"I didn't want to disappoint my parents," she sighed. "My dad was the one who set us up in the first place. He loved Ben, but he never saw the person he really was—the person he became when we were alone. It only took a couple months for me to realize that he wasn't right for me, but I couldn't bring myself to end things. At least until…"

"Until?"

Elsie shook her head, the wall that protected her heart slamming back down as her eyes shuttered. "Nothing." She shrugged. "It's not important now."

There was more to the story, so much more she wasn't telling me, but after this night's ordeal, I wasn't going to push. She would tell me when she was ready.

Hopefully.

Wrapping my arm around her shoulders, I pulled her against my chest, and she melted into me. If all I could do to comfort her was hold her, then I would do it all night. If that was how I proved I wasn't like her ex, that I was a safe place and a man she could rely on, then I would stay here as long as I needed to.

I lost track of how much time passed as we sat there curled together, Luna sprawled across both our laps.

Eventually she yawned and said, "I should probably head home."

My arms tightened around her automatically. *Don't let go.* I wished I could say the words out loud, wished I could ask her to stay.

I gave Luna a pat and she stood, tail wagging as she sauntered out of the room. With a groan, I pushed to my feet before helping Elsie up. Every instinct within me wanted to pull her back into my arms, but I let her head for the front door instead. Her floral shampoo wafted into my nose as she walked past.

"Thank you for dinner, Jameson," she said as I reluctantly helped her into her coat.

"Anytime, Elsie. Text me when you get home?"

She cocked her head as if that was a strange request. *I'm worried about you.*

"Sure."

I worked to put a smile on my face, hoping it would inspire one of her own as I brushed my fingers against her palm. "May I kiss you goodnight?"

An emotion I couldn't name flashed in her eyes, perhaps equal parts surprise and hesitation. I expected her to say no, but she tilted her chin up, leaning closer. It was the most natural thing in the world to brush my lips against hers, once, twice. I couldn't escape how *right* this felt.

"Goodnight, Elsie," I murmured against her mouth.

Her lips twitched, the first signs of a smile since her ex had interrupted our dinner, and it felt like I had won the lottery for causing it.

Elsie opened the door to leave, stepping out into the chilly air. "Goodnight, Jameson."

23

Elsie

By the time I made it home, I had a slew of angry text messages, including two voicemails from Ben. It had been years since I had heard from him. I didn't even know he still had my number.

I found it ironic that he was bothering me now when he hadn't even bothered to fight for me when I broke things off four years ago.

I couldn't bring myself to tap the screen to see what vile words he had sent to me, nor did I want to hear his voice saying the same things in a voicemail. So, instead, I muted notifications from his number, ignoring him entirely.

Give him a taste of his own medicine for once.

I was about to crawl into bed and bury myself beneath the blankets when my phone buzzed. At first, I thought it was Ben's notifications still coming through somehow, but then I saw Jameson's name on the screen.

Heart in my throat, I tapped the screen to open his message.

JAMESON

Hey Elsie :) I just wanted to say goodnight. Please don't worry about what happened tonight. My neighbor has always been a pain and he had no right to speak to you like that. And I certainly don't think any less of you. Despite the rocky end to our date, I greatly enjoyed spending the evening with you.

And that kiss— *mind blown emoji*

I can't wait to see you again.

Sweet dreams, Els.

How was he still so kind to me after everything that had happened? How could he still want anything to do with me after seeing the baggage I carried?

His words were dangerous, weakening my resolve, sending it sliding away like sand in the ocean tide. And yet, it felt like a lifeline, like getting that first breath after being submerged under water for too long.

Ben had both broken and hardened my heart, and added with the heartbreak of watching what my parents went through, I didn't know how to let Jameson in. But if I was painfully honest with myself, Jameson was everything I had always wanted Ben to be, and it left me confused, unsure what to do next. I had to keep him at a distance.

This thing between us wasn't worth the risk, right?

And what if I let Jameson in and then he rips off that mask like Ben did, like my parents did, and he becomes someone else entirely? He hadn't given me any reason to suspect that would happen, but it was hard to silence the voice of the past.

Think about it tomorrow, Elsie. No sense trying to make sense of it all when you're exhausted.

I sighed, sinking deeper into the bed, reading Jameson's last text over and over before slowly drifting off into a deep, dreamless sleep.

The next morning it all came rushing back.

Dinner at Jameson's. Ben showing up and yelling at me. That kiss. It was like a cyclone of pleasure and irritation spinning in my head.

The only thing that made it better was waking up to a text that said:

JAMESON

Good morning. Check your front door :)

Blankets were flung, a robe was donned, and my feet slapped against the cold wood floor as I hurried to the door. Sitting on my green doormat was a paper bag with a hot cup of coffee next to it. Taped to the top was a note with the DoorDash emblem. It read:

Good morning, sunshine.

I couldn't help but giggle at the term of endearment because I was likely the last person anyone would consider "sunshine".

Maya told me how you like your coffee and gave me your address so I could send you something to wake up to. I hope you don't mind. Please enjoy a breakfast of chocolate-glazed donuts and a mocha with an extra shot of espresso and cream. Have a great day! :)

The scent of coffee and sugar wafted into my nose as I plucked up the bag and cup, taking a sip. Immediately, my spirits lifted. Ben had never made me feel this way—not even when we first started dating, when everything was new and supposed to be fun. He had always made me feel like an afterthought; meant to be seen and not heard. I vaguely remembered him using the term "arm candy" at one point.

I had been on two dates and a handful of spontaneous non-dates with Jameson, and he had never made me feel that way. Quite the opposite, honestly.

Racing back inside, I grabbed my phone, settled on a barstool at my peninsula, and pulled up the text thread with Jameson.

ME

Thank you for breakfast :)

It only took seconds for him to respond.

JAMESON

You're welcome. I wanted to give you a reason to smile :)

ME

You definitely did.

JAMESON

Good. You have a beautiful smile.

I wasn't sure how to respond—nor could I remember the last time a man had given me that kind of compliment. Getting compliments from Ben had been like pulling teeth, which always made me self-conscious and insecure.

When a minute passed without me responding, my phone buzzed with another message.

JAMESON

Do you have plans tonight?

Was he already wanting to have the third date? My mind instantly went into a downward spiral of worst-case scenarios. Maybe last night had told him all he needed to know about me, and he wanted to get the last date over with so he could wipe his hands of me.

That was fine. Better for me in the end. I was already getting too attached.

But why did the thought of parting ways after our

last date fill me with an aching loneliness that brought tears to my eyes?

JAMESON

It's not our official third date, but I'd like to see you tonight.

And just like that, my tears transformed into a smitten grin, vanishing all those doubts having a rager in my mind.

Smart Elsie was screaming at me to say no, to keep my distance, to keep myself safe, but being near Jameson was as addictive as a drug, and I wanted another hit. So, instead of telling him we should wait to see each other for our final date, I texted back:

ME

I'm free. What did you have in mind?

24

Jameson

For the record, going to a beach at the height of fall was probably not the smartest decision. The wind coming off the water was icy, biting beneath my layers, despite the lingering warmth of the sun. The local beach, Meridel's Tide, was deserted, though the sun warmed the sand enough that I took my shoes off to walk barefoot.

In one hand I carried an enormous blanket and two giant hoodies and, in the other, a big basket full of hot foods perfect for such a chilly day. Only a fool would have a picnic on a windy beach on a cold fall day, but that's what Elsie had turned me into. A fool in—

Nope. Don't go there, Jameson.

I let out a sigh. My feelings for Elsie had grown fast, much faster than I'd ever experienced. I was certain that if I revealed the depths of them to her, she would run and never look back. *I* was resisting the urge to run. We had only known each other for a few weeks now, but every time I walked away from our time together, I had fallen a little bit more.

Falling was scary. Falling was dangerous.

It was like sliding down an enormous water slide not knowing if there'd be a pool of water or concrete at the bottom. One had the power to save, while the other had the power to destroy.

Apparently falling for someone felt a lot like that.

And yet, I'd never met someone I was so willing to risk it all for.

Yes, Elsie was gorgeous but that was only a bonus. Behind the barricade surrounding her heart was a kind, sweet soul that I couldn't get enough of. I loved her grumpy firecracker personality, especially when her feisty side came out and I caught a glimpse of her quick wit. She genuinely cared about everyone she encountered, even if she kept them all at a distance. The way Elsie bit her lip when she concentrated, or how she pressed them together while trying not to laugh constantly replayed in my mind.

Maybe some people would be scared away by all the defense mechanisms she used to protect herself, but I only wanted to dismantle them, brick by brick.

On top of it all, I had read the articles and blogs she had written recently, and they were *good*. So good that I couldn't believe she had never tried to publish anything of her own. Elsie was beyond talented, and the world only saw tiny fragments of her ability.

But I saw every piece, and the world needed her writing. I saw every dream she kept hidden, even in the silliest articles. Her heart was on display even if she didn't know it, and it was beautiful.

I rubbed a hand over my face, trying to quell the rush of emotion that made me want to leap headfirst into a serious relationship with Elsie.

One thing at a time, Jameson.

Fighting against the wind, I spread the blanket across the sand, setting the picnic basket in one corner and my shoes in the other to hold it down. I was pulling the hot dishes from the basket when someone spoke behind me.

"I can't say I've ever had a beach picnic in October before."

My grin was automatic as I stood and turned to face her. She was bundled in a long peacoat, a cute little beanie on her head. It was around fifty degrees, but she was dressed like the middle of winter. I chuckled as I reached for her, pulling her into a hug.

"What? It's the best time of year for a picnic," I whispered into her ear. Elsie leaned her head back with a smile, and it was only natural to press my lips against her cheek. It lasted a split second, but when I pulled away, her eyes fluttered open slowly as if the light kiss had put her in a trance.

Taking a step away, I gestured to the blanket. Dishes

of hot food—steam rising into the rays of sunlight—warm drinks, and two giant blanket hoodies, were carefully spread across it.

"You've been busy," she commented.

I smiled before handing her one of the giant hoodies. "It's a little chilly so I thought you might want this." I slipped the other over my head. It was a long blanket that ended at the knee with sleeves and a hood. Those infernal social media ads had gotten me to buy two of them a while back when I couldn't sleep and was doom scrolling instead. Hers had a cute dog pattern that looked like Luna, while mine was plain blue.

"Thanks," she replied, giggling when she got her head stuck in one of the arm holes. Why was she so cute? She snuggled deeper into it and my insides squeezed at the sight of her wearing something of mine, even if it was only a blanket hoodie. A bloodie? Or would it be a hanket?

"Have a seat. I brought broccoli cheddar soup, three different kinds of bread, chicken pot pie, and because I'm not *completely* unhealthy, roasted veggies. I also brought hot chocolate for dessert."

She eyed the dishes as if they were sent straight from heaven.

I handed her a bowl and spooned in some soup, then sliced her a small chunk of each of the different breads. One was French Bread, another was some sort of Italian herb bread, and the last was a cheesy bread that made my mouth water. Elsie dunked one straight into her soup before stuffing it into her mouth, which was followed by a quiet hum of approval.

"Good?"

"Mmhmm," she said around a bite. "It's perfect."

"I wish I could take credit for it, but I cheated a little. Work went longer than expected today, so I picked the food up from Dina's." Even though my mom had taught me to cook as a kid, I wasn't *that* good, and I hadn't anticipated having to squeeze in extra patients today. Otherwise, I probably would have…no. I still would've picked up Dina's. I would do anything to impress this girl.

"Whether you made this, or picked it up from Dina's doesn't matter. It's hot and delicious, and I'm happy."

Her words sent a thrill through me, and I felt like I had won a gold medal at the Olympics. Elsie froze mid-chew, eyes widening as if her words had surprised her, too.

I couldn't hold back my grin. "Then mission accomplished."

Her throat bobbed as she swallowed, eyes lighting up at my words. Sparks shot up my legs from where our thighs touched, and my traitorous eyes strayed to her lips. We moved identically, like puppets controlled by the same desire. She leaned closer to me, her hot breath puffing against my lips. Then a loud buzz came from my pocket.

We both flinched, pulling apart, and I didn't miss the disappointment that flashed in her eyes. Elsie picked up her bowl and resumed eating, a pretty blush coloring her cheeks. For a moment, I didn't move, letting the call go to voicemail. I didn't want to be *that* guy. I didn't want her to think whoever was calling was more important than she was. But as soon as it stopped, it started again.

"I'm sorry," I apologized, fishing the phone from my pocket, frustrated by the interruption. "It might be an emergency," I added, hoping she'd understand.

Angel's Hearth flashed across the screen and my stomach dropped. Jumping to my feet, I walked a few feet down the beach. Why was my mom's assisted living home calling? A thousand pounds settled on my shoulders, and I ran a nervous hand through my hair as I pressed the green button and held the phone to my ear.

"Hello?"

"Mr. Beck?" a woman said. It sounded like Rhonda, the receptionist.

"Yes?"

"Mr. Beck, are you able to come to Angel's Hearth?"

"Is everything all right?" I asked. Anxiety gripped me by the throat, squeezing the air from my lungs. Had something happened to my mom?

"Mr. Beck, your mother had a little accident. She's fine, no serious injuries, but she's a little frazzled. It might be good if you came to see her."

Nausea instantly filled my stomach. "What happened?"

"She took a tumble on the way down to dinner. Her legs gave out beneath her. I think it startled her more than anything, but it would be a good time to visit if you're able."

"All right. I'll be there as soon as I can."

My finger slammed on the end button, and I shoved the phone back in my pocket. As much as I hated the thought of ending my non-date with Elsie early, my mom needed me. Would Elsie be mad? I hoped that she would understand this wasn't a case of which person I cared about more. It was simply that my mom needed me right now, and I would do whatever I had to in order to be there for her.

My hands shook at my sides as I returned to the picnic and started packing up the food. "I'm so sorry, Els. My mom…" I blew out a breath. I didn't know how to voice my fear or tell her how scared it made me that my mom had an accident. My hands trembled as I picked up the bowl of soup, almost spilling its contents.

Elsie put her hands over mine, steadying me. "Jameson, what happened?"

I met her concerned gaze. "My mom fell."

As much as I hated pulling away from her, I returned my shaking hands to the dishes, shoving them into the basket, not caring if I spilled the leftover food.

Elsie placed her hands on my chest, forcing me to still. Her touch grounded me, forcing the anxious thoughts pummeling me to abate ever so slightly.

"Hey," she whispered. "It's going to be okay. I'll finish cleaning up. Go see your mom."

My hand settled over hers, rubbing her soft skin. It calmed me, if only for a moment.

"Will you come with me?"

Panic clouded my mind, and it was the only thought I had. I wanted Elsie there with me. I wanted her calming presence. I needed her hand in mine as I walked down the hallway to my mom's room.

Her gaze softened. "Are you sure that's a good idea?" she asked.

"I want you to come," was my only reply.

She hesitated a moment longer before nodding. "Okay. I'll come."

I sagged toward her. "Thank you," I whispered, pressing my lips to her forehead. Together, we finished packing up the picnic remnants before I laced my fingers through hers and led her up the beach toward my truck.

25

Elsie

A slight drizzle started falling from the sky as we parked in front of Angel's' Hearth. Instead of rushing inside, Jameson stared at the red brick building with glazed eyes, a heavy silence filling the cab of the truck. I wanted to reassure him, but I wasn't sure how.

On the drive over, Jameson had explained that his mother fell on her way to dinner and that, though she was only in her early sixties, the combination of cancer treatment and medicine weakened her body, making it difficult for it to heal properly as a result. A simple fall like that might not have been a big deal for most people, but for her it could've meant a trip to the emergency room.

"Should we go in?" I asked, breaking the silence.

His eyes slid closed and his throat bobbed before he gave a small nod. His chest rose and fell in deep breaths, hands clenching his knees.

I reached across the space between us, putting my hand on his. "I'm sure she's fine, Jameson. Your mom is strong. Look at all she's fought through." How could anyone survive the battles she had faced and not come out stronger in the end?

I pressed my lips together to hold back a question that formed, not wanting to take the focus away from his mother or reveal my insecurities. Unfortunately, my mouth had other plans.

"Do you..." I started before I sighed. "Do you want me to stay in the car?"

Jameson's eyes popped open, narrowing as they focused on me. "That's the last thing I want," he replied. "I want you here with me."

It was such a simple statement and yet it meant everything. Those six words eased my anxiety like nothing I had experienced before. It felt like sinking into a warm bath after a long day of physical labor, soothing all the aches and pains of the past.

Jameson climbed out of the truck before opening the door for me, and I wiped my clammy hands against my pants as I slid out of the cab. I'd be lying if I said I wasn't nervous to meet his mom, and I was certain that it would be a shock for her to see a strange woman walking in with him.

Nerves prickled like needles under my skin. It took a full year into my relationship with Ben before he ever invited me to any family function and, even then, he didn't really want me spending time with his family. It was rare for him to invite me to family events, dinners, or vacations. I always assumed it was because he was embarrassed by me.

Jameson slipped his hand in mine as we entered the building. Why did our fingers intertwined feel so *right*?

The scent of overcooked food and that distinct smell of elderly people permeated the lobby. The thermostat was clearly set too high—my coat suddenly felt too heavy and sweat slid down my spine.

"Hi Rhonda," Jameson said as we arrived at the front desk, where he signed both our names on a visitor sheet. The lady behind the counter appeared to be a few years older than us. She wore pink scrubs and her black hair was tied into a high ponytail. Her face was bare aside from a swipe of eyeliner on each lid. She eyed our linked hands and her lips pressed together, giving us a nod.

With a tug, Jameson pulled me down the hall. In the truck, he had explained that this wasn't a typical assisted living home. It wasn't only for the elderly but also for people who had suffered through severe illness, and family wasn't able to care for them. Or in Jameson's case, his mother had wanted him to have a life that didn't revolve around taking care of her day and night.

I could only imagine how hard that decision must have been. It spoke volumes of their relationship and how much they cared for one another.

The distinct sting of loss pierced through me. My parents had been my favorite people in the world once upon a time, but then the arguing started. And the yelling. I'd barely had any contact with them in four years, and it was their divorce that made me no longer believe in love. How could there be real love when everyone was fake?

I banished all thoughts of my parents as Jameson stopped in front of apartment 306. A cute little fall wreath hung on the door, with a few tiny gnomes on a ledge in the corner. I couldn't help but smile.

He knocked twice before unlocking the door with a key he pulled from his pocket.

"Mom?" Jameson called, poking his head in.

"Jamie?" a voice responded.

"It's me." He stepped inside, pulling me with him.

I was half expecting it to smell like an old person's home, musty and stale, but instead, the scent of baked apples filled the air.

Jameson slipped off his shoes and went to kneel in front of his mom who was propped up in a recliner. She had bandages on her left arm but showed no other signs of injury. Her salt-and-pepper hair was meticulously curled, and she wore a pretty red sweater, and loose, wide-legged yoga pants. Though she appeared frail, she was still quite beautiful, her hazel eyes identical to her son's.

"Are you okay, mom?" Jameson asked, gently setting his hand atop hers.

She waved the other hand. "I'm fine, Jamie. The

nurses made a fuss over nothing."

With gentle fingers, he picked her arm up to inspect it. "This is not nothing."

His mom rolled her eyes which had me biting back a snort. "I'm fine. It was just a few scratches from the ridiculous excuse for carpet they have here. Quit your fussing." She gave him a soft pat on the cheek.

Then her eyes snapped to mine, and I froze like a cornered animal. I suddenly wanted to run for my life as though a lion stalked toward me, preparing to eat me. What had I been thinking? Meeting Jameson's mom was a huge deal—dating or not.

Her eyes held me firmly in place, my feet frozen to the carpet. "Who's this lovely lady?"

My ears burned, and I was pretty sure I had Niagara Falls pits again. I squeezed my arms tighter against my sides. *Please stop sweating, armpits.*

Jameson turned toward me, a soft smile on his face. "Mom, this is Elsie. A...friend of mine."

Yeah, that's right, Jameson. Friends. Nothing more.

I wish those words relaxed me, but they seemed to have the opposite effect, winding my body tighter and tighter.

"A friend, hmm?" she said, looking between the two of us, though what she saw with twenty feet between us, I couldn't say.

Jameson stood, gesturing for me to come over. I tried to discreetly wipe my sweaty palms against my thighs before I had to shake his mom's hand.

Jameson put his hand on my low back and said, "Elsie, this is my mom, Margaret."

I offered a hand to her. "It's nice to meet you, Mrs. Beck."

"Oh, please call me Maggie, dear," she replied, giving me a loose handshake. "Mrs. Beck makes me feel old."

Jameson snorted, rubbing at the back of his neck.

"What brings you here, my dear? Surely Jameson didn't drag you along simply to check on his poor mother?"

The words tumbled from my lips before I could stop them. "We were having a picnic when he heard about your accident. He was really worried about you."

Her eyes widened, and I immediately second guessed my decision to tell her about the picnic. Was she the super protective type that would think I would never be good enough for her son?

But then she said, "A picnic you say?" A sly smile split her mouth, eyes sliding to her son. "Have you been hiding this delightful girl from me, Jamie?"

It was the first time I had witnessed Jameson Beck blushing, and I had to admit, I liked it. A lot.

"We're just getting to know each other, Mom."

She tutted, fixing him with a *look*. "I hope my Jamie is treating you well, dear."

I chuckled, both from her words and the sheer embarrassment written all over Jameson's face. "Don't worry, Mrs. B—Maggie. *Jamie* has been nothing but a gentleman. You raised a fine man.”

A mischievous gleam appeared in her eyes. “He *is* fine, isn’t he?”

Jameson gave a startled laugh. “All right, I think that’s enough. How much pain medicine do they have you on, Mom?”

“Oh hush, Jamie. You ended your date and ran all the way here for nothing.”

“It wasn’t a date,” we blurted at the same time.

She gave us each a wry grin. “Keep telling yourself that, dears. I know two people who are smitten with each other when I see them.”

“Mom…” Jameson said, exasperated, running a hand over his face before locking his eyes with mine. Heat crawled over my face.

“Well, you’ve come, you saw that I’m perfectly fine and that the nurses bothered you for no reason, and now you can get back to your date.” Maggie grabbed a book sitting on the table next to her, effectively dismissing us.

Neither of us bothered to correct her this time.

He shook his head. “I’ll drive Elsie back to her car and then I’ll come stay with you for a while.”

“Nonsense,” she barked. “You go finish your date, young man.”

“Mom—”

“Jameson Henry,” she middle-named him.

I had to cover my mouth with a hand to hide my smile. He sighed, the tips of his ears turning scarlet.

"Okay, Mom. We'll go finish our...date."

He pressed a kiss to the top of her head, and I didn't miss the smug smile on her face as she gave me a secret wink.

"It was nice to meet you, Maggie."

She smiled and gave me another wink. "Likewise, my dear. You take care of my boy, you hear? I'll see you soon."

I worked hard to keep my expression neutral, but my stomach sank.

I wouldn't be taking care of her son. I *wouldn't* be seeing her again.

The thought of letting down this woman I had just met, and hardly knew, had me biting at my nails as Jameson pulled me into the hallway, locking the door behind him.

I started the trek back to the entrance when warm fingers wrapped around my wrist, stopping me.

"How did you do that?" Jameson asked, voice uncharacteristically hoarse.

"Do what?"

He shook his head, stepping toward me, slowly backing me against the wall of the empty hallway. "My mother is very picky. She's never liked anyone I've introduced to her. Not that there's been many," he hurried to add, wincing. "But you...you completely enchanted her."

My back hit the wall, Jameson's hands landing on

either side of my head, blocking me in. His mouth was only inches from mine, and my chest heaved from the sudden closeness, my body begging for him to move closer. His fingers trailed across my cheek, down my neck, and lingered on my collarbone, setting me on fire.

"You're…" he sighed. "You're incredible."

And then his lips were on mine.

Despite knowing that our relationship had an expiration date, that kissing him would only lead to getting more attached, I leaned into the kiss. His body pressed into mine, chest to chest and hips against hips. His fingers tangled into my hair, and mine skimmed the skin at the bottom of his shirt. I was making out with Jameson Beck…in an assisted living home.

Was it weird? Maybe. Was it also hot? Most definitely.

But then someone cleared their throat, and we jumped apart. The receptionist, Rhonda, stood a few feet away with crossed arms. Her foot tapped against the floor.

Had I just gone for a swim in a pool of fire? That's how my body felt—everything was burning.

"H-hey, Rhonda," Jameson stuttered through a sheepish smile. "Mom is doing well, so we're going to go now. Okay? Okay, bye!"

He grabbed my hand and pulled me along at a pace that had me skipping to keep up. An absurd giggle bubbled out of my throat. I felt like a teenager again, stealing kisses and secret moments with a boy.

It made me feel…alive.

When was the last time I had felt like this?

Jameson looked over his shoulder at my giggle and gave me a crooked smile that had me laughing harder. When we made it out to his truck, he backed me against the door and kissed me again, though much slower this time, savoring every moment.

Like kissing me was the most important thing in the world, in *his* world.

"Elsie…" he whispered against my lips, sending a shiver through me. "I need to tell you something."

I was lost in his breath on my lips, in the feeling of his hands on my waist, that it took a moment for his words to sink in. Then my stomach fell to the cement beneath my feet, my brain immediately jumping to conclusions. Was this it? The end of whatever *this* was? He saw how much his mother liked me and decided that I couldn't get closer to either of them? This was where he was going to walk away, cut all ties?

I knew the end was coming. I expected it. I kept telling myself I *wanted* it to end. So why did it feel like I was losing something special? Why did it hurt to think of him saying all of this was over and that he didn't want to see me again?

Because you're falling for him, you fool, Smart Elsie barked in my mind.

I held my breath as I met his hazel gaze.

Was I?

Was I falling for Jameson Beck?

"Elsie..." Jameson repeated, halting my spinning thoughts. "I...I know I said that I wanted you to give me just three dates—and then we'd part ways if you wanted."

Here it comes.

"I know I said that but..." He exhaled, brushing his lips against mine, leaving me lightheaded when he pulled away. "I want more than three dates, Elsie." He took my face gently in his hands. "I want more with you."

My heart stuttered to a halt before doubling in tempo. He wanted *more*?

"I can't stand the thought of saying goodbye. I..." His eyes moved back and forth between mine as if he were searching for something. "There's something here..." He exhaled, his breath clouding in the chilly air. "Elsie, I'm falling for you."

I closed my eyes at his words. I was imagining this. I had to be.

How had he fallen for me?

I was grumpy and insecure, with enough baggage to fill an airport three times over. How could anyone fall for that?

But what scared me even more than his declaration were *my* feelings.

Because if I had been able to utter a single word, I knew I would've said it back.

Because, despite Smart Elsie's protests, I was falling for Jameson, too.

Jameson had wriggled his way inside my heart like a worm in an apple.

How did I get him out? Or the better question was… how did I get myself to *want* him out? Because if I were being honest, I desperately wanted things to work between us.

Dang it, Elsie. Why did you have to fall for this man?

My thoughts spun in circles about masks, and resentment, and feelings I shouldn't have while Jameson patiently waited for me to say something, but no words would come. After another moment he touched his forehead to mine.

"You don't have to say anything now." His fingers ran through my hair before tucking it behind my ears. "There's no pressure. I'm not going anywhere."

He pecked a kiss on my forehead before stepping back to open the car door. His endless patience and understanding rendered me speechless, and I slid into the seat, numb. He drove me back to my car at the beach, his hand intertwined in mine, while my brain warred with itself. By the time he dropped me off, I still couldn't formulate words, unable to quiet every doubt and insecurity running rampant in my mind.

What was I supposed to do now?

26

Jameson

Elsie didn't say anything when I confessed my feelings, and to say her silence was a sucker punch to my stomach was an understatement. I knew she was hesitant about dating, and I kept telling myself it was okay. If I were honest, I never thought that agreeing to do a silly couples photoshoot with someone I had never met, would end with me falling for the girl.

And yet, here we were.

Elsie was full of life and sass, and I loved every bit of it. Even in the brief interaction with my mom, she had sensed something special in Elsie. I had never seen my mom take to a girl like that. My mom was unafraid to say what she was thinking, and most women would have been scared away.

But not Elsie.

She had laughed, blushed, smiled, even played along when my mother ribbed at me.

I ran a hand through my hair. *I really like this girl.* There had been a spark from that very first meeting in the sunflowers, but never had I imagined it would turn into *this.*

Elsie had to feel something between us. She wouldn't kiss me like that—dig her fingers into my skin and hold me tighter like she had—if she didn't feel *something* toward me. The question was…was what she felt strong enough to counteract whatever fears and reservations she had about me to begin with?

After I dropped her off at her car, I went home, mind spinning. I thought about going back to spend time with my mom, but she had middle-named me in front of Elsie and insisted she was fine. I couldn't argue with being middle-named.

Even at almost thirty years old, my mother still had me wrapped around her finger.

So now, here I sat on my leather couch, nursing a warm mug of coffee, thoughts of Elsie incessant in my mind.

Her soft floral scent.

The tender press of her lips on mine.

Her fingers in my hair, on my neck.

I rubbed my face. I was a goner.

This girl had me hook, line, and sinker.

I tried not to think about the flash of fear in her eyes when I told her how I felt. I chose to be optimistic that she was only scared by what she felt for me in return. But the practical part of me couldn't help but worry about whether I had made a mistake in telling her. What if she didn't reciprocate? What if my declaration scared her so much that she ended things?

I couldn't let that happen. She meant too much to me, and there was no way I would let her go without a fight.

Her ex may have been a coward who let her walk away, but I would not be like him.

Elsie was worth the fight. *We* were worth the fight.

I just hoped she let me prove it to her.

27

Elsie

"Elsie," Maya sighed, coffee cup in hand. "Jameson said he has feelings for you. This is amazing. Why are you freaking out?"

Why was I freaking out? Because, despite my efforts to keep Jameson at a distance, to protect my heart, I had fallen for him. I kept picturing my future with him, which was a huge problem knowing it would all come crashing down at some point.

I liked him too much to allow that to happen. I liked him too much to not be broken if—and when—he revealed his true self.

My mind was a mess. Hence the freaking out.

I squinted at her, pursing my lips as I glanced around. Though it was noisy in the coffee shop, it didn't stop her voice from carrying. I didn't need all of Meridel hearing about my boy problems, and I especially didn't need word getting back to Jameson...or worse, Ben. Ben was the type to be vengeful and vindictive, and I wouldn't put it past him to do something to hurt me or Jameson.

"Because," I said around a bite of a cinnamon chip scone, "this isn't what we agreed on. It was supposed to be three dates, and then it was supposed to end. There weren't supposed to be feelings involved. He wasn't supposed to *like* me."

"But *you* like *him*," Maya was quick to point out. While I hadn't said those exact words out loud, my best friend knew me far too well, and it was impossible to hide the truth from her.

I pressed my fingers against my eyes, trying to stop the tears that wanted to fall. "What am I going to do?"

"Oh my gosh, Elsie. You act like a man falling for you is the equivalent of your cat dying. You both like each other, so just date! *Really* date!"

I dropped my hands, clenching them into fists. "You know I can't do that."

Maya rolled her eyes. "Look, Els, I'm going to give you some tough love because you need it, and I know you can handle it. You and Jameson are *not* your parents. Their divorce was awful, yes, but that doesn't mean it will happen to you two. You'd really miss out on the chance at an incredible guy because you're scared things will end like your parents?"

"Twenty-nine *years*, Maya," I snapped. "They were

married for twenty-nine years, and they just gave up on each other. They were always yelling, always fighting. By the end, there was so much resentment between them, I felt like I was choking on it when I was around them. They used to be crazy about each other. Now look at them. If it could happen to them, it can happen to me, and it's not worth it. It's not worth it to fall in love with someone, build a life together, then grow to resent them each day, until you both just…give up."

Maya sighed. "Els, you can't look at your parents as the be-all end-all. Not every relationship and marriage ends like that. Your parents stopped choosing each other. They stopped choosing to fight for their marriage. They let resentment stop them from working things out."

I took a long drink of my coffee, scalding my tongue as her words settled. I had never thought about it like that before.

"Don't do that with Jameson. See where things can go. And if it works out, take it one day at a time, choosing each other each day." She paused, studying me. "Have you even told Jameson about your parents?"

I avoided her eyes, which must have been answer enough because she scoffed.

"Elsie, you need to tell him. How can he fight your fears and prove his feelings when he doesn't even know what beast he's battling?"

I winced. I supposed she had a point, as much as I hated to admit it.

Could I tell Jameson about my parents? Would he understand why I was so scared of relationships? Would he do as Maya suggested and help me fight those fears? Or would he see my baggage and run away? The baggage from Ben was one thing, but adding my parents' brutal divorce into the mix, and how it skewed my belief in love? Who would want that?

"I don't know if telling him would change anything."

"Well, you'll never know unless you try. You're calling it quits before you even give him a chance. That's worse than what your parents did if you ask me."

Outrage filled my veins before it settled into a dull simmer. As much as those words hurt to hear, maybe she had a point.

I eyed her. "When did you get so...relationship-y?"

She shrugged. "Just call me Love Guru Maya."

"You're not even dating anyone."

Maya rolled her eyes. "I don't need a man to know that you're being ridiculous. I'm serious, Els. Give Jameson a shot."

I sipped my coffee, rubbing at the ache in my chest. "I'll think about it."

JAMESON

Hey.

Do you have plans tonight?

I'd like to see you.

Jameson's texts came through right as I finished a freelance blog piece about the health benefits of pumpkin pie and sent it off for approval. Was it mostly made up? Sure, but at least I *tried* to make people feel less guilty about indulging in that pumpkin goodness. Besides, pumpkin pie season only came around once a year. Might as well help people enjoy it to the fullest. YOLO, right?

Snapping my laptop closed, I stared at the phone on the counter like it had grown horns and a mustache, debating how to respond.

Did I have plans? No. When did I ever?

But that wasn't the big question here, was it? The question was: did I *want* to see him tonight?

I shouldn't.

I absolutely should not want to see him.

But Jameson had quickly become a normal part of my daily routine after spending nearly every evening and weekend with him for the past month. It felt...wrong to think about not seeing him tonight. I sighed. These were the exact feelings I was trying to avoid.

I blew out a long breath, putting my face in my hands. How did my heart develop feelings when my mind had only experienced fake people and false love? How could I yearn for him while waiting for the other shoe to drop?

The rug would get pulled out from beneath me eventually. Wouldn't it?

But...what if it didn't? What if Maya was right and I had it all wrong? Yeah, what I went through with Ben and what I witnessed in that mess of a divorce was terrible, and I *thought* that meant real love couldn't exist. The two relationships that had meant the most to me ended in disaster. It was a logical conclusion to reach.

Maya's words echoed in my mind. *Give him a chance.*

What if...what if I *did* give Jameson a chance?

Then you'd be opening yourself up to get hurt again, Smart Elsie snapped. *What happens when you two get in a fight and he turns into someone else entirely, like Ben always did? Someone cruel who says awful, hurtful things?*

But there's no guarantee that Jameson is like that, Smitten Elsie retorted. *Not once has he given you any sign he's that kind of man. I think he's genuine.*

With a frustrated groan, I shoved their unhelpful words away and tapped out a reply:

ME

Yes, I'm free.

I didn't have a response to his confession yet, at least

not one I could voice out loud, nor was I sure what I wanted to say about these confusing feelings swirling inside me. I was as conflicted as a squirrel running back and forth in the middle of the road, unable to make up its mind before a car ran it over.

JAMESON

[excited GIF]

Would you rather go out or have a night in?

I didn't want to admit it, but I loved that he was thoughtful enough to ask such a question. I was a home-body to the core and always preferred a night of relaxing at home to going out somewhere loud and people-y. Ben never bothered to ask—always taking me to noisy, crowded places, as if he couldn't wait to flaunt how big his wallet was.

If only he had noticed that I couldn't care less.

ME

Let's stay in.

You bring the food, I'll provide the couch and movie.

JAMESON

Deal. I'll be there around 5. See you soon :)

P.S. this isn't the third date yet :)

At five on the dot, Jameson knocked on my door. The smile on his face was like a million-watt light bulb, and darn if it didn't make my knees wobble...just a little bit.

"Hi," he breathed, scanning me from head to toe, setting every inch of me on fire. He needed to stop or I was going to spontaneously combust.

"Hey," I replied, unable to keep the smile from my lips. I stepped aside to let him in, and he pressed a kiss to my cheek. He had a blue insulated bag in one hand and a bottle of wine in the other. I gestured at the peninsula for him to set everything down.

I had frantically cleaned the house after inviting him over, scrubbing every single surface. Though I wasn't a messy person, I often went too long between rounds of cleaning. A thick layer of dust had built up on every surface, and there was an embarrassing number of dirty dishes in the kitchen sink. But now, everything was spotless and my home smelled like caramel apples thanks to the wax melt in the corner of the room. Jameson shucked off his shoes and crossed my little living room to set the food bag on the counter.

I couldn't help thinking he looked like he belonged here.

I shook my head, banishing the thought. Maya's

words had gotten to me, but the fear was still very real, and I couldn't quite reconcile the two yet.

Jameson turned to me, opening his arms for a hug. My feet moved of their own accord as I walked straight into them, inhaling his woodsy, leather scent, relishing the feel of his arms as they wrapped around me.

Why did this feel so good? So right?

"How was your day?" he asked, planting a kiss on the top of my head.

"Oh, you know. Just saving the world one pumpkin pie at a time." I pulled back a little to look at him. "How was your's?"

Jameson's eyes creased in the corners as he smiled at me. "It's better now."

Butterflies awoke in my stomach as he leaned down and brushed his lips against mine. He pulled away too soon, turning to pull containers of food out of the bag.

"I hope you like Thai food?"

I stepped up to the counter, inhaling the delicious combination of scents. "Love it."

If his smile could make a sound, it would have been the most beautiful symphony.

I forced my eyes away before I face planted into his lips and grabbed a couple plates from the cabinet, followed by two wine glasses.

"I got panang curry, chicken fried rice, and drunken noodle. I wasn't sure if you liked spicy or not, so I got an array of spice levels."

My mouth watered. "It's perfect, thank you." I smiled, and his answering grin was almost enough for me to forget my fears.

Popping the cork on the wine bottle, he poured each of us a glass. We took turns piling food onto our plates before nodding my head toward my big comfy couch. Most of my furniture had been thrifted or given to me by friends or family, but the couch was the one thing I had splurged on. It was long, L-shaped, and the squishiest, most luxurious piece of furniture I had ever sat on. It was perfect for naps.

Or cuddling.

But I'd keep *that* little tidbit to myself.

"We can eat on the couch," I replied to the question in his eyes. "The fabric is indestructible."

"Indestructible, huh?"

"Yep. When you have a cat, it's non-negotiable."

He chuckled before sitting down, and I didn't miss the way he eyed Rhys on the cat tree in the corner. The cat's green eyes glowed in the dim light as he watched us, eyeing Jameson as though he was a snack he wanted to indulge in.

Me too, Rhys. Me too.

I plopped down next to Jameson, leaving several inches of space which he quickly wiggled over to erase. His smile reminded me of an excited kid, and I couldn't help but laugh. I flipped the TV on and turned it to reruns of *Friends*.

"Break or no break?" Jameson asked as Ross and Rachel talked on the screen.

"Huh?"

"The age-old question for *Friends* fans. Were Ross and Rachel on a break?" His eyes twinkled at the joke.

Eep! He knows Friends! Smitten Elsie squealed in my mind.

"Hmm. Not a break."

He smiled. "They were always meant to be together." He nudged me with his elbow.

He's perrrrfect! Smitten Elsie was enjoying this a little too much.

I had a feeling if my cat could talk, he'd be purring, "he's puuuurrrfect," too.

When the food was gone, Jameson took my plate and glass and brought them to the kitchen. Over the back of the couch, I watched as he quickly scrubbed down the plates and dried them with a towel.

"You didn't have to do that," I called.

"I wanted to," he said, returning to my side and pressing a kiss to my forehead. He scooted us into the corner of the couch and then tucked me into his side. I loved those small, seemingly insignificant touches that spoke things that words never could.

"What are you in the mood to watch?" I asked, flipping through the channels.

"Anything you want."

I looked at him out of the corner of my eye. "Be

careful what you wish for."

His whole body shook as he laughed. "Do your worst, Elsie."

My cheeks warmed at the sound of my name on his lips. I skipped through the channels until I finally landed on something that would be distracting but not *too* distracting. Jameson raised his brows at my choice.

"You said do my worst," I taunted, crossing my arms, smug.

"Never in a million years would I have expected you to turn on Hallmark Christmas movies." He playfully nudged my nose, and I melted a little bit more.

"I can change it," I replied, suddenly self-conscious. Ben always hated these movies. He thought they were stupid, cheesy, and unrealistic. Fairytales for royalty, not people like us.

Jameson snatched the remote from my hand and held it out of my reach. "Nope, too late. You already picked."

Indignant, I tried to reach for the remote, but his arms were too long, and it ended with me partially straddling his lap before I finally stole it back.

Too late, I realized what I had done.

Our faces were inches apart, and all it would take was for me to swing my leg the rest of the way over to be in his lap. My breathing was suddenly too loud in my ears, coming in quick gasps like I had just finished a workout. Jameson relinquished the remote into my hands but placed his on my waist before they slid to my back and pulled me toward him.

Tension crackled between us, hot and heavy, before his lips crashed into mine.

My hands were instantly in his hair and his skimmed the skin at the hem of my shirt, setting me ablaze. His tongue traced my lip before he bit it lightly, eliciting a small noise from my throat had him smiling against my mouth.

A romantic Christmas movie played on the screen in the background, but all my thoughts were consumed with the feeling of him holding me, his fingers pressing into my skin and tangling in my hair. The way his lips moved in perfect synchronization with my own.

By the time we pulled apart, we were breathless, and I barely registered that the movie was over and the next one had started as my mind spun, high on Jameson's kisses.

I half-expected Jameson to finish what he started, and I worried that I would have to pump the brakes a bit. But instead of pushing me farther than I was comfortable, he flipped me around, tucking me into his side. My head nestled beneath his chin as he draped the fleece blanket from the back of the couch over us and held me tight, turning the volume up on the TV.

"Now, let's see what these Hallmark movies are all about."

The world outside my windows was dark, rain pattering against the glass, when I finally pried my eyes open. It took several moments of blinking in the dim light of my living room for reality to come into focus.

Jameson and I had fallen asleep cuddled on my couch. His face was peaceful as he slept, a slight shadow of scruff lining his jaw that I wanted to run my fingers over. My admiration quickly turned to horror as I noticed a distinct wet mark across his shirt from where my head had been laying.

I smacked myself in the forehead, my face blazing.

I *drooled* on Jameson.

Jameson stirred, peeking an eye open, before he stretched, his body wiggling beside me.

"Why are you blushing?" he asked, voice hoarse from sleep.

At that moment, he ran a hand over his chest, stopping on the damp spot. I didn't wait to witness his reaction, or how mad he was about to get. Surely, the mask would come off now. I curled into a ball next to him, hiding my face in my knees.

He didn't miss a beat, sitting up and pulling me closer.

"Hey, what's wrong?"

All I could think about was the one single time Ben

had ever let me cuddle with him. I had fallen asleep then, too, and when I woke up, he was livid. He was angry that not only had I fallen asleep on him, but that I had drooled on his extremely expensive shirt, creasing it.

In hindsight, the whole thing was ridiculous, and Ben had been an idiot to react that way, but the damage had been done. My insides coiled tight, waiting for a similar reaction from Jameson.

"Els, talk to me." He tucked my hair behind my ears, eyes roving over my face.

Unreasonable tears spilled onto my cheeks.

It was then that I realized how much Ben had really screwed with my head, and being single for four years had provided zero opportunities for me to work through any of it. The fear of what happened to my parents only exacerbated all of it. Only now, with Jameson, was I forced to finally face those issues.

I let out a shaky breath. "I drooled on you." My shoulders tensed, waiting for his anger.

His body stilled next to me. Then his hand was under my chin, forcing me to look at him. "Elsie, it's just drool."

I shook my head, still waiting for the anger, for awful words to be spoken.

Jameson cradled my face in his hands. "Els, I'm not mad. I think it's sweet."

My brows lowered at his words, and he huffed a laugh.

"It's sweet that you felt comfortable enough to fall asleep with me. Who cares about a little drool? That's what a washing machine is for." His finger brushed across my cheek. "Please don't hide from me. I'm your safe place, remember?"

The memory of him saying those words days ago, right before Ben had interrupted the evening, echoed through me. It settled the anxiety eating away at my stomach, smoothed the sharp ridges trying to poke their way out of my skin.

More and more, Jameson proved that he was nothing like Ben—or my parents. Maybe, just maybe, Maya was right, and this thing between us *might* work.

Jameson kissed me softly. "I'm not going anywhere, Elsie," he whispered. "Even if you drool on me every night."

A smile cracked across my lips.

Sensing victory, Jameson kissed the tip of my nose before glancing at his watch. He gave a low whistle. "It's after eleven. I should probably get home."

I nodded, unfolding myself from my spot next to him.

"Thanks for spending your evening with me, sunshine," Jameson whispered, pulling me against him.

I smiled. "Thanks for putting up with my crazy."

He pulled back to look at me, face serious. "I don't see crazy. I just see you."

Warmth flooded through me, an unfathomable joy spreading through my veins at the thought of being seen for the first time in years. Ben certainly had never seen the real me.

Jameson tugged me to my feet, and I stood on tiptoes to kiss him, hoping to express my feelings even though I didn't know how to *say* them.

"Sweet dreams, sunshine," he said against my lips. "I'll talk to you tomorrow?"

I nodded, sliding my arms around his waist one last time, letting his woodsy scent settle into me, calm me.

"Goodnight," I squeaked.

He opened the door and pressed one last kiss to my lips. "Goodnight."

Through the window, I watched him drive away, confused at this strange emotion settling on my chest. Was this…happiness? Joy over feeling accepted for the first time? Whatever this was, I could get used to it.

I went through my nightly routine, brushing my teeth, and slipping on my pajamas with the cute fox print. Not long after Jameson left, as I was about to crawl into bed, a knock sounded, and I scanned the living room, wondering if he had forgotten something. Head still spinning from the night, I crossed to the door and opened it with a smile, expecting to see Jameson standing there.

The smile slid from my face, like I had seen a ghost.

But it was worse than a ghost.

It was Ben.

28

Elsie

Ben stood in my doorway, his blonde hair and long black coat dripping water onto the ground. Rain fell in blowing sheets behind him, and I couldn't help seeing that as a bad omen.

"What are you doing here?" I asked, wishing the words had come out stronger, snappier than an unsure, breathy whisper.

"Can I come in?"

The absolute last thing I wanted was to let him inside my house, but at that moment, the wind shifted, blowing the rain directly at my door. I had no choice but to step back and let him in. Ben shook his wet hair like a dog, flinging water all over me. I didn't even attempt to hide my scowl.

"Could you get me a towel or something?" he demanded, not even bothering to look at me as he wrung his coat out on my floor, soaking the rug beneath him.

"Why?" I snapped, anger filling me like hot fire. "You're just going to get wet again when I kick you out in..." I looked at the invisible watch on my wrist. "Thirty seconds."

Ben narrowed his eyes. "Don't be like that, Els."

"Get to the point or get out."

He let out an exasperated breath, running a hand through his hair. "What happened to you? You used to be a sweet, quiet wallflower."

I shook my head in disgust. "It's amazing what happens when you leave a relationship with a guy who keeps you in a box until it's convenient for him to let you out."

"Don't be like that, Elsie," he repeated, reaching for me.

I took a step back, crossing my arms. "Don't touch me."

"You used to like me touching you." He had the audacity to sound wounded.

I bit my cheek to keep from voicing that I never did. His kisses were sloppy, and his hands were too grabby—when he bothered to show any type of affection at all.

I wasn't about to fall for his fake hurt. "Twenty seconds, Ben."

He threw his hands into the air. "Fine. Stay away from that Beck guy."

"I don't see how it's any of your business whom I do or don't spend time with."

"You told me when you *left me* that you didn't want anyone at all. So why are you wasting time with that guy?"

"Like I said, it's none of your business, Ben. You lost the privilege of any information on my life a long time ago."

He drove the blade home in my heart. "Do you really want to end up like your parents? Isn't that why you dumped me?"

I ignored his question, blinking against the burning in my eyes. I refused to play his game. "It's been four years, Ben. Move on with your life and leave me alone." I didn't miss this—him. I didn't miss the way he always made me feel small, how he discounted my feelings. It only illuminated how *different* Jameson was, how much *better*.

Ben dared a step closer, the rug squelching beneath his shoes as he ran his cold finger up my arm. "Come on, Elsie. We were always good together."

I jerked away from his touch. "According to whom?"

The skin between his eyebrows creased, and his lips twisted into a snarl. "You belong with me, Elsie. Forget about that Beck guy."

"Why, Ben? Give me one good reason."

He sniffed and rubbed at his nose. "He's irritating and his dog is a menace."

For a moment, I stood in stunned silence before my

voice returned. "That's it? That's the best excuse you could find for why I shouldn't be spending time with Jameson? For why we should be together instead?" His answer told me all I needed to know—he didn't *actually* want me. He simply didn't like that someone else had me instead.

Ben shook his head, pointing a long, bony finger at me. "You belong with *me*."

"No, Ben. The only person you belong with is yourself. Until you pull that stick out of your butt and realize that women are human beings, and are worth more than being your *arm candy*, you will always be alone."

Ben took a menacing step toward me, clenching his hands into fists. "If you stay with him, you'll just end up in the same situation as your parents." He gave me a villainous grin. "I know you don't want that."

Though Ben spoke my greatest fear, reinforcing those thoughts I had battled since first meeting Jameson, I refused to react to his words. I didn't want to give him the satisfaction of knowing he got under my skin. "Get out, Ben. I want nothing to do with you, so leave me alone. We're done and you need to get on with your life."

I gave his shoulder a shove, nudging him toward the door.

"Elsie—"

"Get. Out." Rain blew inside, but I ignored it, unwilling to back down until Ben was gone.

"You're making a mistake."

"Even if that were true, which it's not, it's my mistake to make."

He opened his mouth to spew more poison, but I interrupted him.

"You have five seconds to leave or I'm calling the police."

Ben's eyes widened and he looked at me in disbelief. "You wouldn't."

"Do you really want to test that?"

He huffed out a breath as I pointed to the door. "Wow."

"Have a good life, Ben," I snapped, putting my foot against his backside and kicking him out of my house.

He turned around with a glare, giving me a once over, his lip curled in a sneer. "Good riddance."

I gave a crude laugh. "Feeling is mutual, Ben. Buh-bye."

Then I slammed the door in his shocked face and waited for his footsteps to fade off my porch, quickly drowned out by the pouring rain. A moment later his headlights flashed through the window before his car disappeared down the road.

I sank onto my couch, Rhys curling up next to me, as a strange feeling settled over me.

For the first time in four years, my lungs felt free, unrestricted, like I was finally able to breathe again. So, why did a part of me still feel so uneasy?

"Ben did what?" Maya shrieked into the phone.

I called my best friend over lunch the next day, needing to sort through my spinning thoughts after lying awake most of the night. I had explained how Ben showed up last night, and all the words he had spewed at me, glossing over the fact that Jameson had left minutes beforehand.

"Why that pathetic excuse for a man..." Maya snapped, mumbling several unintelligible curses. I swear I heard her mutter, *let me at him.* "What the heck was he hoping to accomplish?"

I shrugged even though she couldn't see me.

"He's such a liar, Elsie. Please don't even think twice about the poisonous things he said. He's just angry that you turned him down four years ago, and now you're into someone else. Little boys get mad when they think their toys have been stolen."

I snorted. She wasn't wrong.

"I mean it, Els." Her voice grew louder, her mouth likely right on the microphone, trying to make her point. "Don't listen to him. He's wrong about you and Jameson. I told you before, you are not your parents."

Despite knowing there was truth in her words, and feeling like I was starting to accept the possibility of me and Jameson, I still couldn't stop doubt from seeping into me. It was like venom, filling my veins inch by inch, killing the notion of us until we no longer sounded like a good idea.

He said he would be my safe place.

But how long would that last? Until the first fight? Or would he make it twenty years before he became so resentful that he walked out the door?

I shook my head. As much as I liked Jameson, and as much as I wanted to believe that maybe we could make things work, I didn't know if I could do it.

"Elsie…" Maya said, sensing my inner thoughts over the phone through some crazy best friend Spidey sense. "Don't shut down."

"I'm not shutting down," I retorted, even though it was a bald-faced lie.

"You're letting Ben ruin your chance at happiness, and he's not even the one you're dating. Don't let him have that power over you."

My body went still. Was that what I was doing? Was I still giving Ben power over my life, my mind?

"I'm not." The lie was automatic, though my insides were twisting and unsettled.

Maya sighed. "Don't do anything rash, Els. Let this settle. Calm down before you make a decision you'll regret." The phone crackled as she sighed. "I got to go, Els. I'll talk to you later, okay?" she said, adding, "I mean it, don't make any decisions about Jameson until you've calmed down."

"Yeah, yeah," I replied. "Talk to you later."

We hung up, and I dropped the phone on my couch with a *thud*, collapsing onto my side.

Frustrated was not a strong enough word for how I was feeling. I had finally started to come to terms with giving a relationship a try, with risking everything for Jameson. He hadn't given me a reason to believe it was a bad idea, yet I couldn't stop my walls from rising again. Brick by brick, they encased my heart, and only a wrecking ball could bring them down.

And I'd had enough wrecking to last a lifetime.

Fear and logic warred for control of my brain, my resolve teetering like a see-saw.

As much as I wanted to believe things with Jameson would work out and have a happy ending, the uncertainty was too much for me to overlook; too much to risk.

Instead of sitting at the kitchen counter and working on an article I had been putting off for days, I turned my phone off and spent the day in bed, curled next to Rhys, trying to make sense of the scrambled eggs my mind had become.

29

Jameson

I felt like a little kid about to enter a candy store.

It was the night of my third official date with Elsie.

This was it. Our last date and then I'd lay it all out there—more than I did when I had her pinned against my truck. Everything I was feeling, everything I wanted with her. Women liked feelings talk, right?

It had been two days since I had last seen Elsie. She had been strangely distant through text messages, but work had been so crazy I couldn't spend a lot of time decoding why. I was still on a high from leaving her place the other night, though I couldn't get the tear-stained look on her face out of my mind, couldn't forget her thinking I'd be mad at her for a little drool either.

I wanted to wipe those memories from her mind. I wanted to make sure she never felt small, diminished, or self-conscious again. I wanted her to see what I saw, to feel confident and important, not like someone who needed to hide.

I dug my phone out of my pocket.

ME

You ready for tonight? :)

A few seconds later a response popped onto the screen.

ELSIE

I guess so. What are we doing?

I arched a brow at her lack of enthusiasm. *I guess so?* I thought I was finally making progress with her, that her walls were beginning to crumble, but this felt cold and closed off. Grumpy.

That was okay. I liked a challenge.

ME

It's a surprise :)

ELSIE

[skeptical GIF]

ME

[GIF of raccoon rubbing its hands together]

I'll pick you up at six.

Originally, I had planned to drive us into the city,

treat her to a nice restaurant, and we'd see where things went from there. But she wasn't the type of girl who liked fancy restaurants or expensive evenings. She was a Chick-Fil-A cookies n' cream shake, picnic on the beach, cuddling on the couch while watching Christmas movies type of girl. She preferred a quiet night at home to busy, loud places with lots of people.

Maybe her ex missed that bit about her.

But I didn't.

So, instead of doing a typical "date" to try to impress her, I was going to keep it simple. We'd do something I hoped she'd enjoy and wouldn't make her uncomfortable. Something that might bring out the smile that made my knees tremble and stomach clench. Something that let me wrap my arms around her and kiss her every chance I could get.

ME

Wear something you don't mind getting dirty :)

ELSIE

Should I be nervous?

ME

You never need to be nervous with me, sunshine.

But you might want to bring a spare change of clothes.

Just in case :)

ELSIE

I'll see you at six.

I blinked at her response. I was trying to be playful and make her smile, but she didn't even attempt to flirt back.

Rubbing at my chin, I was overcome with anxiousness about tonight, even though I'd been looking forward to it for days. After a long week, I was excited to spend time, just the two of us, hopefully with lots of laughter and kisses involved, too.

All that was left was a last-minute run to the store after work to get a few things for our date. Then I'd get to pick up my grump-who-was-secretly-a-sunshine-in-disguise.

Maya's name flashed on my phone, and I debated not answering it. It wasn't that I didn't want to talk to my cousin, but more that I wasn't sure I was up for any more of her meddling. Besides, I was at the store and needed to get my butt back home to set things up.

I didn't have time for a phone call with Maya right now, so I let it go to voicemail. A second later, it rang again. This repeated two more times before I finally gave up and answered with an impatient huff.

"Yes, Maya?"

"Jam-Jam! Were you ignoring me?"

Yes.

"Of course not."

"Didn't your mother ever teach you where liars go?" she retorted.

Apparently not away from you.

I sighed into the phone. "Now isn't a good time, Maya. What do you need?"

"Are you seeing Elsie tonight?"

"That was the plan."

A beat of silence and then, "Jameson, I need to tell you something about her. It's important."

Every muscle in my body clenched tight. She used my full name which told me this was serious. My mind took a deep dive off a cliff, coming up with endless awful scenarios. The store was loud around me, but it did nothing to drown out my thoughts, nothing to settle my churning stomach.

"What about Elsie? What's wrong? Is she okay?" I asked, gripping the phone tighter.

Maya's exhale made the phone crackle. "I'm assuming Elsie never told you much about her past."

Of all things I expected her to say, *that* never crossed my mind.

"She told me about Benjamin who, unfortunately, is my neighbor."

"Ben is your *neighbor*?" Maya shouted, and I pulled the phone away from my ear, wincing.

"Can you not break my eardrum? Thanks."

"Sorry," she said, and I could picture her rubbing the bridge of her nose like she always did when she was thinking. "Elsie didn't tell me that." Another beat of silence. "Ben is a deadbeat," Maya muttered. "But that's not what I'm talking about. Elsie has a fear of relationships because of her parents."

"Her parents?"

"Yeah." Maya sounded out of breath as if she were pacing back and forth. "Four years ago, her parents suddenly divorced after almost thirty years of marriage. They went from fine to...really bad, but Elsie never expected for them to just split up. Their divorce hit her hard."

Understanding settled over me.

"It ruined her belief in love, and she's afraid if she gets in a relationship, if she lets herself love someone, that they'll grow to hate one another and everything will end. That was one of the reasons she broke up with Ben. Although, that ended up being a blessing in disguise because Ben is a loser who never treated her well. On paper he was perfect, but behind closed doors..." Maya sighed. "He wasn't a good guy."

"No argument there." I rubbed at my forehead, my mind spinning. "So, that's why she has so many walls... why she won't let me get close."

"Yeah," Maya admitted. "I told her to talk to you about this, but she refused. I wanted you to know why she is the way she is. I don't want her to make a rash decision to end things between you guys when anyone can see how crazy you are about each other. You both deserve happiness, and I don't want her fear of getting hurt to end something so good."

Everything suddenly made sense. Why she wouldn't let me in, why she was determined not to date, not to let anything between us go farther than the third date. It made sense why her walls were so thick, and why she shut down any time I caught a glimpse of the Elsie she constantly kept hidden.

"Thanks for telling me, Maya," I responded after a lengthy silence.

"I'm trusting that you'll use this information for good, Jam-Jam. Elsie deserves the world, and so do you."

"I know."

"Don't let her get away, you fool."

"I don't plan on it."

We quickly said goodbye and I forced my mind to focus, returning to the duty at hand—getting the supplies for tonight.

Tonight was everything. Knowing about her past changed nothing and everything.

Maybe it would scare some people away, but learning how hurt Elsie had been in her past didn't scare me. It only made me want to love her more. To show her that she deserved the world, deserved to be treated like the queen she was.

What happened with her parents was awful, yes, but that didn't mean we would end up the same way. Elsie had to know how crazy I was about her. I couldn't imagine a world where she wasn't in my life.

I wanted her. All of her.

And no amount of fear, insecurity, or past trauma would change that.

30

Jameson

The clock on the dashboard of my truck read 5:59 as I pulled into Elsie's driveway. My limbs tingled, my heart racing like a kid on a sugar high as I climbed out and headed for her door. I jogged up the short walkway, leaped up the two steps to her front porch and gave three quick knocks. The night was cold, the air clouding as I fought to catch my breath, not from exertion, but simply because I was excited to see her. It had only been two days, but it felt like weeks.

When the door opened, all the air in my lungs whooshed out. Elsie's dark blonde hair was pulled back in a messy ponytail, her curves on display in a pair of leggings and a cropped sweatshirt with a graphic that said "donut worry about a thing" over a box of donuts. A hesitant smile spread over her beautiful face before narrowed her eyes at my heaving chest.

"Did you run here?" she deadpanned.

With a huff, I pulled her into a hug. "I'm just happy to see you." I wanted her to melt into me, for her to press her nose into my neck, but instead she froze in my arms, turning into a rock.

"Everything all right?"

Elsie's eyes stayed on my chest as she pulled out of my embrace, avoiding my gaze. "Yes. Let me grab my purse. Be right back."

Unease settled in my gut. Elsie hadn't been that cold toward me since we met at the photoshoot a little over a month ago. As if her house would tell me her secrets, I scanned the cottage themed living room, neutrals and light pastel colors littering the space, eyeing the couch where we had fallen asleep. I smiled at the memory. I wanted more of that, more of her and I together.

Elsie rounded the corner, a baggy denim jacket now thrown over her sweatshirt. "Ready," she said, still avoiding eye contact.

Maya's phone call replayed in my head. She had been worried Elsie would make a hasty decision and end things between us because of her past. I had hoped that my cousin was wrong, that love would win, silencing Elsie's fears so we could move forward together. But seeing her now, the way she was acting, her tense shoulders, how she avoided my gaze...Had she already decided?

If she had, why go through the motions of another date?

I wanted to dig my heels in and ask what was bothering her. I wasn't afraid of confrontation, but after Maya told me about Elsie's parents, I wondered if confronting her would do more harm than good. I needed to get her back to my house and remind her how good things were between us. I hoped tonight would show her, once and for all, that we belonged together. I cared about her—more than I thought possible after such a short time.

I didn't want this to end.

So, I laced my fingers between hers, kissing the back of her hand before leading her to my truck. True fall weather had finally descended upon Meridel, the brisk air hinting at the winter to come. She burrowed into her seat, pulling her jacket tight as I backed out of the driveway.

"Where are we going?" Elsie asked.

"My place."

She relaxed back into her seat. "What are we doing there?"

I gave her a quick smirk before looking at the road again. "It's a surprise."

Elsie squinted at me. "A good surprise?"

"Aren't all surprises good?"

"No."

At her tone, my eyes snapped to hers. There was no amusement on her face, and I wondered what experience made her dislike surprises.

"Well, this is a good one." I forced lightness into my tone, nudging her arm with my elbow.

Elsie crossed her arms, leaning away from me.

Well then.

I was not an insecure person. I wasn't afraid to admit that I was a good guy, and I was confident—not cocky. Even so, her coldness had doubt inching under my skin like a knife. I thought we had moved past this.

Ten minutes later, we pulled up to my house, silence descending as I turned off the truck. I felt the need to say something, to reassure her somehow, but I didn't know what to say. I wasn't sure how to crack her cold facade and get to the warmth and laughter from the other night.

Clearing my throat, I walked around to open the door for her, and she slid out of the cab, ignoring the hand I had offered to help her down. I stared at my outreached hand, brows lowered.

"Is something wrong, Elsie?"

"No," was all she said before she turned on her heel and headed for the front door.

Running a hand through my hair, I blew out a breath. *Later,* I told myself. We could talk about whatever was bothering her later. There would be plenty of time for it. First, I wanted to get her inside, out of the cold, and surprise her with what I had planned for the evening.

Unlocking the door, I pulled her inside, and led her straight into the kitchen. Luna bounced around our feet, happy to see us. Eggs, flour, sugar, vanilla extract, and bottles upon bottles of decorative icing were laid out on the counter. Luna circled us, tongue lolling and tail wagging.

Elsie's eyes widened as she patted Luna on the head. "And what are we doing with all that?"

"Having a bake-off of course."

Her brows inched up her forehead. "What?"

I grinned. "We're going to bake cookies and decorate them. Whoever has the best ones wins." Something akin to happiness flashed across her eyes before she mastered it, hiding it away. "And then we'll take all of them, both ugly and pretty." I paused as she let out a small laugh and my insides melted at the sound. "And eat all the cookies our stomachs can handle."

This time, Elsie didn't try to fight her smile. "This is…not what I expected for a date," she admitted.

"What were you expecting? Noise? Lots of people?"

She narrowed her eyes but nodded.

I stepped closer, putting her between me and the counter. "But you don't really like that, do you?" Her throat bobbed as I pinned her between my arms. "You prefer simple, quiet nights in, don't you?"

"How do you know that?" she whispered, eyes glistening.

I brushed her hair over her shoulder, my fingers trailing across her neck, and I didn't miss the way her pulse stuttered beneath my touch. "I see you, Elsie."

A shuddering breath slipped through her lips as I pulled her into my arms, relaxing as she *finally* melted against me.

"Besides, I'd rather have you all to myself tonight. No distractions."

She tilted her head back to look at me. "What about dinner?"

"Cookies *are* dinner," I deadpanned.

A wide grin spread across her face, and I had that ecstatic lightweight feeling, like when I brought Luna home for the first time and knew I was no longer alone.

"I wholeheartedly agree with this plan," she finally admitted, eyeing the cookie ingredients on the counter.

"Shall we get started?" I said, leaning in to whisper against her ear, eliciting a shiver from her. I opened a drawer and pulled out a bunch of cookie cutters in various shapes, though most of them were Christmas themes: trees, stars, a few leaf shapes, and a snowman.

She arched a brow. "Christmas cookies in October?"

I shrugged. "There's never a wrong time for Christmas cookies."

A laugh bubbled out of her, and I wanted to bottle up that sound and carry it with me everywhere. Grabbing a few different recipe cards from the box I had borrowed from my mom, I spread them on the counter.

Elsie listed them off. "Lemon cookies, toffee nut gingerbread, butterscotch chip crunchies?"

"My mom loved to bake cookies when I was a kid. These were a few of her favorites."

Elsie flipped through the cards while I turned on some music. She decided on the lemon cookies while I opted for the gingerbread. We each set to gathering and measuring ingredients, and I purposely bumped into her often—taking advantage of every chance to touch her. Elsie appeared to be having a good time, even singing along with Bing Crosby as he crooned about a White Christmas but, as time passed, she seemed to get more into her head.

Every time a smile curled her lips, or amusement and joy lit her eyes, she shut it down, turning it off like a light switch.

I hated it, but I didn't know how to stop it. It was clear she felt something between us. It was in the way she looked at me when she didn't think I was looking, the way she brushed against me, lingering a second longer than necessary. How her gaze darted to my lips before she looked away, her cheeks turning pink.

Elsie felt something for me, but that fear Maya had told me about—it was strong. By the time the cookies were out of the oven, cooled, and decorated, all the joy that I had worked so hard to put on her face had disappeared.

Slight change of plans, then. Trying to make her smile was now my top and only priority.

I looked around, trying to think of something, when my eyes landed on the tubes of icing. Without thinking, I grabbed the green one, popped the top off, held it to her face, and squeezed. Green goo smothered her nose.

She froze, wide caramel-eyes meeting mine.

"What—"

And then I kissed the frosting off her nose.

I gave an appreciative hum, licking the sugary goodness from my mouth, satisfied when her eyes tracked the movement.

"Did you just…squirt icing on my face…then lick it off?"

"I *kissed* it off," I mumbled, smacking my lips. "But yes."

Come on, Elsie. Play with me.

Elsie froze for another second before she lunged for a different tube and squeezed it onto my face with a smug smile. She didn't just aim for my nose but slathered it all over.

I pursed my lips and gave her a fake glare when she finished. "Are *you* going to lick it off now?"

Fire burned in her eyes. "You'd like that, wouldn't you?" she retorted.

I stepped closer. "What if I would?"

Come on, Elsie. I know you feel this too. Get out of your head.

Her gaze flicked to my lips, chest heaving as tension built between us.

And then she did the last thing I expected from her.

She jumped—literally jumped—into my arms, wrapping her arms around my neck and her legs around my hips and kissed me.

My arms circled her waist, holding her tight as I set her on top of the counter. Her fingers scraped against my scalp, and I dug mine into her waist. Her lips tasted like frosting. She leaned into the touch, pressing harder against me.

I could get used to this—the way she kissed me, her skin on mine, her fingers in my hair. The scent of her floral shampoo and cookies in the air.

I never wanted to let her go.

There was something different in her movements, in the way her mouth crushed into mine. Something almost...desperate. As much as I didn't want to stop, I forced us to slow, cupping her face in my hands. I gave her one last lingering kiss before pulling back.

Elsie's lips were covered in the red frosting that was still all over me. Her stomach gave a fierce rumble, her cheeks warming beneath my hands.

"Is it time to gorge ourselves on cookies?" I asked her, nodding toward the counter full of terribly decorated cookies. Instead of cute Christmas trees and Frosty the Snowman, they looked like a toddler had squeezed globs onto each cookie and hoped for the best. Elsie wasn't any better than I was at decorating, and I secretly loved it.

Her fingers dug into my neck as if she wanted to say something else, or maybe keep kissing, but she dropped her hands and nodded. Wetting a cloth in the sink, I wiped my face clean before handing it to her. A faint green tint sat on the tip of her nose, and it might have been the cutest thing I'd ever seen.

"Will you grab our jackets and I'll box these up to

take outside?"

"Outside?" she asked.

I nodded. "The rest of the surprise is out there."

She arched a brow. "Isn't it a little cold?"

I whispered against her ear. "It won't be for long."

The same desire that burned in me blazed in her eyes, and it took everything in me to let her leave the kitchen and not drag her back into my arms. A moment later, Elsie reappeared, handing me my jacket. I shuffled into it and grabbed the thermos of hot chocolate I had made while the cookies cooled.

Box of cookies in one hand and thermos in the other, I offered my elbow to her. With a shy smile, she looped her arm through mine.

I leaned closer. "Shall we?"

She nodded and I pressed a light kiss to her lips before heading outside. Elsie skidded to a stop when she saw what I had done.

In the middle of my fenced in backyard was a huge tent with a mesh ceiling, perfect for stargazing. It was positioned between two large maple trees where I had hung bistro lights back and forth between the branches. It had taken hours, but the effect was beautiful and romantic. Bright red and orange leaves that I hadn't had a chance to rake yet littered the yard around the tent.

Inside was an unreasonable number of soft, fuzzy blankets and pillows, and a small space heater in case she was still cold. My laptop was set up in the corner with

Return to Me already cued up. She had told me it was one of her favorite rom-coms while playing a game where we guessed each other's favorite things.

Setting the box and thermos on the ground, I unzipped the tent and gestured for her to crawl inside. Elsie slipped her boots off and rolled in, instantly cocooning herself in the blankets. My heart squeezed at the sight.

She belonged here.

The thought panged through my mind before I could stop it.

I cleared my throat against the tightness threatening to bring tears to my eyes and crawled in after her. I settled next to her and wrapped a green blanket around my shoulders, then poured each of us a mug of steaming cocoa. After handing one to her, I opened the box of cookies.

We looked inside and burst out laughing.

"I don't think cookie decoration is a future career path for either of us," she wheezed out between laughs.

"At least they taste good?" It came out as more of a question. Truthfully, I had never made my mom's cookie recipes myself before, and I did not excel at baking. For all I knew they were disgusting.

"Let's find out," she said, grabbing a sugar-cookie snowman that looked more like the Joker rather than Frosty, and took a hearty bite.

Elsie chewed in silence for a moment before meeting my eyes.

"Delicious." She smiled at me with bulging cheeks.

Needing no further encouragement, I took a bite of the toffee nut gingerbread and found those were equally tasty. We gorged ourselves on cookies until we had a sugar hangover, then flopped back onto the pile of blankets. The lights overhead disrupted the view of the night sky, but I had planned for that. I snatched a tiny remote from the corner of the tent and hit the power button. The lights blinked out, settling us in the pitch-black night. One by one, the stars winked into the sky, and Elsie shifted closer to me.

"As a kid, this was one of my favorite things to do," I explained. "Since there's less light pollution in Meridel, I used to lay in the hammock, staring at the constellations, trying to find new ones, and naming my own. There's something peaceful about staring up at the wide expanse of dark sky and just…watching."

Then a shooting star streaked across the sky. "Make a wish," I whispered, squeezing her hand. My wish was simple: to spend every second I could with this amazing girl.

Elsie closed her eyes, breathing deeply. I wanted to ask what her wish was, but when she opened them, I was surprised to find a tear streaking down her cheek.

"Elsie?" I immediately rolled onto my side so I could look her in the eye. "What's wrong?"

She shook her head, closing her eyes against more tears. I wiped them away as they fell.

"Sunshine, what's wrong?"

"Jameson, I..." Her voice choked on whatever she was about to say.

I leaned forward, wanting nothing more than to kiss away whatever was worrying her, whatever was bringing those tears to her eyes, but she lifted a hand to stop me.

"Jameson, I don't think we should see each other anymore."

31

Elsie

The words were physically painful to say.

When he told me to make a wish, I wished with all my heart that I didn't have to say those words—that we could be together without my fear getting in the way—but wishes were for children, and it was time to be an adult.

As the words left my mouth, Jameson went so still I thought he might have stopped breathing, but then he recoiled, his face scrunching in disbelief.

"What?" He pulled himself onto his knees.

I shook my head, sitting up. "This was the third date. I never promised anything more than this."

"But—" he started, stopping himself when his voice cracked. "I told you I wanted more with you. I thought you did too." He pointed at his house. "You wouldn't have kissed me like that if you didn't feel this thing between us."

All I could do was shake my head again, shutting out his words. This entire evening had made this decision so much harder. Jameson had been determined to make me smile, and after fighting it for so long, I finally gave in, deciding to enjoy my last moments with him.

But I had to say goodbye. This had to end.

As much as I liked Jameson, and as much as I wanted to believe that things could work out for us, my fear had won. This was better than what would come later—the heartache, the resentment, the pain.

"You know we're good together, Elsie." He tried to take my hands, but I slipped out of his grip. "Why are you doing this?" His hands clenched into fists in his lap.

"I can't be in a relationship."

"Why?" he demanded. "Because of that fool, Benjamin?"

"No."

"Is this about what happened with your parents?"

I flinched. "How did you…"

He sighed. "Maya called me earlier. She…she told me about your parents, and how you don't want to risk falling in love because of it."

Fury at my best friend made my stomach clench, and my hands fisted at my sides. "She had no right to tell you—"

"She was worried about you," Jameson interrupted, crawling closer, taking my face in his hands. "Elsie, I know you're scared of ending up like them, but what happened to them won't happen to us. It'll take work, like any relationship, but I know that we can figure this out. You don't have to face your fear alone. Let me help you shoulder it."

I closed my eyes against his words, against the hope flaring in my chest.

"I'm crazy about you. Don't walk away before we've even tried."

His words broke something in me. "And what happens when we end up fighting, Jameson? Will this nice guy façade disappear, replaced by vicious, cutting words?"

"*Façade?*" He gaped at me. "I have been nothing but sincere with you, Elsie. I've given you every reason to trust me, every reason to show you I could never treat you like your ex. Every couple fights. You will never find anyone who doesn't. But we'd face it together—not with raised voices and hurtful remarks, but with patience and a desire to fix things. *That's* how you make real love work." His thumbs wiped the tears from my cheeks. "Don't walk away from this."

Jameson's words simultaneously soothed my every fear while stabbing my heart into a million pieces. I wanted to believe him. Smitten Elsie was practically begging me to give in, to stay here with him. My thoughts grew jumbled in my head, confused and swirling, and I couldn't think straight.

Jameson must have taken my lack of response to mean I was sticking with my decision because he begged, "Please, explain this to me, Elsie. I need to understand why you're putting an end to something so good. So *right*."

"But it won't always be good, will it?" I demanded, a last-ditch effort to stick to this plan. "Eventually, one of us will hurt the other, and I would rather end things before that happens."

He shook his head side to side. "Elsie, just because your parents gave up on each other, doesn't mean that I would ever give up on *you*."

"Jameson," I started, pulling out of his grip. I needed to get out of here. I needed to *think*.

"No," he interrupted. "What do I have to do to prove to you that this will work? I've never been more certain of anything in my life. I want every day with you. I want frosting kisses, and nap cuddles, and Hallmark Christmas movies with you. I want your laugh in my ear, and your fingers in mine. I want *you*, Elsie."

Tears glistened in his eyes, and I had to look away.

"I have to go. I need to think," I whispered, not missing the flash of hope in his eyes that I hadn't outright said no before it was replaced with hurt.

"Elsie..."

With a shake of my head, I slipped on my boots and crawled out of the tent, forcing myself to not look back as I headed for the sidewalk. My heart ached, and it hurt to breathe. It didn't matter that I didn't have a car, or that I had to walk home in the dark. Nothing mattered.

Because I left my heart, and all the feelings with it, inside the tent in Jameson's backyard.

"You did what?" Maya screamed in the middle of Chick-Fil-A, earning annoyed looks from everyone around us.

I nibbled on a chicken nugget, not meeting her eyes after telling her how I left Jameson in that tent a week ago, sort of breaking up with him.

"Noo," she whined, smacking the table. "Why would you do that?" She chucked a fry, and it bounced off my cheek. "He's perfect for you."

I scoffed, glaring at her.

"Name one thing wrong with that man."

I huffed out a frustrated breath, not a single thing coming to mind. He wasn't like Ben, who had more faults than redeeming qualities. Jameson had been sweet, gentle, patient, and attentive. He was everything I had always hoped Ben would be. He was everything I had once wished for. He was everything I *had* wished for beneath the stars.

"See, you can't do it," Maya snapped, crossing her arms.

"It doesn't matter, Maya."

"Yes, it does!" Maya yelled, earning more irritated looks from other customers. "You fell head over heels for him, and you just walked away without even trying!" She took an angry slurp of her Cherry Coke. "I can't believe you."

"And I can't believe you told him about my parents. You had no right to do that."

"I was trying to help you."

"And how did that turn out?"

She shook her head, avoiding my gaze. "I can't believe you just walked away."

"Well, sorry to disappoint you," I snapped, shoving an entire nugget into my mouth. I hated that I had let her down, disappointed her, but in that moment, I had been so conflicted I couldn't even think straight. And now that a week had passed, and my thoughts were somewhat coherent again, I couldn't bring myself to pick up the phone—to tell Jameson how I really felt.

Her face softened. "Elsie, I'm not disappointed in you so much as I'm *sad* for you." She reached across the table to grab my hand. "Everyone could see there was something special between the two of you, and you just walked away."

I shrugged, sniffling to hold back the tears.

"Sometimes love is worth taking a risk on, Els. Jameson is worth risking your heart for." She sighed. "I told you before and I'll tell you again. You are not your parents. They stopped *choosing* each other. They stopped communicating and fighting for one another. That's not you. That's not Jameson. You're taking the choice away from him—the choice to love you. He would never hurt you the way your parents hurt each other—or the way Ben did."

She stopped to take a deep breath. "Look at what *he's* been through. He lost his dad when he was a kid, and his mom got so sick that he had to give up everything in his life to take care of her. Any normal person would have bent under that pressure, would have given up and stopped fighting. But Jameson didn't. He did what was needed to take care of his mom and sister. He didn't give up when things got hard. He kept fighting because that's the kind of man he is, just like he would keep fighting for you and your relationship if you would stop being so dang stubborn."

Then she drove the blade home. "Jameson is not fake, he's not wearing a mask, and he's nothing like Ben."

"You don't know that," I muttered.

Maya took the chicken nugget out of my hand and slammed it down. I watched it bounce off the table and onto the floor. I wished she'd stop taking her anger out on my nuggets.

"I *do* know that. I grew up with Jameson. I've seen the man he's become, and I would have *never* tried to put you two together if I didn't think it was in your best interest. You're being a coward."

Ouch.

Maya's chest heaved as she glared at me, my mind spinning. Was she right? Was I so scared of turning out like my parents that it had forced me to walk away from the one thing, the one person, that gave me hope for something better?

He had laid his feelings out for me, and I stomped all over them. Was I taking his choice away? Would he *choose* me, no matter what the future held? When things got hard, when we faced the difficulties that life would inevitably bring, would he *still* choose me?

My parents had been so in love...until they weren't. They went from adoring looks and caresses to scathing remarks and glares of hatred. Was it possible to have a relationship that *wasn't* like that?

I think Jameson would be worth taking a chance on and finding out, Smitten Elsie said.

As much as you don't need anyone else, he's a good man and maybe Maya is right. Maybe you should give him a chance to prove that he won't hurt you. Let him have the choice to love you. I was dumbfounded by Smart Elsie's words after she had been so vocal about staying away from Jameson.

"The truth hurts, doesn't it?" she asked, not missing my wince.

"Maya..."

"Don't *Maya* me. You need to go see him. Apologize for being a fool, and ask him to give you another chance."

It had been a week since I had seen Jameson, and I missed him something fierce. But was I ready to forget all the pain and heartache I had both witnessed and experienced? There really *was* no guarantee that Jameson would give up on me. He hadn't given up on his family when life got hard, and they needed him. Could I trust that Jameson would do the same with me?

I had been trying to protect my heart in the process… but what if what was best for my heart was Jameson?

I blew out a breath, finally meeting Maya's gaze. She had a smug smile on her face.

"Have you finally come to your senses?"

"What if he doesn't want me now?" I asked.

"Trust me, he does." Maya stood and yanked me out of the booth. "Now go get your man!"

32

Jameson

"Mom?" I called, cracking the door to her apartment open.

"Jamie?" A soft voice answered.

"It's me. I brought cookies." I walked in, slipping my shoes off before I brought the remaining cookies from the last date with Elsie over to my mom. I had put them in the freezer, saving them for a rainy day, but I couldn't stand to look at them anymore. I couldn't stand to see the remnants of such an amazing evening that ended so horribly. To me, the box of cookies was nothing more than a box of brightly colored ash.

Part of me was still in denial, that I had dreamed her leaving me in that tent, and that any minute she'd walk through the door and into my arms, but I knew that was a fool's wish. When Maya had explained about Elsie's parents, it all made sense. All of her insecurities, all of her walls, every time she pushed me away when I knew that she wanted me closer…I understood.

And yet, I still couldn't believe that Elsie had just walked away from us.

The fact that she wanted time to think somehow made it worse. Instead of being able to actively help her fight those fearful thoughts, she was facing them alone. I didn't know where that would leave us in the end.

"Those are the ugliest cookies I've ever seen," my mom chided when she peered into the box, breaking me out of my thoughts.

I winced. "Elsie and I made cookies the other night."

She pursed her lips. "Well, I wouldn't put much hope in a cookie decorating career," she laughed.

Her words were so close to what Elsie had said that night that I flinched, like I had been punched in the gut. Mom's eyes narrowed as she studied me, her laugh trailing off.

"What's wrong, dear?"

"Nothing, Mom."

"Don't lie to me, Jamie. The last time I saw you, you looked like you were on top of the world. Now you look like a pop can that was emptied and crushed."

I winced. "I suppose that's an accurate description of how I feel."

"What happened?"

I sighed. "Elsie sort of ended things." The words

spilled out of me like water waiting to burst from a dam.

"Why?" My mom seemed genuinely surprised. "And how does one 'sort of' end things?"

I shrugged, running a hand through my hair before sitting in the chair next to my mom. "She tried to call things off at first, but after I tried to convince her not to, she said she needed to think about us. But I haven't heard from her since. She has some things from her past that have made it difficult for her to trust that I wouldn't hurt her," I explained.

"Oh?" Mom raised an eyebrow.

"Her parents' divorce was brutal, and it convinced her that real love doesn't exist, and that a relationship isn't worth risking her heart on. Elsie thinks she's destined to end up like them."

My mom hummed, fiddling with her fingers while she considered my words. "It sounds like you need to give her a reason to put her heart on the line."

"I thought I had."

Mom waved a hand. "It's going to take more than a couple dates, Jamie. Why did you let her walk away?"

Her question caught me off guard. "She wanted time…I wasn't about to force a relationship on her—"

"That girl wanted you," she interrupted. "I saw it plain as day on her face. Why did you let her walk away? Why didn't you fight harder?"

This time her question had my stomach dropping. I had *wanted* to fight harder, to grab her hands and try to make her see reason. But I didn't know how at that moment and, if I was being honest, I was hurt that she was so willing to give up what we had, even if I understood why she did.

"She's scared, and rightfully so, but I didn't raise my son to be a quitter."

I opened my mouth to object, but nothing came out.

"Go get her," she demanded.

"What?"

"Jamie, you are a bright man, but sometimes you are duller than a box of rocks." She rubbed a hand over her face before looking me square in the eyes. "Go get Elsie. Tell her how you feel and don't let her go. Perhaps she's the type of girl who needs someone to fight for her, to prove that *she's* worth the risk before risking her own heart."

The words hit me like a bag of bricks. Her ex hadn't fought for her and let her walk away, but hadn't I done the same thing by letting her leave that tent?

"Mom—"

"Don't *Mom* me," she snapped. "I've already discussed this with Maya and Emma, and we all agree that you're being a fool. I'm kicking you out of here until you convince that lovely girl that you belong together."

Of course, she had been talking to my sister and cousin about this. I ran a hand through my hair, sighing. "Mom—"

"Go." She pointed at the door. "Get going." She

shook the box of cookies, threatening to chuck it at me.

"Don't come back until you've kissed that girl senseless and convinced her you're meant to be together."

33

Elsie

I tossed and turned all night long. Not only had Maya's incessant text messages telling me to make up—and make out—with Jameson plagued me for hours, but...I missed him. I hated not waking up to a good morning text from him, or wondering what sweet date he'd take me on next, or when we'd fall asleep cuddling on the couch again.

I missed the way he looked at me, the way he held my hand and called me sunshine. I missed the way he saw through my insecurities to the person underneath and didn't shy away but, instead, helped me battle them. He accepted all of me and didn't force me to hide pieces of myself.

Maya had suggested that I show up at his house and make a big dramatic gesture, like bringing him a box of donuts that spelled 'I'm sorry' like Mia did with the pizza she sent to Michael in *The Princess Diaries*. But I wasn't really the big gesture type of girl.

I thought about texting him, like the coward I was, but apologizing in a text wasn't my style, either. At the very least, he deserved a face-to-face conversation. And so, I somehow convinced myself to climb in my car and drive to his house. What I did *not* convince myself of was getting out and knocking on his door.

Soft rain pinged against my car as I rested my forehead on the steering wheel for several moments, fighting the urge to bang my head against it. Was I a fool to come here? What if, during my week of thinking, he had decided I wasn't what he wanted after all? I bit my lip against the tears that threatened to fall.

A tap came against the window, and I let out a little scream, jumping so high I bonked my head on the ceiling.

"Elsie?" a muffled voice came through the glass, and my heart gave a little flop. "What are you doing here?"

Rubbing my head, I turned to face Jameson, who was standing on the outside of my car. His arm was propped on the top as he bent down to peer in the window. Word vomit immediately spewed from my mouth, and I spoke so fast, it came out a jumbled mess that didn't make sense.

Jameson shook his head. "I can't hear you through the glass, Elsie."

"Oh. Right." My cheeks blazed. Only I would try to confess all my feelings through a closed car window.

Bravery was in limited supply, so instead of getting out, I rolled down my window.

"Why are you here, Elsie?" he repeated, his voice barely more than a whisper. His shoulders were stiff, and the same pain in my chest was reflected in his eyes.

"I..." The words were stuck in my throat. How hard was it to say I was sorry? That I had feelings for him... that I had fallen for him, too? I tried to speak but the only thing that came out was a choking sound.

After another moment of struggling to apologize, Jameson sighed and opened my door. "Come on, let's go inside out of the rain."

I barely noticed the brisk autumn wind cutting beneath my jacket or the rain clinging to my face as I stepped out and followed him to his door. The woodsy leather scent crashed over me once we were inside, simultaneously comforting me and making me want to cry.

Jameson stopped in the middle of his living room, not bothering to shed his jacket. His hands flexed at his sides as if he were fighting the urge to touch me and waited for me to speak with way more patience than I deserved.

"I wanted to talk to you," I said quietly, fixing my eyes on the rug beneath my feet.

Jameson headed toward the couch, running a hand through his hair. "Did you do your thinking?" he asked. I expected to hear derision in his voice, perhaps how Ben would have spoken to me in such a scenario, but there wasn't any emotion at all. He took a seat on the leather cushions, then patted the seat next to him.

With a nod, I shuffled over to him, settling onto the very edge.

"I..." Why was this so hard?

Because he could reject you and crush your heart.

Jameson put a hand on my knee, sending a million bolts of lightning through my veins. "Elsie?"

You can do this. Jameson is worth it.

I took a deep breath. "I'm sorry."

He removed his hand, taking my heart with it.

No, come back! Smitten Elsie cried.

His gaze went to his hands in his lap, giving me space and time to formulate my words.

I took a steadying breath. "I shouldn't have walked out on you the other night. Ever since my parents...I couldn't stomach the thought of having the same thing happen to me—of falling in love with someone only to find they weren't who I thought, and then watching it all crash and burn. Their relationship taught me if that was real love, I didn't want any part of it. It's not worth the pain just to have a few moments of happiness."

Tears filled my eyes, and he finally looked at me. "After you left the night we fell asleep on my couch, Ben paid me a visit. I told him I wanted nothing to do with him and kicked him out, but not before his cruel words were able to get inside my head."

I let out a long breath. "I let my fear ruin everything.

I don't want to end up hurt and I don't want to hurt you. The only way I could see to avoid it was to end things before they went further. But I took away *your* choice in the process. Didn't I?"

When I mentioned that Ben had come to my house, anger twisted his face, but then it was quickly replaced with a blank expression. I couldn't tell if my words were having any effect on him. I couldn't stand the emotionless look on his face, so I looked down, wringing my hands in my lap as a tear slid off my cheek and hit my wrist.

I took a deep breath before whispering, "I'm falling for you, Jameson, and that terrifies me."

For a long moment, Jameson was still, unmoving next to me. My heart stuttered in my chest, thinking maybe he wasn't responding because he no longer wanted me. But then a warm thumb brushed the next tear away.

His touch spurred me to keep talking. "But I know I have a lot of baggage and I understand if—"

"We all have baggage, Elsie. I'm not afraid of yours. Only a coward would be."

Could he really mean that? Ben hadn't been interested in helping me deal with any of it. He was more content to sit on his phone, only paying attention to me if I did something that embarrassed him. He would have let my heart rot away in grief, insecurity, and fear rather than helping me face it all.

But Jameson wasn't Ben. Not once had he made me feel less than, small, or like my fears weren't valid. He helped me through my fears rather than making me hide them away from the light of day. Ben never *saw* me. But Jameson had—from the very first moment we met. Maybe I just hadn't seen *him*.

"Elsie…" His voice was so heart wrenchingly soft that I was certain he was about to tell me to leave. His thumb skimmed across my face, and he scooted closer. "Elsie, I can't promise that we'll never hurt each other because we're human and that's what we do…but I *can* promise that, despite any future hurt, I will never give up on us. When I told you I wanted you, I meant it. I know you haven't had the greatest examples of what a relationship is supposed to look like, but if you're willing to try, I'd like to figure it out together. I…"

He sighed, leaning forward so his forehead rested against mine.

"I don't want us to have an end. I want to find out where this can go. I know you're scared of the future, but I think it's worth it, Els. *Our* love is worth the risk. It's worth fighting for."

The feeling his words elicited brought me back to when I had played with a bunch of puppies several years ago. They had jumped all over me, licking the heck out of my face, and were desperate to love me and be loved in return.

That's how Jameson's words made me feel.

Desperately loved; like nothing could ever ruin it because he was happy to simply be with me.

I was expecting to have to beg him for another chance, to try to convince him that I truly wanted to try this, but I didn't have to.

He wanted to be with me, despite my fears and reservations.

That alone proved that he wasn't like my parents, or Ben. Jameson knew that there were likely difficult times ahead for us, but instead of giving up and refusing to face it, he wanted to walk through it with me.

The thought had my lips curling into a smile.

He arched a brow. "You're…smiling?"

A half laugh, half sob broke out of my throat before I launched myself into his arms, bringing my lips to his. He held me with gentle, reverent hands.

"Does that mean you want to give this a shot?" he murmured against my lips.

I giggled, tightening my arms around his neck in response. "Yes."

His hands pressed into my sides as he laid me back on the couch and lowered himself next to me. With gentle fingers, he brushed the hair from my face, and I shivered as they ran through my hair.

Jameson took his time, kissing me like I had never been kissed before. Each of his movements were confident, slow, savoring. When we finally broke apart, he smiled the sweetest, most breathtaking smile I had ever seen.

"We're worth it, Elsie. I promise," he whispered as his lips brushed the shell of my ear, sending a shiver through me. "We'll take it one day at a time. We'll tell each other about our days, how we're feeling, if we're angry."

He pulled away from my ear to look me in the eyes. "This only ends if we stop fighting for each other. It's a choice, and I choose you, sunshine."

Elsie

The smell of cider and apple donuts filled the air as Jameson and I walked, hand in hand, across Beck's Pumpkins and headed into the little shop.

I still couldn't believe it.

Jameson was mine. We were together.

"Well, well, well. Look who it is," a familiar voice rang out. Aunt Jo came around the corner, eyeing our hands before looking between the two of us.

"Well, what do you have to say for yourselves?" she demanded. If I hadn't already had an encounter with her, I would have thought she was angry.

Jameson tugged me forward before pulling me against his chest and wrapping his arms around me. His woodsy cologne made his hug even better. I loved being in his arms. There was no other place I felt so treasured and loved, so wanted, so *safe.*

"Aunt Jo, I'd like you to meet my girlfriend, Elsie."

For a minute, Aunt Jo just stared at us before she squealed. Yes, *squealed,* and ran toward us, folding us in a big bear hug.

"It's about time," she muttered.

I couldn't help but laugh at how similar her reaction was to Jameson's mom's. We had told her a few days ago, and she had been absolutely over the moon for us. At first, I was afraid she would be upset that I had tried to break up with Jameson, that in doing so I had proven I wasn't right for her son, but Maggie had simply pulled me into her arms, squeezing the breath from my lungs.

"All that matters is that you came to your senses. All the rest can be figured out along the way," his mom had said. "I'm happy you gave Jamie a chance, my dear."

Aunt Jo planted a kiss on my forehead, pulling me out of the memory, before doing the same with Jameson.

"Now," she barked, clapping her hands together. "To what do I owe this pleasure? The patch is about to close, you know."

It was the last weekend of October, and we wanted to come back to the place where we had our first date one last time before it closed for the season.

Jameson ran a hand through his hair. "We know. I wanted to show Elsie the stars from the best place in Meridel."

According to Jameson, the patch had the best view

of the stars at night, completely unobstructed by lights or trees. He claimed it was like staring at the entire universe.

Aunt Jo nodded and threw a thumb over her shoulder. "There are some extra blankets in the back. Feel free to take them and some cider with you."

Jameson nodded his thanks before ducking into the back and emerging a moment later with an arm full of multi-colored blankets. I filled two Styrofoam cups of cider, and we headed for the door when Aunt Jo stopped me.

"Elsie?"

I stopped mid-step, looking at her over my shoulder. "Yeah?"

"You take care of my Jamie, you hear?" Her gaze was stern, but the love she had for her nephew was evident in each word.

I didn't pretend to have everything figured out yet, nor had my fears vanished overnight, but I did know that Jameson and I had something amazing that I couldn't imagine giving up now. It wouldn't always be easy, but like Jameson had said: we were worth fighting for.

Real love always was.

I smiled. "Don't worry, Aunt Jo. There's nothing I'd rather do."

We said goodbye to her before heading outside. The late October air had taken a turn for the brutal and bitter, but Jameson was adamant that this was an experience not to be missed. Especially when our previous stargazing night had ended in a not-so-pleasant way. I winced at the memory, thankful I had decided to give a relationship with Jameson a shot.

In the two weeks since we made up, he had done nothing but prove to me that I had made the right decision, and now I couldn't imagine my world without Jameson in it. Though I still had a lot of fear and insecurity to work through, there was no one else that I'd rather have by my side while I faced down the beasts within my mind.

We crossed the pumpkin patch by the light of the moon, my foot snagging on vines once or twice, before he helped me climb up the steps onto the hayride. His muscles flexed as he rearranged the hay bales into a bed-like rectangle before he spread one of the blankets down and then gestured for me to crawl on. Settling down next to each other, he planted a kiss on my cheek.

Everything was silent as we sipped on our cider and munched on the donuts he had swiped while Aunt Jo wasn't looking. It was perfection: sitting here with Jameson by my side, listening to the sounds of nature, the wind blowing through the trees.

Once the treats were gone, he curled me into his arms, and we stared up at the stars.

Jameson was right. This was the best view of the night sky I had ever seen. It felt like we were floating through the galaxy, watching stars shoot by every few seconds. I was lost in the warmth of his arms, in the beauty of the sky, so when he spoke, I almost didn't hear him.

"There's no one I'd rather be here with, Elsie. No one I'd rather have in my arms."

His smile had my heart stuttering in my chest as he pulled me impossibly closer. Tears filled my eyes, and I bit my lip to hold them back. I wasn't sad—not in the slightest. No one had ever made me feel so treasured before. I loved how he truly cherished me with every moment we spent together.

I loved his kind heart. His sweet soul. The way he desperately loved those he cared about.

Jameson was a rare find, and I was so, so lucky he was mine.

I brushed my lips against his, knowing it would say more than simple words ever could. He kissed me through his grin, and I knew in that moment that I had found something irreplaceable. A love like pure magic—one I never thought existed or dared to dream of.

The last two months had been an absolute whirlwind, but I couldn't stop thinking back to that moment in the tent when we watched that star shoot across the sky—when he told me to make a wish.

I pulled away just enough to look into his hazel eyes, which flickered in the moonlight, running my hand through his hair as his smile lit my insides on fire. Jameson's arms tightened, wordlessly telling me that I wasn't going anywhere—and neither was he.

"Thanks for making my wish come true," I whispered against his lips.

And then I kissed him beneath the starlight.

EPILOGUE

Jameson

Fourteen Months Later

I was back in the sunflower field where I had first met Elsie over a year ago, only this time, snow covered the ground.

I never thought I'd come back to the place where I posed for a silly couples photoshoot with a stranger. Maya's meddling was to blame, though I couldn't even be mad at her because it brought Elsie into my life. Maya had gotten the two things she wanted—us together and beating her photography classmates for the most unique photoshoot, temporarily boosting her business afterward.

Even though she ended up losing the final class competition, which would have come with an award and more exposure, I was still insanely proud of my cousin; even if she wouldn't stop complaining about the guy she lost to.

I pulled my phone out of my pocket and glanced at the lock screen—which I did far too often—just to see my favorite picture Maya had taken. The setting sun cast the perfect glow over the photo, sunflowers looming overhead, as Elsie stood front and center with me behind her, holding my arms across her chest. Her dainty hands gripped my forearms, and my lips were pressed to her cheek in a kiss. The smile on her face made me unfathomably happy whenever I looked at it.

Snow started to fall in fat, drifting flakes, as I put the phone away and waited, my nerves distracting me from the cold.

This was it.

I had spent weeks planning this, months thinking about this moment, and it was finally here. Maya was hiding somewhere, camera in hand. Though, with the field barren, I had no clue where she could be.

The last year with Elsie had been an absolute dream. A little bumpy at first as we worked through a lot of her fears, but we did it together, and it only made our relationship stronger.

She was my best friend, my girlfriend, and now, I hoped to add fiancé to that list. She was everything I ever dreamed of in a partner, and I couldn't wait for what the future had in store for us.

A few months ago, I had convinced her to *finally* submit one of her novels to a few literary agents. It was her dream—to publish her own books—and I fully believed she was talented enough for it to happen. She just needed a little nudge.

The nudge had paid off. Elsie recently signed a contract with an agent, and a publishing house bought her book. Her first romantic comedy was set to release later next year. Her dreams were coming true, and now, it was my turn.

I ran my hand across my coat, checking for the hundredth time that the little ring box was still inside. I couldn't wait to give it to her. The ring was perfect and fit Elsie in every way. It was a beautiful pear-shaped diamond with a rose-gold band. It was elegant but simple in the best way—just like her.

I found it six months ago and had been holding onto it ever since. I had wanted to ask Elsie to marry me for months, but I didn't want to rush her, so I had been waiting to pop the question for what felt like years, ignoring every impatient hint from my mom to hurry up.

Every moment with Elsie wasn't long enough. I wanted every second, every day, every year, for a lifetime. I hated having to say goodbye every night, letting go of her, missing her.

I couldn't wait to wake up to her morning grumpiness, or kiss her goodbye before leaving for work, or fall asleep cuddling to cheesy Hallmark movies. I couldn't wait to grow our family together, create new memories and traditions. I wanted it all with her.

And I didn't want to waste another second.

The crunch of footsteps in the snow had me turning to find my little bundle of grumpy sunshine trudging toward me, her hands shoved into the pockets of her gray peacoat. She wore a matching gray beanie with a big poof on top that immediately brought a smile to my face.

How did I get so lucky? Elsie was everything I always wanted, and everything I never knew I needed. If there were such a thing as soulmates, there wasn't a doubt in my mind that Elsie was mine.

As she grew closer, a slow smile spread across her face as she took in my tux.

Yes, I was wearing a tux in December on a snowy, barren sunflower field.

I was a romantic. Sue me.

Elsie stopped in front of me, looking up with those caramel and jade-flecked eyes that pierced my soul.

"Hi," she whispered.

"Hi," I whispered back, our breaths fogging in the air in front of us.

She cocked her head. "Aren't you cold?"

"Not when I'm with you."

Her face brightened even more. "What are we doing here?" she asked after a moment, her teeth chattering.

"Do you remember when we first met?"

She scoffed. "How could I forget? I had to pretend to be in love with a stranger."

I smiled, taking her hand in mine, running my thumb

over her gloved knuckles.

"No pretending anymore," I replied, kissing the back of her hand.

Her smile was soft, the kind only reserved for me. "No pretending."

I took a deep breath before dropping onto one knee in the snow. Her eyes widened, and she covered her mouth with her other hand.

"Elsie Feran," I began, "I never imagined that a couples photoshoot with a stranger would result in me falling in love. I never imagined that I would find someone so special, so perfect, so *right* for me. But here you are." A single tear slipped down her cheek. "Elsie, I love you with all my heart, and I want to love you for the rest of my life." I paused, willing the emotion to leave my voice so I could finish. "My love, my sunshine…will you marry me?"

A laughing sob broke out of her, and she flung herself at me, tackling me to the ground. We rolled together, like two kids playing in the snow. I wiped my fingers across her cheeks, staring into those brown eyes that I loved so much.

"Is that a yes?" I asked, bringing my lips to hover right above hers.

Her hand cupped my cheek, and she gave me a smile that made my knees weak. "There's nothing I'd rather do, Jameson, than spend forever loving you. That's a yes."

I couldn't hold back my grin as I pulled the ring box

out of my pocket and popped it open. Elsie took off her glove, gaping as I slipped the ring onto her finger. It was a perfect fit.

I tucked her hair behind one ear before I tugged her forward and pressed my lips to hers. "I love you, Elsie."

She smiled. "I love you, Jameson."

I rubbed my thumbs over her cheeks and said, "Now, prepare to be thoroughly kissed."

THE END

A Note From Emily

Hi there! I hope you loved reading Elsie and Jameson's story! I wanted to write a book that not only made you laugh, but also portrayed just a little bit of the struggle that insecurity and past trauma can play in a new relationship. That's why Elsie tends to go back and forth so often, fighting against all those negative inner thoughts. Growth and healing aren't always linear, and sometimes we take steps backward instead of forward. But despite all the hurt in her past, Elsie still found real love that was worth risking her heart for. I sincerely hope this book gave you hope and reminded you that real love exists and is worth taking a chance on.

THE HEART SHOT PLAYLIST

The following songs encompass all the vibes and feels of *The Heart Shot* and are in no particular order. Enjoy!

Someone to You - BANNERS

The Bones - Marren Moris, Hozier

Celestial - Ed Sheeran

Glad You Exist - Dan + Shay

Like No One Does - Jake Scott

Black and White - Niall Horan

Lose Somebody - OneRepublic, Kygo

I Found You - Andy Grammar

CWJBHN - Jake Scott, Josie Dunne

Lease on Life - Andy Grammar

Like This - Jake Scott

Best of You - Andy Grammar

Whole Lives - Jake Scott

Safe With Me - Gryffin, Audrey Mika

DID YOU LOVE THE HEART SHOT?

Please consider leaving a review on Amazon to help other readers discover the magic of Elsie and Jameson's story too!

Maya

At the risk of sounding jealous, let me preface this by saying I was happy for them. I really was.

Jameson was like a brother to me, Elsie like a sister.

I had never seen two people so perfect for each other—so smitten, too.

I was hidden across the field, the proposal over, with a camera full of photos. I was so happy that they had found love and yet...

My stomach twisted. It wasn't exactly jealousy—at least, I didn't think so. It was more than that.

I wanted what they had found. Sure, I had gone on my fair share of dates over the past year, but nothing ever went past the one date.

Elsie had found her Jameson.

But where was mine?

I packed up my camera gear and prepared to leave the two lovebirds to make out in the snow. I didn't need to see any more of that than I already had.

The snow crunched and creaked beneath my boots, the cold December wind battering against me as I trudged to the parking lot. I was just about to crawl into my car when I noticed a huge scratch in the door.

"What the heck?"

Had someone keyed my car?

I groaned. This was not what I needed right now. Between my photography classes and the shiny new lens I put on my credit card when I had an influx of inquiries on my website, I had enough debt. And now, I apparently had to pay for a new paint job for my car.

I fought the urge to kick the tire, knowing that would likely only hurt me instead of making me feel better. Grumbling under my breath, I opened the door and slumped into my seat. Then I noticed a white napkin shoved under my windshield wiper, and I stood, reaching my hand out to grab it. I uncrumpled it as best as I could to attempt to read the chicken scratch scrawled all over it. Who had written this? A two-year-old?

Sorry about your car, mate! I promise I'll pay for the damages. Give me a call and we can figure things out! Happy Christmas!

A phone number was below the words, but it was barely legible.

Mate? Who was this? An image of the British guy,

Oliver, from my photography class flickered through my mind, but I shoved it away, along with the surge of anger that accompanied the memory of him. There was no way this was him. He had gone back to England when the class ended.

Although…how many British guys had been in the town of Meridel in the past year? As far as I knew, it was only him. Besides, if it *was* him, I wanted absolutely nothing to do with him. If we had lived in a world with superheroes and villains, Oliver Lewis was without a doubt my arch nemesis.

I rolled my eyes, crumpling up the napkin. Forget it, I'd pay for the stupid scratch myself. Maybe I'd send the guy a nasty text as a thank you for putting me further into debt.

I pulled out of my parking spot and onto the snowy road, starting the wipers to clear the flakes off the glass. At each light I was forced to stop at, I couldn't help but glance at that napkin, wondering. Would it really hurt to make the stupid guy pay for the damage? Why should I fork over the money when it was his fault?

That's assuming it even was a guy.

I glared at the napkin on my seat. "This is all your fault," I snapped at it.

Great. I was yelling at a napkin.

I sighed as I pulled into my designated spot outside my apartment building, resting my head against the steering wheel.

I was single, in debt, with a scratched car door and, possibly, a British guy I despised promising to pay for it. All happening in December, the worst time of the year.

I muttered a curse into the cold air as I crawled out of my car.

Happy Christmas, indeed.

Acknowledgements

Wow, what a crazy journey writing this book has been. Trying to write a new genre after publishing a YA fantasy series is one of the scariest things I've ever done. In a way, writing a rom-com was easier than writing fantasy, but in some ways, it was so much harder. While there wasn't a need for major world building or fancy magic systems, coming up with a unique story that was sweet, funny, but also had depth and heart was incredibly challenging.

I absolutely loved being able to write a story with many of my favorite things, while sprinkling in little pieces of myself too. I love *The Heart Shot* and I really hope y'all enjoyed Elsie and Jameson's story too.

Writing and publishing a book can be a lonely journey, but it really takes a village to make the magic happen. There are a few people I could not have done this without:

Thanks be to God—for His never-ending faithfulness throughout this entire process. Whether I needed peace or provision, He always came through. He never failed. I'm so thankful for this gift that He has given me, and may He get all the glory from this book. I would not be where I am without Him.

To my husband, Cody—Thank you for pushing me to keep dreaming, and reminding me that the doubts and fears in my head are all lies to keep my stories away from those who need it.

To Brittany Cox—thank you for keeping me sane and for not letting me get away with believing all the lies and fears I had about this book. Your friendship is irreplaceable and I'm so thankful to have you in my life.

To The Authorteers—I am so blessed to have found writer buddies like you. Thank you for your constant encouragement, talking me off many cliffs, and for helping me stay somewhat sane. I couldn't have gotten here without you!

To Vanessa, Katie, Natalia, and Angelica—thank you for beta reading the scary draft of my book, for all your constructive criticism, as well as your encouragement. It's terrifying having readers see my story for the first time, but your feedback has been invaluable and you helped me make *The Heart Shot* what it is. Y'all are the best!

To all my author/bookstagram friends—I'm so thankful for each of you! Your excitement, encouragement, and every like, comment, and share mean so much to me. I feel so blessed every day to have found a community of people who are so supportive and that cheer me on, even when I pull a 180 and write a new genre lol.

To Amanda Chaperon—thank you for all the work you put into editing my book and encouraging me along the way. You helped me make this story what it is, and it never would have been possible without you.

A special shoutout to @apetersonimagery on Instagram

whose stranger photoshoot inspired me to write *The Heart Shot*.

And to my readers—I am beyond honored that you chose to give me a chance and pick up something new. It was terrifying to take this leap, but I hope this story made you smile and reminds you of how precious love really is. I hope you walk away from this book feeling uplifted, hopeful, and have a big old grin on your face. Thank you for giving *The Heart Shot* a chance. It means the absolute world.

About the Author

Emily Schneider is a multi-award-winning author who grew up in Minnesota where she spent most of her life studying music and singing, which ironically has nothing to do with writing fantasy novels and rom-coms. While music had always been a passion, Emily could never get away from her love of reading and writing books full of dragons, Fae, monsters, magic, and romance. When she's not writing, you can find Emily chasing around her two dogs, Pixel and Frodo, playing Mario Kart with her husband, or watching The Lord of the Rings for the one-hundred-and-eleventh time.

emilyschneiderwrites.com

 @emilyschneiderwrites